Sea Music

Briege Brannigan

August 2015

Sea Music

BRIEGE BRANNIGAN

Matador
9 Priory Business Park
Kibworth Beauchamp
Leicestershire LE8 0RX, UK
Tel: (+44) 116 279 2299
Email: books@troubador.co.uk
Web: www.troubador.co.uk/matador

ISBN 978 1784623 708

British Library Cataloguing in Publication Data.
A catalogue record for this book is available from the British Library.

Printed and bound by CPI Group (UK) Ltd, Croydon, CR0 4YY
Typeset in Aldine401 BT Roman by Troubador Publishing Ltd

Matador is an imprint of Troubador Publishing Ltd

In memory of my parents,
Vincent and Winifred

Part One

Chapter One

Jess laid her vase of sweet pea by the remembrance stone. The inscription was succinct:

Anna Katherine Cooper
10 June 1944 – 21 July 1991

Seeing the bouquet of red roses, she knew that her father had been there already. She stood for several minutes in silent communication and as the heavy rain mingled with her tears, she wiped her face with the palms of her hands.

As she retraced her steps through the memorial garden, the rain stopped abruptly, the sky lightened and the sun came out. Walking between the horse chestnuts and sycamores she stared in wonder at the magical transformation that was taking place. Thousands of tiny raindrop jewels shimmered in the sun's rays, with all the colours of the spectrum and a group of blue tits flew in and out of the branches, feeding on some nourishment unseen by her. With renewed hope, she got into her car and began her journey to Northumberland.

It was the tenth anniversary of her mother's death and as she drove east and then north, she contemplated the life of the woman who had died at the age of forty-seven, wondering yet again what had changed her from the positive person she had once been to the woman intent on self-destruction. She had asked her father this question many times over the years but he was reluctant to talk about it. All he disclosed was that Anna was unable to have any more children after Jess.

'She really wanted three or four children and she never came to terms with not being able to have more.'

Jess was satisfied with that explanation for a while but she had long suspected that there was something else. Her father, however, would not be drawn further on the subject.

For as long as she could remember, she had had an awareness of a void in her life. It was a strange, vague feeling that she couldn't put into words. Sometimes she put it down to the fact that she had no relatives. Neither of her parents had siblings and her grandparents were dead. But mostly she sensed that it was something much more profound than a mere absence of family. There were times when she was enveloped in a deep sadness and she would find herself so close to tears that, if she was in company, she would have to excuse herself and go to the bathroom or her bedroom to have a quiet weep. It was at these times that she felt as if a vital part of her had been torn out. She knew she was grieving but for what?

Early memories were sparse and for the most part, nebulous. Some friends had very clear memories of when they were three or four, but her clearest memories began when she moved from London to Manchester a couple of months before her eighth birthday. One substantial memory from London was of her mother teaching her at home. She knew she had attended school at one time, for she had a hazy but warm recollection of being in a classroom with her friend Cathy and other children. When she'd asked her parents why she no longer went to school, she was told it was because she had been very ill and needed to build up her strength before she returned.

'But I don't remember being ill. Was I in hospital? Did I nearly die?' she'd asked, wide-eyed with a delicious mixture of horror and glee. Her parents explained that part of the illness was losing her memory of it, hastily changed the subject and refused to discuss it thereafter.

They had arrived in Manchester in June 1979. The home-tutoring continued after the move because it was nearly the end of the summer term. Jess was happy with this for she was filled with fears, some indeterminate, others very clear, like the thought of facing a class of new children in a strange city. Lonely for Cathy, she created two playmates, Lily and Gwen.

Jess closed her reader and looked hopefully at her mother. 'Can I go out to play now?'

Anna smiled. 'Yes, I think we've done enough for today; your reading's coming on a treat.' Jess gathered up her books and having put them away in the sideboard, ran outside. Lily and Gwen were waiting for her by the shed at the bottom of the garden. She greeted them, folded her arms and screwed up her face. 'Now what are we going to play today?'

'What about shop?' suggested Lily.

Jess took on a superior air. 'As long as I can be the shop keeper. I'm a greengrocer.' And she set about collecting stones for potatoes, grass for spring onions, dock leaves for cabbage.

'Who are you talking to?'

Jess jumped at the sound of the voice coming from the fence. She had become used to her playmates sounding only in her head. Turning, she saw a mop of blonde curls, a pert nose and two big blue eyes staring intently at her. Embarrassed to admit that she was talking to herself, she said nothing, wishing at the same time that she could disappear.

'Were you talking to yourself? I do that sometimes when I have no one to play with. My name's Tanya, what's yours?'

'Jessica,' she replied, thankful that she did not have to answer the girl's first question, 'but I'm mostly called Jess.'

'You've just moved in, haven't you? When we went on holiday your house was empty and now you're here. Can I come round and play with you? That's if my mum lets me. I'll go and ask her.' Without waiting for an answer, Tanya disappeared.

Jess had mixed feelings about the newcomer for, although she was lonely, she'd got used to being in charge of Lily and Gwen who joined in her games without demur. She continued her search for produce for the shop.

'Jess, there's a little girl here, she lives next door and she wants to play with you. Says she's already spoken to you over the fence.' Anna was halfway down the garden.

Entering the kitchen, Jess saw Tanya and a blonde woman, very like her in appearance, seated at the table.

'Hello Jessica, Tanya's told me you've already met. We're your next door neighbours. We've been away on holiday. Is it alright if Tanya plays with you?'

Stricken by shyness, Jess put her head down and made circles on the floor with the toe of her right foot before murmuring her assent.

It turned out that Tanya was also an only child and she and Jess forged a firm friendship that summer. Jess felt her shyness and fears diminish and she began to look forward to going to school, feeling very excited when she went with her mum to buy her uniform and other requirements.

But as the start of term approached, she began to worry about being disliked, bullied even, by the other children. Tanya had a different way of talking; she sometimes said things that Jess didn't understand and she knew that Tanya didn't always understand her. What if the other children made fun of her because she was different? She resorted to biting her nails, something she hadn't done for several weeks, as she sat staring through the window, pondering these things.

'You all right love? Not playing with Tanya today?'

She jumped at the sound of her father's voice. 'No, she's gone to visit her gran.'

'Are you looking forward to school tomorrow?'

'Oh yes.' She knew it wasn't exactly a lie because, in spite of her anxiety, she had a certain curiosity about the place Tanya had told her so much about and she wanted to be with her friend.

At the back of the garden shed, she spoke to Lily and Gwen who had not been around since she'd met Tanya.

'I'm going to school tomorrow so I won't be able to play with you. I know I've not played with you for a while and that's because of Tanya. You see she doesn't know about you and I don't think she would like it if she did...because... she likes to keep me to herself, so I've not told her.' She looked sidelong at them to see how they were taking it and when there was no reaction, she continued. 'Tanya loves school and I want to go with her but I hope I won't get sick again like I did before and I hope the other children will like me.' Her voice quivered, then in a brighter tone, 'But Tanya likes me and Cathy, my friend in London liked me and you like me,' she gave a loud sigh, 'so maybe they will.'

She was interrupted by her mother's voice, calling down the garden. 'Jess, where are you? It's nearly teatime, come in and wash your hands.'

Her fears were unfounded. Tanya was very popular and her many friends gathered round the newcomer with interest, asking questions about London: Had she been to Buckingham Palace?

Had she seen the Queen? They commented admiringly on her 'posh accent'. Tanya was very assertive and fielded any adverse remarks with aplomb. Even the rougher boys appeared to be in awe of her. The teacher, Miss Harris was kind and welcoming and her work had in no way suffered in her absence from school. She was well ahead of many of the other pupils. At half-term, she and Anna spent happy days exploring their new area.

—⚎—

Just north of Leeds, Jess stopped to buy petrol, also picking up a sandwich and a bottle of water and as she continued her journey, she recalled the day she first became concerned about her mother.

As usual, she came in from school like a whirlwind, the latest happenings already on her lips. Normally Anna would be sitting at the kitchen table, drinking coffee and eager to hear her news. Today the kitchen was empty.

'Mum?' She went into the sitting room. 'Mum?' She looked in the dining room, called up the stairs. There was no reply and she could feel her anxiety growing as she raced upstairs and burst into her parents' bedroom.

'Mum? Mum?' There was a note of panic in her voice. Anna was in bed and she opened her eyes as Jess came in.

'Oh there you are Mum, I thought you'd gone. Why are you in bed? Are you poorly?'

Anna sat up and gave her a startled look, shook herself and swung her legs over the side of the bed. 'No darling I'm fine, just a bit tired. Come and give me a cuddle.'

She put her arms round her mother but something was amiss. There was a very odd smell about her. She leaned back and looked closely at her.

'What's that funny smell? I don't like it.' She pulled a face.

'Oh, eh…it must be that stuff I was feeding the houseplants. Now let's go down and get you a drink and you can tell me about your day.'

On the landing, she noticed that the step ladder was in place under the open attic hatch, a cardboard box next to it.

'What were you doing in the attic Mum?'

'I was just looking through some business papers.' Anna hastily lifted the box and proceeding up the ladder, shoved it inside and slammed the hatch shut.

In the kitchen, Jess cuddled her again. 'I really thought you'd gone Mum.'

Anna held her tightly. 'I'd never leave you Jess, you know that, don't you?'

She nodded her head vigorously. 'I do know,' she said, 'I don't know why I thought that.'

She knew in her heart that her mother would never leave her, so it puzzled her that from time to time she had a fear of being deserted by one or both parents; at that moment, the feeling of an absence in her life was stronger than ever and despite what Anna had said about being tired, she had a niggling worry that she might be ill. She just wasn't her usual self.

That night she had a dream about a house of many rooms and stairs where she wandered about searching for someone. She had no idea who the person was, just that they were important to her. And, as she was neither able to find them or to find a way out, her frustration grew. It was a recurring theme in her dreams and she always woke in tears.

As the weeks went by and Anna seemed back to normal, her anxieties dissipated. Then in September she had the shock of her life. Returning from her dancing class one Saturday afternoon, she was met by her father, looking grave.

'I need to talk to you Jess. Let's go up to your room.'

She felt uneasy; something was wrong. Was her mum poorly after all?

'What's wrong Dad?'

'We'll talk upstairs.'

As they passed the sitting room, she thought she heard a sob. Was that her um crying? She sat on her bed and looked anxiously at her father who sat next to her. He ran a hand through his thinning fair hair, took off his glasses and held them up to the window, inspecting them for smears, rubbed them with a hankie, put them back on.

'There's no easy way to tell you this Jess,' he hesitated but his next words came out in a rush, 'you see, me and your mum, we've not been getting on well recently and… well… I'm going to move out for a while. I'll only be about a mile away. I've got a flat with two bedrooms and you can come and stay whenever you want. I love you very much Jess and I'm going to miss you but things are too difficult here and I think this might be the best way of sorting things out.'

Unable to believe she was hearing this, she stared at him, put her head down and began to pull at a loose thread on her cardigan, twirling it round her forefinger.

'I don't want you to go Dad. Don't you care about me and Mum anymore?'

John sighed. He reached over and stroked her long, dark hair.

'Jess, Jess have you listened to a word I've been saying? Of course I care, nobody could love you more and I still love your mum but, as I said, we've been having a difficult time and I think a separation might help us. I'm hoping it won't be forever.'

She looked up then. 'So I can come and stay whenever I want?'

'Yes, well at weekends of course when I'm not at work.'

She pulled the thread tighter until the tip of her finger went blue.

'Is Mum very upset?'

'Well yes, I'm afraid she is but she will be okay.'

'I wouldn't want to leave Mum too often if she's really upset but I would want to come and stay with you…oh Dad I'm going to miss you.' And she flung herself upon him as the tears began to flow.

John was crying too. 'Oh I'll miss you darling. And you know this has nothing to do with you. It's between me and your mum and…oh how I wish things were different.'

She had no understanding of what had happened between her parents. She had never heard them argue, never mind row; she'd always believed them to be happy and she had been so happy since coming to Manchester, meeting Tanya and going to school and her dancing classes. She'd had that period of worry about her mother's health but that had been short-lived. Now she felt as if her beliefs had no substance, like sandcastles she had built with pride and care, only to see them decimated by the in-coming tide.

After her father left, she sobbed herself to sleep every night for weeks, even though she did go to stay with him most weekends. This was not the complete desertion she had feared but it was bad, very bad. The dreams of futile searching haunted her regularly.

One day in February, Jess returned from school to find Anna sound asleep on the sofa.

'Mum! Mum are you alright?' Anna didn't stir. A little apprehensive, she went over and shook her shoulder. 'Mum?' There was still no movement and, as she shook her again, she noticed a bottle tucked between her and the sofa back. She picked it up. It was empty. She read the label: Vodka. So her mother was drunk! She had never seen either of her parents drunk; had never seen them drink much. She shook Anna more forcefully and this time she opened her eyes and a look of horror passed over her face.

'Jess! Oh my God Jess! Is it that time already?' She groped for an alarm clock on the coffee table. Jess's face was furrowed in consternation.

'Mum why have you been drinking? I didn't know you ever got drunk.'

Sitting upright now, Anna patted the sofa. 'Come and sit next to me Jess.' She put an arm round her.

'As you know, I don't drink much and I certainly don't get drunk. I've not been sleeping well recently and I thought I'd take a nap. I thought a drink would help me to relax. I only had a couple – this bottle of vodka's been in the house for ages – and I'm so unused to drinking that it knocked me out. I was planning on being up before you got back but I even slept through the alarm. Just shows how tired I was. Well I won't be doing that again in a hurry.' She laughed.

Jess accepted her explanation but she wasn't completely satisfied and her mother's next words gave her more cause for anxiety.

'Oh by the way Jess, promise me you won't tell your dad about this. I know he would worry, even though he has no need to and he would be angry.'

Jess shook her head. 'I won't tell him but promise me it won't happen again.'

'I promise. I've learned my lesson.' Anna laughed again. 'Now what shall we make for tea?'

Jess said goodbye to Tanya and went round to the back door.

To her surprise it was locked. Anna never locked the back door unless she was going out and she was always in when Jess returned from school. She began to feel uneasy as she knocked on the glass and called for her mother. No reply. She was just going round to the front when Anna came through the gate.

'Mum where have you been? I was wondering why the back door was locked.'

'I just went round to the shop for something. I thought I'd be back before you got here but there was a queue.'

Ushering Jess inside, she asked her to go and change out of her uniform. Jess obeyed but she was puzzled. Her mum didn't usually ask her to change straight away and there was something odd about her. When she came down, she found Anna mopping the kitchen floor and there was a strong smell of disinfectant.

'Be careful not to walk in here in your bare feet Jess. I broke a bottle of milk and there may still be some small pieces of glass around.'

'Okay Mum, I'll be careful.'

After tea, she helped Anna to clear up and as she scraped the plates into the pedal bin, she noticed a jagged piece of glass behind it. Picking it up, she saw that it had a torn red label. There was something familiar about that label and then she recognised the letters – Vod…Vodka! So it wasn't a bottle of milk that her mother had dropped. She was still drinking and what's more she was lying about it.

Although Jess had previously had no experience of drunkenness, she'd heard rumours from girls in her class. When Tracey Carter came in with a black eye, it was whispered that one of her parents had done it.

'Her dad doesn't work you know. Neither does her mum. My mum says they spend all day drinking.' Arms akimbo, Jackie

Smith was censorious. Her friend Michele Edwards agreed.

'Yeah, that's right, my auntie lives next door to them and you want to hear the stories she has to tell. She says they're always fighting.'

Jess was appalled. And that was before she found her mother asleep on the sofa with a vodka bottle nearby.

A few weeks after the rumours, Tracey was no longer in school and those in the know spread the word that she and her younger brother Michael had been taken into care.

Jess's mind was in turmoil: would her mother start to hit her? She had never had as much as a tap from either parent. Should she now break her promise and tell her father? Surely if she did, her mum would be very angry with her and worse still her father would surely be very angry with her mum and maybe they would start to row. Should she tell her mum what she had found or would that also make her angry? She needed time to decide what to do. Lost in thought, she was still staring unseeingly at the shard when Anna turned from the sink.

'What have you got there Jess?'

She started, 'Eh…nothing…just some rubbish.'

'Let me see.'

She felt the heat rise in her face and cast her eyes down as she handed over the piece.

'Where did you get this?'

'Be…behind the pedal bin. I…I know it's part of a vodka bottle and I know it was a bottle of vodka you dropped – not milk!'

Anna threw it in the bin and led Jess into the front room.

'I think I have some explaining to do.'

She told her it was the first time she'd bought alcohol in ages and when the bottle had slipped from her hand she was glad. She would buy no more and she didn't want John to be worried or angry so she hoped that Jess would keep to her promise not to tell him. It was their secret and from now on she would only have the occasional glass of wine in the evenings. There was no need for her to be concerned.

Jess was unconvinced. After all her mother had made and broken that promise before.

For a time it seemed that Anna was keeping her word. She was alert and cheerful when Jess came home but after a while, she suspected she was drinking again because sometimes her eyes were bloodshot and her speech sounded odd; she had taken to chewing gum, something she disliked in other people, but underneath the smell of peppermint, Jess sometimes got a whiff of that peculiar smell, like the stuff the doctor rubbed on her arm before giving her an injection. Often the kitchen was untidy with the breakfast dishes still in the sink, the bin overflowing. On one occasion she asked Anna outright if she was drinking but she quickly denied it.

'I'm just a bit tired Jess. That's why I'm not doing as much housework as usual. I think I must be run down.'

'Why don't you go and see the doctor Mum? I'm worried about you.'

Anna promised she would go soon and a few days later she told Jess that she was anaemic. 'That means that the iron in my blood is low. It's why I've been feeling so tired but Doctor Jones has given me some iron tablets and I'll soon be as right as rain.' She smiled.

Jess breathed a sigh of relief but one sunny day in late June, she came home to find her mother sprawled on the sofa once more. This time she was not asleep but her eyes were glazed and there was a half-empty vodka bottle by her side. Her speech was slurred.

'Well Jesh you caught me out. I can't deny now that I've been drinking. I'm really sorry love.' She lay back and closed her eyes, then lifted her head again. 'What do you want for tea? Thersh not much food in, you might need to go to the shop.'

Jess was frightened and near to tears. What if she said the wrong thing and her mother got violent like Tracey Carter's mother?

'What would you like for tea Mum?'

Anna gave an odd-sounding laugh.

'I don't want to eat love I jush want to drink.' And she took a great slug from the bottle. Jess opened the fridge which was almost empty: a quarter bottle of milk, a piece of mouldy cheese, a wilted lettuce and some soft tomatoes. Well there was bound to be something in the freezer. Her mother kept a well-stocked chest freezer in the garage.

She lifted the lid to find that it was also almost empty and what was in there was at the bottom where she couldn't reach. She looked around and saw a plastic crate. Maybe if she stood on that she could reach. But what was the point? She knew little about cooking but she did know that some foods must be defrosted and that it took a long time.

Returning to the kitchen, she noticed an egg box on top of the fridge. She would try to make scrambled eggs on toast but was there any bread? Opening the bread bin, she found a mouldy end of loaf and two reasonable-looking slices. Now how did you make scrambled eggs? But when she opened the box it was empty. Well beans on toast would be easy and she knew there were tins of beans in the cupboard.

When she went back to the sitting room to see if Anna had changed her mind about eating, she found her fast asleep. She ate her beans on toast ravenously leaving some beans and a slice of bread for Anna. She was still hungry so she helped herself to some cornflakes.

She knew now that her mother had been drinking for some time and it looked like it was getting worse. Her mind teemed with questions. Would she get taken into care like Tracey Carter or would they let her go and live with her dad? She didn't want to live with him; she didn't want to live with Anna. She wanted them all to live together. She wanted everything to be the way it used to be. When had her mum started drinking? Why was she drinking? Had her dad known all along and was that the real reason he had left? But surely he wouldn't leave her on her own with a drunken mother, would he? Should she now break her promise to her mother and tell him?

Unable to face sitting with her mother, she retreated to her bedroom, where she comforted herself by cuddling Danny, her favourite teddy and rocking back and forth on her bed. There was a tap at the door. 'Can I come in?'

Anna looked worse than she had ever seen her: dress crumpled, hair wild, eyes bloodshot and baggy, face white and drawn.

'Can I sit with you?'

She said nothing but made a space on the bed. Anna sat down and put her arms round her but she pulled away, partly because of the smell: that doctor's surgery smell again, mixed with sweat, but also because she was in two minds about being touched by her. Part of her longed to be held and loved, told that everything would be alright but another part felt angry and disgusted. Anna folded her arms and when she spoke, Jess could hear she was on the verge of tears.

'I'm so very sorry darling. What can I say? If I promise to stop, you won't believe me. But I'm promising anyway because this time I'm going to get help.'

Jess clutched Danny even tighter and turned her face to the wall.

'Look at me Jess.'

When she didn't move, she continued. 'I've found an organisation which helps people like me who drink too much.' She reached out and touched her lightly on the shoulder but she pulled further away. Anna began to cry.

'I'm going to ring them tomorrow and, if you don't believe me, you can be there when I make the call. I promise I'll be sober when you come home from school.'

Jess jumped off the bed, Danny still in her arms and stamped her foot.

'I don't believe you! Your promises mean nothing. I remember when I was little you told me you should never say *promise* unless you really, really meant to keep your word and all you do is go back on your word.'

She threw Danny on the bed and picked up a slipper which she flung at Anna with as much strength as she could muster. 'I hate you.' Several other objects followed the slipper, anything that was near to hand and she continued shouting. 'I hate you.' Then she crumpled in a heap on the floor and began to sob. Anna quietly left the room.

Jess was munching on a slice of dry toast when Anna entered the kitchen the following morning. There was no butter and she'd finished the milk with her cornflakes the evening before. Anna hadn't touched the beans or bread she had left for her. Ignoring her mother's greeting, she finished her toast, put her bag on her shoulder and went to call for Tanya without saying goodbye.

When she returned that afternoon, Anna was seated at the table in a spotless kitchen with a mug of coffee, looking better than she had seen her in some time. It was obvious she had been to the hairdresser; her shoulder-length dark hair, which had recently often looked lank and dull, had got back its lustre and had been cut into a neat bob. Her brown eyes were carefully made-up and clearer than they had been for some time and she was wearing a cerise shirt that Jess had not seen before, over black trousers. She smiled as Jess came in. 'Hello Jess, had a good day?'

Relieved as she was, she hadn't forgiven her so she mumbled a reply and made her way upstairs to change, noticing as she did so that the transformation extended to the rest of the house and there were flowers in the hall.

When she came down, she opened the fridge, which was full of food, poured herself a glass of milk and was about to make her exit again when Anna spoke.

'I'm going to make that phone call Jess.' She fiddled with the silver chain and opal pendant she often wore. 'You can listen to what I'm saying so that you will know I mean to keep my word. But once again, I'm asking you not to breathe a word of this to your dad.'

Chapter Two

Jess was relieved to turn off the A1. The traffic had been heavy and it was pleasant to be on quieter roads, but her mood was gloomy. It was a mistake to think about childhood and she was determined to enjoy her holiday. Though, having always holidayed with other people, she had reservations about being on her own.

Concentrating now on the directions to Margaret Sutherland's house where she would pick up the keys for the cottage, she at last felt her spirits begin to lift.

Margaret's house looked somewhat out of place in the Northumberland countryside: a large modern detached with portico, painted a garish pink; two stone lions kept guard on the gateposts and two stone deer – a doe and her fawn reclined by an ornate fountain on the front lawn.

Wondering what the occupant of such a house would look like, she rang the front door bell, but she was greeted from behind.

'You must be Jess. Welcome to Northumberland. Margaret Sutherland here.'

The woman extending her hand was, in Jess's opinion, incongruous with the house. Probably around seventy with frizzy grey hair and brown, weather-beaten face, her blue eyes twinkled in a warm smile. She was wearing a floral blouse, a pair of baggy brown trousers and hiking boots.

'I was just doing a bit of digging at the back, when I heard the bell, didn't want to walk through the house in my dirty boots. Come on in and I'll get you the keys.'

Margaret led Jess round the side of the house and after removing her boots, into an immaculate kitchen where, in spite of the warm day, a great heat came from the range, where a large pot bubbled and a rich fruity smell filled the air.

'I was just making some gooseberry jam.' She lifted a wooden spoon and gave the pot a stir.

'Nearly ready. Now would you like a cup of tea?'

'That's very kind, but it's been a long journey. I think I'd rather find the cottage and get settled in, thanks all the same.'

'I can understand that, you must be tired. Now the owners have asked me to leave you instructions about various things in the house and I've been to check that everything's all right.' She held out the keys. 'I've left you some milk and butter, eggs from my own hens and some of my homemade bread. There's tea and coffee and a few other bits already in the house and there's a small supermarket in the village.'

Jess took out her purse to offer payment but she waved it away. 'Now don't hesitate to call me if there's anything you want to know. My number's on a pad by the phone.'

The 'cottage' turned out to be a large dormer bungalow, probably built in the thirties or forties, white with cornflower blue doors, window frames and sills. At the front, the typically English country garden was a melange of pinks, blues, whites and greens. Someone had worked hard to make sure that no other colour intruded. Standing in the warm sunshine, listening to the soporific drone and chirp of insects, the sea's steady rhythm on the shore; breathing the salt air mixed with the scents of rosemary, lavender, thyme, sage and the myriad flowers, she was suffused by a tremendous feeling of euphoria.

At the back, French windows opened on to a terrace with

white furniture and blue and white pots and urns of geraniums, more Hellenic than Northumbrian. The view was spectacular: the North Sea rolled past the Farne Islands and the impressive Longstone Lighthouse from which Grace Darling and her father had set off on their rescue mission; a stone wall with a gate set in, separated the garden from a sandy beach.

In the kitchen she found the promised eggs and bread but she wasn't hungry and she had a sudden longing for the sea's embrace. Impulsively, she rummaged in her bag for her swim suit and a towel, changed, pulled her hair into a pony tail and ran down the garden, through the gate and down the sand to plunge without hesitation into the waves. The icy impact almost took her breath away but she persevered and as the initial shock became exhilaration, she turned on her back and floated, feeling the sun's warmth on her face, totally absorbed in the moment and in the knowing that she had made the right decision in coming away on her own.

By the time she returned to the cottage she was ravenous so she quickly prepared an omelette, buttered some of Margaret's bread and sat at the garden table to eat. Engrossed in her enjoyment of the food, she was startled by the sound of a woman's voice.

'Excuse me. Sorry to interrupt but I saw you swimming and I just thought I'd stop to say 'Hi' as I was passing. I'm Cassie from next door.' Tall and auburn-haired, she was leaning on the gate.

Jess was a little bit irked by the intrusion but she smiled and walked towards her. As they shook hands, she noticed that Cassie was heavily pregnant. 'I'm Jess, nice to meet you.'

'I won't make a habit of intruding on you, I promise. I guess you've come away for some peace and quiet. Just wanted to say if there's anything you need…oh and I hope my boys won't disturb you too much. They can be a bit boisterous.'

Two little boys were running along the beach, shouting and laughing.

'Oh please don't worry about that. I'll be out a lot of the time anyway. How old are they?'

'Tim's five and Jon is nearly three. This one's due in another five weeks or so, end of August.' She patted her bump.

Jess felt a sharp pang. Her own baby would have been due in October.

When Cassie had gone, she went indoors and as she started to unpack, felt despondency descend once more.

So far it had been a traumatic year: a miscarriage in April, leading to the breakdown of her relationship with Max, her partner of five years; resigning her teaching post. The most distressing event being the loss of her pregnancy. It was Max's attitude to the pregnancy that had brought about the demise of their relationship. But she didn't want to think about that now.

She recalled the day in May when, full of confidence, she had marched into the headmaster's office and announced that she was leaving at the end of the summer term. Trevor Goodwood had stared at her, eyes protruding. 'You what?'

'I'm tendering my resignation Trevor.'

'But what are you going to do? And where am I going to find such an inspirational art teacher?'

'Oh come off it Trevor. There are plenty of art graduates around. You'll be inundated with applications.'

'Yes, but how many who can inspire a love of the subject?'

She shrugged, not really knowing what he was talking about. Sure, she loved her subject. That was precisely why she was leaving. She felt stifled in her teaching post and she wanted to go freelance.

'Art is a subject you only do if you really want to,' she said lamely and got away from Trevor as fast as she could.

The resignation hadn't felt at all stressful at the time. It was what she wanted but now she felt fearful. Had she acted rashly? How was she going to earn enough money to keep herself? Going freelance was all very well but she would no longer have a regular income. She had received her last salary and her mother's legacy was in a high interest-paying account but it wasn't a fortune. When the holiday was over she must see about putting up an exhibition of her work and doing publicity. Anyway enough of that, she told herself. She'd come here to enjoy herself and reassess her life. She would go and explore the beach.

While she had been indoors the temperature had dropped, the wind had risen and dark clouds were gathering on the horizon. It looked like a storm was brewing. She felt a little surge of excitement. She loved storms. Halfway along the beach, she heard the first distant rumble of thunder. The wind, increasing in intensity, was whipping up the sand and she could feel its sharpness, even through the heavy material of her jeans. The sea was becoming turbulent, the thunderclaps louder. It was time to go back and watch it from the safety and comfort of the house.

She reached the back door just as the first great drops of rain began to fall and as she went upstairs to watch from the dormer, carrying a cup of tea, there was an almighty boom which seemed to shake the very foundations.

Going to the window, she gasped. She had never seen such a tempestuous sea. Waves, like mountainous green glass towers, shattered and tumbled into a fizzing, frothing maelstrom, then rolled in to crash in foam on the shore, spray dancing everywhere like a blizzard of yellow snow. Intricate blue and white electric branches cracked the dark sky and pierced the islands and the ocean. The trees in the garden, already sculpted into grotesque shapes by previous storms, bowed their heads to the ground as if in deference to the elements.

As she watched enthralled, she was imbued with a feeling of

comfort and well-being; the feelings that, for as far back as she could remember, always accompanied a thunder storm. And this one was magnificent. She wasn't aware that she had ever before witnessed one like it.

The following morning, she opened the curtains on a cloudless sky; sea like an expanse of flawless blue glass. The islands were in sharp focus and she decided it would be an ideal day for a trip there.

Arriving in Seahouses more than an hour before the next boat was due to leave, she set about exploring the town. It was a friend's birthday soon; maybe she would find a present for her. She reflected that it would be her own birthday in less than four weeks – her thirtieth – and she was determined that this birthday would be a success. So far each birthday marking the start of a new decade had been fraught with misery. She cringed as she remembered her tenth birthday.

She had been so excited as it approached. Ten sounded very grown up and Anna had promised her a party. She had no memory of ever having had a birthday party, though Anna assured her that she had had when she was very young. Certainly, since coming to Manchester, she'd had birthday teas with Tanya the only guest.

The summer had started off well. She knew her mother wasn't drinking because she was back to her old self and she went to support group meetings several times a week. Jess was hoping that her parents would be reunited and that soon they would all be living together again.

She rejected the floaty party dress Anna wanted to buy, in favour of jeans, leg warmers and a thigh-length shirt; Anna had finally given in.

Her birthday was on the sixteenth of August, a Sunday, and as usual she was going to John's on Friday evening and he would bring her back on Sunday in time to get ready. Her excitement was such that she got little sleep on Saturday night and that wasn't just because of the party. As she lay awake, she had a joyous vision of her mum and dad's reconciliation. Would it happen on the day of her party? If it did, it would be the best present ever.

When Anna was nowhere to be found downstairs, she was filled with the old fear. Racing upstairs, she burst into her room and her heart sank. Sure enough, she was in bed. She shook her roughly.

'Wha...what is it? Oh my goodness Jess. The party. What time is it?' Looking at the clock she saw that people were due to arrive in less than an hour. Jess looked at her with disdain. 'You're drunk. And on my birthday too. I hate you.'

Coming upstairs, John heard her shout and she nearly knocked him over as she rushed from the room. He held her at arm's length. 'Whoa, what's going on? That's no way to speak to your mother.'

She burst into tears. 'She's drunk. Again. And she promised.'

Anna emerged from the bedroom, dress crinkled, feet bare.

'Is this true Anna? What's going on?'

She sighed and hung her head. 'Yes I'm afraid it's true.'

John stared, wide-eyed and open-mouthed. 'My God! How long has this been going on? No wait, don't tell me. Guests will be arriving soon and you are a mess and so is the kitchen. Go and have a shower and get changed and I'll clear up.' He handed Jess a hankie. 'It'll be alright darling. Wipe your eyes and blow your nose, then go and wash your face and change into your party clothes.'

Jess blew her nose and went towards the bathroom, muttering. 'It'll not be alright, it's spoiled.' She gave her mum a look of contempt.

When she went downstairs, John was still clearing up. 'Jess you can help me by washing your hands and putting those sandwiches on to plates and taking them through to the dining room.'

She clenched her fists. 'I don't want to have a party now. It's all spoiled.'

'Well we can't very well ring the guests at the last minute and ask them not to come. Come on love, it'll be alright, you'll see. But we'd better hurry. I've still got to blow up those balloons we brought.'

Reluctantly, she began to carry through plates of food. Anna appeared. She'd changed her dress and tidied her hair but she was still bleary-eyed and a bit unsteady. John suggested that she go and lie down again. He would explain to the guests that she had a tummy bug. She disagreed. 'No John, I'm not going to miss Jess's party. I'm alright now, honestly. I'll handle it.'

John frowned and shook his head. 'No you're not alright Anna. You're unsteady on your feet and your hands are shaking...' The doorbell rang: the first of the guests had arrived.

As she was presented with gifts and cards, Jess just wanted to run away and cry but she put on a brave front. She took part in the games and all went well until it was time for the food.

Laura Perkins took a bite of her sandwich, grimaced and turned to her mother, saying sotto voce, 'I can't eat it, it's got mustard.' Others weren't as polite and there were cries of 'Yuk, mustard!' 'My mouth's burning!' and 'What's this horrid hot white stuff?'

Jess cowered with embarrassment as Anna said, 'Oh I'm so sorry, I put mustard in some of the ham sandwiches and horseradish in some of the beef. I meant to label them. I'm so, so sorry.' She realised by now that they weren't even on separate plates. One or two people were careful to examine the fillings

27

after that but most gave up and started on the biscuits and fairy cakes.

John uncovered two trifles and the guests began to help themselves. Jess loved trifle and, in spite of everything, she was looking forward to it. Then she tasted it. Ugh! The sponge was saturated with something so strong, it burned her tongue and throat. She pushed her dish aside, fervently hoping that no one else had noticed. But they had. Once more there were cries of 'Yuk' and 'Ugh.' She felt her cheeks flare with mortification as she heard one of the adults mutter, 'Sherry trifle! Not really appropriate for a kid's party.' 'Yes and there's so much sherry, it's inedible,' said someone else. Yet another voice, 'Well there's no sherry in mine.'

'Eh…one's a sherry trifle…for the grown-ups but…I can't remember which one. Again I meant to label them,' Anna said in a small voice and left the room.

'Sorry about that. Anna's not well – tummy bug. I told her to go and lie down but she insisted on not missing the party.' John coughed. No one said anything. 'Anyway she's made a lovely cake. I'll go and fetch it.'

It was Jess's favourite Devil's Food Cake. She blew out the candles and smiled as the guests clapped and sang Happy Birthday, but she had lost her appetite and she just wished everyone would go home. She got her wish. No one lingered after the cake was cut.

'That was terrible Dad. I can't believe Mum ruined my party. I'll have no friends at school after this.' She was near to tears again.

John leant down and put his hands on her shoulders. 'Listen Jess, I know it was awful but, first of all, let me say how strong and brave you were. A lot of children would have thrown a tantrum or gone off sulking but you behaved in a very grown-up way and I'm proud of you.' He pulled her close and held her as she wept silently.

'And don't worry about the kids at school. Anyone who's a real friend will still be there for you.'

She sniffed and wiped her nose with the back of her hand. 'Do you think Tanya will be?'

He hugged her again. 'I'm pretty sure she will. Now Jess, don't be too hard on your mum. She needs help and I need to go and talk to her. Will you be alright on your own for a while? Oh and, by the way, you'll be coming back with me tonight, okay?'

Jess was greatly relieved.

Later, John told her she was to live with him until Anna got her drinking under control and thus began an even more unsettled period in her life: her mother would return to the support group and when she had not been drinking for a few weeks, Jess would go back to stay with her but a few weeks later, sometimes less, she would lapse and she was back at John's. Eventually Anna stopped going to the group, saying she had reached a point where she could control her drinking. It didn't work; on the contrary her alcohol consumption increased.

John informed Jess that she was coming to live with him full-time. She would visit her mum of course but only if he was with her. Whereas once Anna would have been strongly opposed to this idea and returned to the group, she had reached a point where she no longer seemed to care. It appeared that alcohol was the most important thing in her life. She did however make a surprisingly sensible suggestion.

'Well John, if Jess is going to live with you permanently, I think we should do a swap.' She poured herself another drink. John frowned. 'A swap? What on earth are you talking about?'

'This house. I think you and Jess should live here and I should live at the flat. It makes sense. Jess is getting older, she'll want to have friends round, maybe to stay. This place is too big for me, not to mention the garden.'

She never touched the garden which would have reached the height of chaos by now if John had not gone round occasionally to cut the grass and do some tidying to keep the neighbours from complaining.

When she was told about Anna's suggestion, Jess burst into tears.

'That means she never wants me back.'

John tried to comfort her. 'Look love, as I've already explained, you can't keep going forwards and back. It's not good. You need a permanent home. I made that very clear to your mother and I know she was thinking of you when she made the suggestion.'

Jess was not convinced. 'If she really cared about me she would stop drinking,' she said between sobs. John explained that Anna had an illness and couldn't stop just like that. 'You know when you're sick Jess, you need help so you go to the doctor? Well your mum needs help…'

Jess interrupted. 'She doesn't care. If she did she would go back to those meetings.' John said nothing, at a loss to explain something that he didn't understand himself.

Jess visited regularly but her mother was rarely sober and she grew to hate the visits and refused to go. John put no pressure on her. Going with her to see a woman who was just about coherent at best; at worst almost comatose, he fully understood.

She grew into a troubled teenager. The vague feeling of incompleteness that had always haunted her became an overwhelming sense of having been abandoned. She longed for her mother yet couldn't bear to be near her. She did well at school and she had many friends though Tanya remained her closest friend.

For a while she sought consolation in sex, losing her virginity at fifteen and going from one unsatisfactory experience to another, building up a reputation with the boys. Tanya was worried and told her what was being said but she brushed it off.

'Why is it always two sets of rules, one for boys and one for girls? If a girl sleeps around she's called a slag. No one takes much notice if it's a boy, in fact boys can boast about it as much as they like and their mates think they're great. I'm enjoying myself and I'm not doing anyone any harm.'

She cringed at her lie. There was no real enjoyment in what she was doing; she knew she was searching for something she was unlikely to find amongst the boys at Lowhill Comprehensive.

Jess was frantic because her period was late. She confided in Tanya. 'If I'm pregnant I'll have to have an abortion. I couldn't possibly tell my dad.' They were drinking coke in Jess's kitchen.

'Stop worrying Jess, you're only a few days late.'

'I know but I'm always so regular and I need to have a plan, just in case. Do you think I can have an abortion without my dad finding out?' Unthinkingly she twirled her coke bottle round and round until Tanya leaned over and caught her hand. 'Stop it Jess, you're making me feel dizzy. You'd have to go private…I think…you are only sixteen.'

Jess rolled her eyes. 'Private? How much would that cost?'

Tanya shrugged. 'How should I know? You'd have to make enquiries. But just remember one thing – Linda Carr.'

They sat in morose silence as they remembered their classmate who'd been off school for weeks amidst rumours that she'd had an abortion. When she returned, her personality had changed from cheerful and out-going to introverted and fearful.

Finally Jess said, 'Well that was her. I wouldn't react like that.'

'You don't know how you'd react until it happened.' Tanya laid a hand on her arm. 'Anyway why don't you do a test, it might put your mind at rest.'

'Yeah. Or confirm that I'm definitely preggers! I couldn't bear to watch how it was going to turn out.'

'Well, as I said it's early days. Try not to worry about it.'

Jess banged the bottle down on the table. 'Don't worry, don't worry, is that all you can say? It would be a different story if you thought you were pregnant. But then it wouldn't be you would it? Bloody Virgin Mary, never slept with a boy.'

Tanya was unfazed. 'Well at least I'm not worrying about the cost of abortions,' she said as she got up. 'I'm going home Jess. If you are pregnant, then I'll help you all I can. See you later.'

Jess's agitation grew. How would she find out about private abortions? There was no way she could ask their doctor for advice and there was no one else she could ask. She perused the Yellow Pages for Private Clinics and rang to ask how much an abortion would cost. Staggered by the answer, she told herself it didn't matter, she had no money anyway. She remembered there was always a lot of money lying around at her mum's place. Maybe she should go and visit again. The state Anna was usually in, she probably wouldn't miss it. She made up her mind to go the following day.

Fate however intervened. In the morning she awoke with pain in her lower abdomen and uncomfortably damp pyjama bottoms. Could it be? She leapt out of bed and ran to the bathroom. Yes! Yes! Yes! This was no *curse*; it was a miracle. Dancing along the landing singing *I will survive,* she almost bumped into John, coming out of his room. 'Well you're in a good mood this morning.'

She hugged him, 'Yes Dad, isn't life wonderful?' And danced off, leaving a very perplexed parent.

She apologised to Tanya. 'You were right, I did jump to conclusions and panic. And I'm sorry for what I called you. You're right about that as well. In future I'm going to be like you and save myself for *the right man.*' They broke into a fit of giggles. When she had started sleeping around, Tanya had said primly, 'I'm saving myself for the right man' and Jess had said mockingly, 'You mean Bobby Wright?' and they had cruelly laughed hysterically at the thought of their skinny classmate with his acned skin and thick glasses.

—m—

In the autumn of 1989, Jess was due to start university and she went to say goodbye to her mum. She rang the bell and not expecting a reply, looked through the window of the ground floor flat. Anna was as usual sitting, glass in hand. Jess banged on the glass and held up her key. Anna jumped then beckoned to her to come in.

'Well this is a surprise. What's brought this on?'

'I'm going away next week to uni in Liverpool and I just came to say goodbye.'

'Uni? I presume you mean university.' In spite of her slurred speech, Anna still managed to sound pedantic. 'I really hate the way everything is debased these days.'

Jess kept her retort: *So we should still be talking about perambulators and pianofortes?* to herself.

'Anyway,' Anna continued, 'what are you going to study?'

'Art Mum, fine art.'

'Well you always did love your art. Ever since you were a little girl, always drawing and painting,' she paused, looking thoughtful, 'must run in the family.'

Jess was puzzled. 'Really? I didn't know that. Were you good at art at school? Or was it Dad?'

Anna laughed. 'I don't know why I said that. It must be this stuff talking.' She held up her glass and scrutinised it. 'Well I wasn't bad I suppose. I just never pursued it.'

'Is it all right if I make a coffee Mum?'

'Of course – if there is any'

'How about you? A coffee or tea?'

'Oh no, I'll just stick with this.' She replenished her glass.

Opening the kitchen cupboards, Jess found they were almost bare. There was less than a quarter jar of coffee and it had solidified to a sticky mass so she made herself a cup of tea with one of about half a dozen tea bags. There was no milk, no bread, a couple of tins of rice pudding, a tin of soup, half a mouldy Madeira cake, no fruit or vegetables. Flies buzzed round the overflowing bin and several bottles were lined up alongside it. The fridge was well-stocked with vodka, gin, wine and tonic.

Taking her cup of black tea back to the sitting room, she asked, 'Mum when did you last eat? You've nothing in. Tell me what you want and I'll make a list and go and do a shop.'

Anna rose and turned the television off, then slumped back on the sofa. 'I don't want to eat. There's not much I can stomach these days. When I get really hungry, I have some rice pudding or biscuits. Sometimes I manage a bit of soup. If I eat too much or eat the wrong things, I get sick.'

Jess scrutinised her mother. She was so thin now she looked haggard and much older than her forty-five years. Her hair which now had a considerable amount of grey was short and unevenly cut, as if she had been hacking at it herself. She wore navy leggings and a washed-out green T-shirt. Her feet were bare. The gas fire was on and Jess guessed the central heating was as well for the heat was unbearable.

'Mum you need to see a doctor. You're killing yourself.' Anna said 'Humph' and shrugged her shoulders, as if to say 'So what?'

Jess leaned forward and touched her knee. 'I know we've been through all this before but why won't you get help Mum?'

'I've been there, dammit all.' She clenched her fists. 'I've tried! Nothing works. And now I want to be left in peace. If I drink myself to death then so be it. Now just go and leave me alone. You'll never persuade me to change, neither you nor your father so don't waste your energy.'

In the summer of 1990 Anna was diagnosed with stomach cancer. Opportunely John had just happened to call round one day and found her sitting in a pool of vomit, vomit that had blood in it. He had no hesitation in calling her doctor. Jess was working her way round the art treasures of Europe and he was reluctant to put a dampener on her travels so she didn't find out until she came back in late August. Anna was back living at John's. She had given up drinking and was eating better in as much as her stomach would allow.

'All these years,' he said, 'I never stopped loving your mother. It was just that life with her had become impossible, even before I knew she was drinking. I tried to help her all I could but you know how it was Jess.'

She marvelled at the difference in her mother. In spite of the chemotherapy and her subsequent loss of hair, there was a renewed vibrancy in her eyes. She was eager to hear all about her course and her travels; she apologised for the lost years. Jess shook her head. 'Mum you were ill. There's no need to apologise for being ill.' But in her heart she knew there was still some resentment for a childhood, if not lost, at least curtailed.

She went through the next year of her degree with disparate feelings: delight that Anna was not drinking and that she and John had been reunited; delight that she could converse properly with her mother for the first time since she was a young child but also aggrieved about the years she had missed out on and about how Anna had been able to stop drinking now that her life was threatened but had never been able to do that for her sake or, indeed for her father's.

Then in spite of the treatment, the cancer spread. John took some time out of work to care for Anna at home and when Jess broke up for the summer, she took over. Anna died at home on the twenty-first of July. She was forty-seven years old.

What a waste of a life, Jess thought. Once more she questioned John about the possible reasons for Anna's descent into alcoholism but he offered no new explanation. Her twentieth birthday, less than four weeks after her mum's death went by in a confusion of feelings: grief, regret, guilt, resentment and a strong desire to get at the truth, which for years she'd felt was being withheld.

Chapter Three

It was on the fourth day of her holiday that she saw the house. Standing at the bedroom window with her morning tea, she found that the Farne Islands had disappeared. It was as if a giant had thrown his old, grey cloak over them and, if she hadn't already seen them, she wouldn't have believed they were there. Rain was beating on the window pane. This was definitely not a day to be out of doors and the shops were beckoning.

Waterproof-clad, she walked along the main street of the nearest town and stopped to look in an estate agent's window, curious about house prices. Now that she had given up teaching, she could, in theory at least, live anywhere she wanted. She knew she would probably not leave Manchester where her father and most of her friends were but she sometimes dreamed of a house by the sea.

Sea Music. She was charmed by the name. But there was something else: something that resonated at a deep level of her being, stirring a fragment of feeling that she couldn't quite grasp. She studied the photograph: a stone-built, two-storied house, its austere symmetry alleviated by a Virginia creeper. There was something very familiar about it but it was a typical example of early Georgian architecture; she told herself she must have seen many like it in different parts of the country. Nevertheless she had a sudden compulsion to find out more about it and the next moment she found herself in the shop asking about a viewing.

Sea Music was situated at Barrowman's Point, south of where she was staying and the following day she drove there with fifteen minutes to spare. She was due to meet Mr Winton at two-thirty. The house stood not far from the cliff edge. It was raining again and visibility was bad but on a clear day the view would be superb.

Opening the gate, she walked up the gravel path to the panelled front door with its ornate arched fan light, noticing that the date on the lintel was 1718. The interior window shutters were all closed. She wandered round the back, finding a modern extension. Here there were no shutters, but the windows had been whitened. Beyond the small walled yard, she found an orchard with an abundance of trees laden with apples and plums. She also recognised blackcurrant, raspberry and gooseberry bushes.

As she returned to the front garden Mr Winton arrived. Mid-fifties, pristine in dark suit and tie, cream silk shirt with matching handkerchief in his breast pocket, his dark hair perfectly styled; he held out his hand. 'Ah, Miss Cooper, pleased to meet you.'

Forthwith, he addressed her as Miss Cooper at all times.

'Looks like it's been empty for a while.' She surveyed again the unkempt garden and orchard.

'About six months. There's been a lot of interest, but so far, no buyer. May I be so bold as to ask if Miss Cooper is from these parts?' he queried as he unlocked the front door. She suppressed a smile at his curious turn of phrase.

'Oh no, I'm from London originally but I've lived in Manchester since I was a child. It's my first visit to Northumberland.'

The door swung open on a gloomy hall, the floor tiled in red, black and cream.

Mr Wilton opened the door on the right. A large room, dark because of the shuttered windows. Having opened these, he was at pains to point out the decorative cornice and ceiling rose, the elaborate marble fireplace. She wished he would go away and leave her alone to absorb the atmosphere of the place.

'I can just see Miss Cooper in a house like this.'

She smiled not wishing to be rude.

'Would it be all right if I have a wander round on my own? I find it difficult to get the feel of a house when someone else is with me?'

Mr Wilton gave an old fashioned bow.

'Of course. If Miss Cooper wants to have a look round on her own then that is what Miss Cooper must do. I shall go and open all the shutters, then I'll wait here.'

She stood in the centre of the room feeling a strange familiarity but, more than that, a sense of well-being. It began with a warm feeling in the region of her heart, like one might feel on hearing a well-loved voice on the phone for the first time in many years and it emanated from there to suffuse her entire being. Yet the reason for it was unfathomable. *I feel I know this place.* She stood there, reluctant to leave the room until she heard Mr Winton's footsteps on the stairs and remembered that she was supposed to be exploring the rest of the house.

Across the hall she found a similar, slightly smaller room and was pleased to find that the warm feeling remained while she was there and in the other ground floor rooms, including the large kitchen where she fancied she almost felt heat and a smell of cooking coming from its large dark blue range.

Upstairs, things changed. As she wandered from room to room, she began to have a strong sense that she was looking for someone and as the serenity ebbed, it was replaced by a growing feeling of loneliness. It reminded her of the recurrent anxiety dreams she had where she was in a house of doors and stairs, frantically searching for someone and unable to get out.

Uncomfortable now, she decided she'd seen enough and went in search of Mr Winton.

'Well what does Miss Cooper think?' Then without waiting for an answer. 'Any questions Miss Cooper wants to ask me? Oh and there's a cellar, has Miss Cooper seen it?'

'No, I ...' Feeling oppressed by the house now, she just wanted to leave. But Mr Winton was leading her back to the kitchen. 'Come Miss Cooper must see it, it's so spacious and well refurbished.'

When viewing the kitchen, she had been so overcome by the feeling of homeliness that she had failed to notice a door which the estate agent was now opening. He flicked the light switch. 'Just follow me. I think Miss Cooper will be very impressed.'

She stood at the top of the stairs looking down. Suddenly light-headed she was unable to make the move to descend. Something unpleasant was clawing at her mind, like a caged bird trying to escape, but she couldn't bring it to the fore. She sank back against the wall to steady herself as Mr Winton's voice came from below. 'You there Miss Cooper?'

'Sorry Mr Winton, I should have told you, I have a phobia about cellars,' she lied.

Jess had no idea what was going on. It was the strangest thing that had ever happened to her: an unknown house in an area she had never visited before, feeling so familiar and having such a profound effect. She didn't know what to make of it and back at the holiday home she couldn't get it out of her mind. She was hungry and knew she should start to prepare some food but the very thought of food made her feel nauseous.

Looking again at the brochure for *Sea Music* she tried and

failed to recapture the feelings she'd had there. Then, as she closed her eyes, the image of a woman's face flashed into her mind: pale and handsome, deep blue eyes, chestnut hair. A familiar face, yet no one she knew. It was gone as quickly as it had come. She closed her eyes again and again but she could not recapture it. She was becoming quite perturbed. Was this the start of some form of mental illness?

That night unsurprisingly, she had the anxiety dream: searching, searching. But this time she was calling a name. *Lydia*. She awoke in a sweat at two a.m. and lay thinking about the dream and the events of the day – she had never known anyone called Lydia – finally falling into a fitful sleep around four.

The following morning she rang her father while he was getting ready for work.

'Dad I've never been to Northumberland before, have I?'

'Eh…no…why? Is everything all right?'

'Yes…well no, not really. I've had a very strange experience.' And she recounted what had happened, including the dream. Silence. 'You still there Dad?'

'Yes, I'm just thinking about what you said. Dreams can be very weird things as you know. Are you very disturbed by it?'

Yes, I've never experienced anything like it. And that name, *Lydia* keeps going round and round in my head. Did I ever know anyone called that?'

Again the silence. Then, 'I think we need to talk Jess. You're coming back on Saturday, aren't you?'

'That was the plan yes but I don't feel I can settle here anymore and especially after what you've just said. If there's something you need to tell me then I want to know it soon, the sooner the better. I'm coming back today. Are you in this evening?'

As she drove back to Manchester, the image of the chestnut-haired women returned and, for most of the journey, floated in and out of her mind. In vain she desperately tried to grasp it and hold it there. She found it difficult to concentrate on her driving and, as she nipped into the fast lane much too close to another car, the driver made several blasts on his horn.

—⟶m—

When Jess arrived at her father's house, she noticed a bottle of brandy and two glasses on the coffee table. One of the glasses was nearly empty. As she sat down, John lifted the bottle. 'Want some?'

'That bad is it? What you're going to tell me?'

'It's not going to be easy for either of us.' He poured her a measure of the spirit. They were both cautious drinkers after their experiences with Anna. *Must be serious*, she thought as she watched John drain his glass and pour some more. He wiped a hand over his face, took a deep breath and looked straight at her, saying nothing. She looked at him enquiringly.

'You have been to Northumberland,' he spoke rapidly, 'and to that house before. *Sea Music* was your mother's family home and Lydia, the woman whose face you keep seeing was your aunt.'

Chapter Four

'My aunt?' Jess exhaled her shock and incredulity in a puff of air. 'But I thought I had no relatives apart from you and Mum.'

She swallowed some brandy, grimacing as it burned her throat. 'Why have you never told me this before?'

John drained his glass, poured another hefty measure, closed his eyes.

'Lydia died just before your seventh birthday. You had been staying with her while your mother and I went on holiday on our own – first time since before you were born. We came back a few days earlier than we'd planned because we were missing you. We picked you up and returned to London. The following day we got word of her death. It had happened on the Saturday night, a couple of hours after we left. We broke the news to you as gently as we could but you were distraught. You had always been close to Lydia and staying with her on your own for a week had brought you even closer. You were hysterical when we told you and then you developed a high fever. When you recovered from that you had no memory of Lydia or *Sea Music*.' He opened his eyes, sighed and shrugged. 'So me and your mum decided it was best to keep it that way.'

'But what happened? How did she die?'

'She fell down the cellar steps and died of head injuries.'

Feeling that she was in the middle of a nightmare, Jess finished her drink, shaking her head when John went to pour her another.

'Was she on her own at the time? Was it an accident?'

John nodded. 'Yes it was an accident. There was no sign of a break-in, nothing was stolen. The doctor thought death was probably instantaneous. She was found by a friend the following afternoon.' He leaned his head back on the armchair and closed his eyes again.

'None of this explains why I reacted to the cellar in the way I did. Surely you didn't tell me Lydia had been found there?'

'No of course not. We just said she'd had an accident. Maybe you overheard something about the cellar.'

Jess shook her head. 'Well I still have no recollection of staying in that house or of Lydia. As I said, I keep getting flashes of a woman's face and then in my dream I was calling that name.'

'You always called her Lydia, never auntie. She hated being called aunt or auntie.'

'All these years and you never said a word. I could understand when I was a young child but surely you could have told me when I got older. I asked you enough times. And it would have helped me to understand a lot of things.'

John shrugged and spread his hands.

'I...and your mother...we were really concerned when the news of Lydia's death had such a profound effect on you so we were relieved when it became clear you remembered nothing.'

Jess shook her head. 'Surely you must have known it had affected me whether I remembered or not.'

'Well yes, of course we did but we thought that not remembering would limit the damage. All I can say is we had your best interests at heart.'

She was silent while she absorbed this. 'So did you ever find out why she fell?'

'No. The cellar steps were really treacherous. They were extremely steep and they went straight down from the door in the kitchen. There was no landing. I remember commenting on them several times when I went to stay there but Anna and Lydia were used to them. They would laugh off my concerns, though they were very careful not to let you go down there on your own.

'No one knows for sure why she was going down the cellar that evening. I mean she kept a lot of things down there so she must have been up and down there all the time.' He lifted his glass again, put it down without drinking. 'I've had enough of this stuff. I'm going to make some tea, want some?' He stood up.

She nodded. 'Yes please. So who found the body?'

'Just let me go and make the tea and I'll tell you the rest when I get back.'

But she couldn't bear to wait and followed him into the kitchen. He filled the kettle and turned it on. 'It was a man called Luke Matthews. He was a close friend of Lydia's. I don't think there was anything else between them, though there probably would have been given time. Your mother certainly thought, indeed hoped there would be. We hadn't met him then but Lydia spoke very highly of him. He came to her funeral and he made a very good impression on us. It was also obvious, from the way he spoke of her, that he was very much in love with her.'

They took their tea back to the sitting room.

'Was there ever any question of it not being an accident?'

'No. Like I said, there was no sign of a break-in, or a disturbance, nothing was taken. The neighbours were questioned but no one had heard or seen anything suspicious. Well you've seen the position of *Sea Music* Jess. There are no really near neighbours. And Lydia was very popular. She didn't appear to have any enemies. Luke Matthews was questioned by the police but he was on a cycling holiday in Northern Europe and didn't get the ferry back till the day after she died.'

John stretched and yawned. 'Well I'm off to bed. I feel drained. All this has raked up such a lot of emotional stuff. You are staying here tonight aren't you? I think you may be a bit over the limit for driving.'

'Yes of course I'm staying and I'll turn in soon. Goodnight Dad.'

He put his arms round her. 'I hope you'll be able to sleep after tonight's revelations. I wish now I'd told you all this years ago.'

Jess felt weary but her mind was alert and she sat there going over and over what she had been told. She knew now why her mother had taken solace in alcohol. What a terrible loss she had endured and in those circumstances and to have had the added worry of her daughter's illness immediately afterwards; it must have been intolerable for her.

But there were more shocks to come. John and Jess met up again the following evening and he told her that Lydia had had a relationship with a man called Dave Collier and that a terrible tragedy had befallen them.

'Their son Simon was abducted from his pram when he was eight weeks old.'

'Oh my God Dad! That's dreadful!' Jess gasped and put her hand to her mouth.

'Poor Lydia, what a very tragic life. But what about the baby's father – Dave, did you say? What happened to him?'

'Well they split up before Simon was taken but Dave was involved with his son and after the abduction he was a real tower of strength to Lydia even though he was grieving just as much. Eventually they parted again and Lydia went off to *Sea Music*.'

'So how old was Lydia when she died?'

'She'd just turned thirty-one.'

'Dad, I'd love to see some photographs of her. I presume you have some.'

John looked uncomfortable. 'Of course I have but do you think it's a good idea, dredging up the past? Maybe things would be best left as they are.'

'Dad! What a strange thing to say. The past has already been brought up for me by my visit to *Sea Music* and I won't rest now until I fully recover my memory. As you know I've always been aware of something missing in my life.'

'Okay, okay.' John left the room and returned with a cardboard box which he laid on the floor and began removing photographs, some in albums, some loose. He spread them out on the coffee table.

'Your mum and I always made sure we kept these well hidden from you.'

Jess began to peruse the photos: garden scenes – Lydia lifting her from a paddling pool – walks in the park, feeding ducks, swings, slides, birthdays, Christmas, seaside scenes. The early ones were in black and white, later colour took over. She scrutinised her aunt's face. Yes it was the face that had been coming into her mind since her visit to *Sea Music*, so familiar, yet impersonal, like a hackneyed portrait – the Mona Lisa, the Laughing Cavalier. Certainly she was an attractive woman with her glossy, shoulder-length chestnut hair and her deep blue eyes. She could see the resemblance to herself and to Anna, though the colouring was different. She turned to John.

'What did Lydia do for a living?'

He put down the photograph he was holding. 'She was an artist, same as you. And like you, she gave up her teaching job to go freelance…'

'Oh,' she interrupted, 'that's amazing! What sort of artist was she?'

'She did a bit of everything but when she branched out on her own, she illustrated some children's books. One of them was a best-seller, *Tom and the Pterodactyl*.'

Something came back to her then. 'You know, when I went round to tell Mum that I was going away to study art, she said something that I didn't understand at the time, something about art running in the family. So it was Lydia she was referring to?' John nodded.

'What happened to her work?'

'Most of it's here, in the attic, including copies of the books. I'll get them down sometime…that's if you want to see them.' He hesitated, gave her a searching look.

She nodded, excited at the prospect. 'Oh yes, I'd love to.'

In some of the pictures a tall, athletic-looking man with dark hair and a raffish smile had his arm round Lydia; in some he was playing with Jess. She turned one of the images to John.

'I guess that's Dave. There is something familiar about him. Did I have much to do with him?'

'Well yes you would have seen quite a bit of him. You were less than three when he and Lydia separated but he'd been part of the family before that. And then, as I said, he was around again after Simon's abduction. Dave certainly had his faults but I'll never forget how supportive he was to Lydia after Simon was taken. I think she'd have gone under without him. He didn't come to her funeral but he sent us a lovely letter – I still have it somewhere – he sounded desperately upset. Let me see…um… you'd have been about four and a half when he was finally out of the picture.'

She moved photographs taken at *Sea Music*. John picked one up. A sunny summer's day. Anna and Lydia on a garden seat with

Jess between them, he standing behind. All of them smiling and happy-looking.

'This is the last photo of us all together at *Sea Music*. It was taken by Lydia's friend Jane. We'd not long arrived for a holiday and she was about to leave after a weekend. Look there's another one here of Jane with you, Lydia and Anna, taken by me. It was the year before Lydia died.'

Her eyes pricked with tears. What harrowing experiences her family had had. It was on the tip of her tongue to ask if there were any photos of Lydia's baby, then she thought better of it. She didn't feel she could cope with those at the moment.

A thought struck her. 'Was Lydia buried or cremated Dad? Is there a grave somewhere or a memorial stone?'

'She was cremated and we thought of scattering her ashes in the sea near the house but your mother couldn't bear to part with them and she buried them in the casket in the garden in London. Then when we were moving here, she dug the casket up and we brought them with us. They're buried under one of the rose bushes. I'll show you later.'

As Jess continued to study the photographs, she began to have fragments of recall: laughter, play, beaches, stories, cuddles. Non-sequential. Evanescent.

Many things that had puzzled her over the years had begun to fall into place. She realised that the void she'd always felt was caused, not just by her loss of Lydia but also by her inability to recall anything about her aunt. She knew now why memories of her early childhood were sparse and vague.

A few nights later, over a takeaway Indian meal at Jess's, John explained why she had been home-tutored in London.

'We couldn't let you go back to school Jess. People in the neighbourhood knew about the tragedy and we were worried that one of the children would tell you. But the most difficult thing was what to do about your friend Cathy – remember Cathy?'

She nodded, 'Yes, she's one of my clearer memories.'

'Well you two had been inseparable since your first day at nursery and Cathy lived only a few doors away. We felt we couldn't keep you apart. Anyway, your mum had a serious talk with Cathy's mother who understood her concerns and agreed to explain to her that there were things you just didn't mention to you and to be vigilant when you were playing together. But we were on tenterhooks when you went to Cathy's and tried to make sure you nearly always played at ours.'

'So that was the main reason we moved to Manchester?' Jess helped herself to more rice.

'That was the only reason Jess. We wanted to get away to somewhere there'd be no chance of you finding out. And we thought a fresh start would do us all good. It just so happened that a suitable accountancy post came up in Manchester and I applied and got it.'

'A fresh start.' She felt rueful as she laid down her fork and toyed with her water glass. 'It didn't turn out quite the way you hoped, did it?'

John shook his head. 'At the time we thought we were doing the right thing in trying to protect you. But I've often thought since that it was too much for Anna moving away from her friends and the pastimes she had in London.'

Anna waved Jess off to school and returned to the kitchen where she started to wash up. It was a month since term began and, in spite of all their worries about Jess settling into school after being tutored at home for nearly a year – a new school in a new area at that – she and John were happy with the way things were going. Jess had come home on the first day eager to tell them everything that had happened, how nice her teacher was, the new friends she had made and how she'd loved her dinner. It had become apparent from the teacher's comments on her work that it had not suffered from the time she had spent being taught at home.

But Anna missed her daughter and, in particular, she missed the hours she had spent teaching her. When they'd first moved up from London, she had been so busy unpacking, cleaning and sorting rooms and cupboards, contacting utility services and the many other things that come with moving home, there hadn't been enough hours in the day. Jess's schooling had taken precedence however, everything else had to be fitted around that.

Now that everything in the house was sorted and Jess was out all day, she found that the hours dragged. She didn't even need to walk Jess to school as it was less than a quarter of a mile away and there were no major roads to cross.

Putting the last item of cutlery in the drainer, she made herself a cup of coffee and sat down to contemplate the long day ahead. She had never had this problem in London. When Jess was at school there'd always been something to do: gardening, reading, meeting friends for lunch or coffee. She'd attended a Spanish class and a sewing class where she'd found she had a flair for dressmaking and she'd begun to make clothes for herself and Jess. She knew there were probably many classes she could attend in Manchester but she had left it too late to enrol for this year, not having anticipated the emptiness she would feel when Jess was at school. The garden needed attention, she could join the local library, take up dressmaking again, but the truth was, she had no heart for any of these pursuits. The long days gave her time to dwell on the events of just over a year ago and when the housework was done she would go to her room and take out her stash of photographs: the photos that Jess must never be allowed to see, and she would pore over them, recalling happier times and weeping. She knew she was being self-indulgent. It was necessary to grieve but surely this daily routine wasn't healthy; she carried on.

She always made sure to erase signs of her tears and to put on a brave front for Jess and John. Jess took her at face value but John was not to be fooled. He sensed that underneath the bravado lay a deep sadness and ennui. Sadness was to be expected but he felt it was exacerbated by the fact that she had little to occupy herself. His once always busy and interested wife had slipped into apathy.

One evening they were watching a play on television or at least he thought they were both watching it until he looked over and saw that Anna was staring at a spot above the television – a momentary lapse in concentration? When he looked over a few moments later, she was gazing at her hands as she twisted them in her lap. Watching her covertly, he realised that her eyes were anywhere but on the television.

'You seem distracted Anna, are you not enjoying this? We can turn over if you want.'

Anna gave him a wan smile. 'No it's alright love. I'm just not in the mood for television. I can't concentrate. I'll go and make us a cup of tea.'

John said nothing but when Anna came back, he had turned the television off.

'John there was no need to turn it off.' She set the cups down. 'Would you like some biscuits?'

'No just the tea for me thanks. Anna we need to talk.'

'Oh? What about?' Her brow furrowed.

'You're not happy are you? I mean I know you have a lot to be unhappy about but this is different. Are you bored, fed up or is it something to do with me?'

Anna shifted in her chair, took a sip of tea, then put the cup down and turned towards John.

'No point in denying it I suppose. Sometimes I think you know me better than I know myself John Cooper. And no it's nothing to do with you. I am bored. It's a long day now that Jess is at school and I don't know what to do with myself. I might as well tell you, I've been going through photographs and getting upset.' Her voice broke.

John got up, sat on the arm of her chair and put his arms round her.

'Oh love, why torture yourself like that?'

'I know I shouldn't,' Anna said between sobs, 'but the truth is, over the summer I was so busy I didn't have time to dwell on things. Even before we left London I was busy, what with tutoring Jess and everything, but now, now...'

John held her close until the weeping subsided.

'Have you ever thought of going back to nursing?' he asked at last.

Anna dried the last of her tears and blew her nose.

'No, how could I do the shifts with Jess to look after? It wouldn't be possible.'

'Of course you're right. I hadn't thought it through. But what about a doctor's surgery? That would be regular hours, maybe some evenings but I would be home by then.'

'No, I don't want to go back to nursing.' She shook her head.

'Well what about a class...'

'I've left it too late to sign on for this year,' she interrupted.

'Then there's your sewing. You've not had the machine out for ages and you used to love making clothes.'

She stood up suddenly. 'The truth is John, I have no real interest in anything at the moment. But, given time, I hope that will change. Anyway Jess is on half-term the week after next and I look forward to exploring more of this area with her. After that, I'll try and make myself do something. Now let's turn on the telly again. There's a sit com starting on ITV. It might do us good to watch something funny.'

'Okay, but promise me you'll stop going over the photos and the past.'

'I promise and, not only that, I want you to put them away in the roof space so I can't get at them so easily.' She laughed then and kissed him.

Jess looked at her father who had stopped eating, pushing aside his half-full plate of Chicken Biryani.

'Not enjoying it Dad?'

'It's fine, I don't have much appetite these days. All this talk about the past. I know it's necessary but it's not easy.' He pushed his fork through the remainder of his meal, making swirling patterns.

'Shall we leave it for tonight then? Let's have a coffee and watch some telly.'

She stood up and gathered the plates, scraped the excess food into the bin and began to fill the sink with hot water.

John stood now as well. 'It's alright Jess. I'd rather talk about it now than leave it till another time. Why don't we take our coffee into the front room, continue with this?'

She squirted washing-up liquid into the water, put the plates to soak, made coffee and followed her father.

'I got the shock of my life when you and Mum split up. I'd

never heard you argue. I just thought you were really happy. I know you've always denied you knew she was drinking but I've often wondered if you were telling the truth. Surely you can tell me now?

John accepted a cup of coffee and wrapped his hands round it.

—⟋⟍—

John was seriously worried about his wife. It was a year and a half since the traumatic events of August 1978 and there was no let-up in her grieving. She'd tried to disguise her feelings but he was not to be fooled and many a night he woke to the sound of her muffled sobs. She kept the house spotless and there was always a good meal on the table and he knew these tasks were performed with love for him and Jess. But she had no real interest in anything and he wondered what she did all day, apart from the routine tasks. He urged her to see the doctor and she did, coming home with some pills which she took for a week and then discarded saying they only made her feel dull and sleepy. He suggested private counselling but she said couldn't bear the thought of talking to a complete stranger about what had happened.

Anna was always better during school holidays when Jess was at home but he knew she was just postponing her grieving to be resumed when the child was back at school. He was at a loss as to know how to help her. He secretly went to see a therapist for he felt he was slipping into depression himself. The man asked how Anna had been at the time of the event and for some time afterwards. Had she postponed her grieving? John said that she'd been grieving from the start, putting on a brave face for Jess, yes but still grieving when their daughter wasn't around.

John loved his wife but a distance was growing between them and they were rarely intimate. He suggested Marriage Guidance. Anna gave a scornful laugh.

'Marriage Guidance? Are you joking? What can they do? I still love you John. I just need time to grieve, to get over what happened and then we'll be okay, I know we will.' She put her arms round his neck. John held her.

'But maybe if you talk to them about what happened, about how you feel, they may be able to help.'

Anna pulled away. 'No John, I couldn't do that! You know how I feel about talking to strangers.' She left the room.

After much soul-searching, John decided that he had finally had enough and, on a Saturday morning in early September, he told Anna he was leaving.

'I've found a flat, only about a mile from here – two bedrooms so that Jess can come and stay. And I'll want her to stay often. I'm going to miss her so much, but we can't go on like this. It's bringing me down as well.'

Dumbstruck, Anna stared at him. Finally she found her voice. 'So that's it John, you're deserting me when I need you most. What happened to "In sickness and in health"?'

John spread his hands and shrugged. 'Anna I've tried…'

'And what do you think this is going to do to Jess? And after all she's been through? I can't believe you're being so selfish.' She slumped down on the sofa and began to cry.

'Sorry Anna but my mind is made up. I've done everything I can to get you to seek help. I still love you and if you change your mind, I'll be happy to give things another try. Now I'm going to start packing and when Jess gets back from her dancing class, I'll break the news to her.'

'Yeah go on then, break your daughter's heart as you're breaking mine!' Anna shouted after him.

—⁄⁄⁄—

John set his coffee cup down. 'I don't think Anna started drinking seriously until after I moved out. Certainly if she was drinking before that I had absolutely no idea. As I've reiterated over the years, there is no way I would have left you with her if I'd known. I had no idea until the day of your party.'

'Yes my notorious tenth birthday party,' Jess said, cringing again at the thought of it.

'Looking back on that time, I think your mother was right. It was selfish of me to walk out like that. I should have given her more time to grieve and I guess I'll always feel guilty about it but, honestly Jess, I would never in a million years have believed that she would resort to alcohol. She was always a moderate drinker.'

Anna had first found comfort in alcohol about four weeks before their first Christmas in Manchester, the day she made the Christmas cake. She had always remained true to her mother's recipe which called for whisky and she had always recoiled at the smell of that spirit but for some reason, when she'd looked at the bottles in the supermarket, she had decided to try brandy for a change. When she had removed the top and sniffed, she had been pleasantly surprised by the smell.

With the cake in the oven, she decided she would clear up, have a rest and a cup of coffee before starting on the Christmas pudding.

As she'd turned from the sink and reached for the kettle, her eye had rested on the brandy bottle. *Why not have a drop of that instead?* Anna wasn't a drinker. She and John shared a bottle of wine occasionally and she would have a sherry and a G&T or two at Christmas but that was all. Now she saw no harm in having a nip of brandy. Maybe she wouldn't even like it. Sitting at the table, she poured herself a small measure, took a sip and held it in her mouth for several seconds before swallowing to feel a delicious heat suffuse her. She remembered she should have diluted it with water but she didn't want to; she liked it as it was. *Why not have another?*

Anna opened her eyes and wondered where she was. Rubbing her stiff neck, she looked around and realised that she had fallen asleep with her head on the kitchen table. Then she saw the brandy bottle. She held it up – about half an inch left. She'd only used three tablespoons in the Christmas cake which meant she'd drunk nearly all of the quarter bottle.

She felt no remorse as she remembered the euphoric feeling it had given her. It was a one-off, no harm in that. Glancing at the clock she saw that she'd been asleep for over an hour. She'd better pull herself together. Jess would be home soon. Getting to her feet she felt groggy and her mouth was dry. The pudding could wait till the weekend when Jess could help her.

But the following day found Anna at the local off-licence, buying brandy for the pudding which she had decided, after all, to make today. Much as she had enjoyed the experience of the previous day, she had no desire to repeat it, particularly as the after effects had not been so pleasant so she had decided on a miniature, which they didn't have, so she came away with another quarter bottle.

She added a couple of tablespoons of brandy to the pudding mixture, replaced the top and set the bottle aside, finished stirring the pudding and put it on to steam. She sat down and eyed the bottle. It would do no harm surely to have a small amount, replicate yesterday's feeling of warmth and euphoria. She poured a measure, retreated to the sitting room with what was left and once again fell asleep.

With the approaching festive season, Anna had less time to dwell on past events. There were presents to be bought, cards to be sent. Jess was in a school play and, at her teacher's request, Anna got out her sewing machine and made her costumes. Seeing her seemingly happily occupied, John's anxiety lessened.

—⁓—

A January day. Mild, damp and so dark. At two in the afternoon Anna had still not turned the light off. At the best of times she had hated this time of year; now it was worse than ever. She was having another attempt at reading a library book. Those she had borrowed so far had been returned unread; she was determined to give it another go but, as usual, she was finding it hard to concentrate.

She stood up, casting the book aside. She had an overwhelming urge to look at the photos again. Going upstairs, she got the step ladder from the spare room and placing it under the hatch on the landing, she climbed up, opened the hatch and felt around for the box of photos. The roof space was not floored so things were left near the opening. Having located it, she climbed down, leaving the hatch open and the ladder in place. She would have to put the photos back before Jess returned.

Seated at the kitchen table with a cup of coffee, she lifted out an album and began to peruse it. Stopping at an image she gazed lovingly at it until she felt the tears begin. Wiping her eyes with her palms, she took a mouthful of coffee and it occurred to her that it wasn't coffee she needed but something stronger. She remembered the days of the cake and pudding making, the delicious warmth as the brandy slid down her throat. She knew there was no brandy in the house but surely something else would have the same effect. Going into the front room, she opened the sideboard: sherry, gin, a bottle of red wine, a bottle of white. She reached for the gin. There was no tonic but there was orange juice in the fridge.

The gin and orange didn't have quite the immediate effect as the neat brandy but after a couple of hefty measures, Anna began to feel the numbing sensation she so desired and she put the photograph albums back in the box. She would put them away now. Having mixed another gin, she picked up the box and, a bit unsteadily, made her way upstairs. She put the box down, looked up at the hatch and felt dizzy. Maybe she should have a lie-down first. Anna sat on her bed and drained her glass, lay down and fell asleep immediately.

That was the day when Jess first became concerned about her.

Chapter Five

In the two weeks since John's disclosure, Jess continued to have fleeting memories of Lydia but she had a great desire to remember as much as she could about the woman whose short, sad life had been pivotal to her own. John had brought some of her paintings down from the attic and, though she had been looking forward to seeing them, she now felt such overwhelming sadness that, after looking at only two or three, she dismissed the others to view at a later date.

There was a niggle at the back of her mind which would not go away. Why had she been so frightened of the cellar? Would overhearing that Lydia had been found there, cause such a strong reaction? Had something else happened in the cellar when she was staying there? She asked John if he knew of anything but he said no, Lydia had told him and Anna that Jess had enjoyed her stay and had been no bother. There was only once when she had said she was missing them but she was soon distracted.

'I think you should stop tormenting yourself about the cellar Jess. I'm pretty sure nothing happened there.'

Jess thought that if anything frightening had happened there, Lydia might not have told her parents.

She considered returning to Northumberland. She could not bear the thought of contacting the unctuous Mr Winton again but decided she could go round the outside of the house, explore the garden further and get a feel for the surrounding area.

Having packed a bag in preparation for leaving the following morning, she rang John to tell him of her plans.

'I don't know why you're pursuing this business of the cellar. As I've already told you, I don't believe anything happened there. You seemed perfectly happy when we picked you up. You were pleased to see us but you were also reluctant to leave. I think you would have liked us all to stay on for a while.'

'Well Dad, apart from the cellar, going back might help me to remember more of Lydia.'

Jess sat up abruptly at the sound of an almighty bang. Glancing at the clock, she saw that it was 3 a.m. There was a flash of bright light and, as there was another crack of thunder, she threw back the bedclothes and went to the window.

This was no dramatic storm like the one she had witnessed on holiday. There was nothing to be seen through the torrential rain but the red brick houses opposite, identical to her own, which were illuminated now and then by the sheet lightning. Nevertheless, as she went back to bed, she felt the familiar feeling of peace encompass her and, as always, she asked herself why thunderstorms had this effect on her: excitement, mingled with a sense of security, of love.

At that moment she had her first really strong memory of Lydia.

She is standing by her bedside. Her chestnut hair tousled, her eyes bleary from sleep; she is wearing a deep blue dressing gown and she is holding a sketch pad and a pencil. Thunder booms and Jess is crying.

'It's all right Jess, there's nothing to be afraid of. It's only the elements.' Lydia pulls back the covers, gets in beside her and cuddles her.

'Look I'll show you what's going on up there.' She points towards the ceiling, starts to draw: cartoon ice crystals and raindrops with facial features, stick arms and legs. They are dancing and the ice crystals are

bumping into the rain drops sending out flares of light. As she draws Lydia explains that the storm is caused by a build-up of electricity when these particles of ice and water collide. The light is the electricity. 'Remember when I was brushing my hair really fast so you could see the sparks of electricity? Well it's a bit like that only there's so much electricity it makes a really big flash of light.'

Jess squirms. 'I don't mind the light it's the noise I don't like. Sometimes it feels like the house is falling down.' She snuggles closer to her aunt as there is another clap of thunder, albeit not quite as loud. Lydia explains that the noise is caused by the explosion of electricity and that it is harmless. She goes on to explain that lightning, like all electricity can be dangerous but, viewed from a safe place it can be both beautiful and exciting. 'Light travels faster than sound so you see it first and then hear the noise. Shall we go to the window and I'll show you?' Jess is still a bit fearful as she takes Lydia's hand and together they sit watching the jagged forks run down to the dark sea. Lydia is exhilarated. 'Here's another one Jess, oh this one's amazing, truly beautiful, now count how long it is till you hear the thunder.' Lydia's enthusiasm is infectious and soon Jess is enjoying herself. They sit until the storm subsides. She feels herself grow sleepy in Lydia's arms. When she wakens, it is morning and she is back in bed.

Sitting in her bed in Manchester, she realised that she hadn't always loved thunderstorms. She had been frightened once, like so many other children – and adults. It was Lydia who had taught her to love them and who had given her a feeling of peace and security when she was most fearful. She remembered her parents' cuddles and words of reassurance at those times but no one had ever explained things the way Lydia had.

She reckoned that that storm must have happened when she stayed with Lydia just before she died. According to John, she had only stayed there once without her parents.

Gradually other events of that time began to seep into her recall.

She loves staying with Lydia. She remembers a lovely day out in a big town. Lunch in a restaurant, a visit to an art shop where Lydia lets her choose some paints and crayons, the cinema where they see Snow White.

After the film her aunt's mood has changed. As they walk into the car park, she is holding uncomfortably tightly to her hand, then she hastily bundles her into the car and closes the door, saying she'll be back in a minute. Jess is frightened. Has she done something wrong? She has never known Lydia be less than gentle.

When Lydia returns to the car, she can see that her hands are shaking. Is she ill? Lydia says she has a headache, suggests they go for chips before returning to Sea Music. Jess's worries dissipate at the very rare treat of one of her favourite foods. They go back to Sea Music and she goes to play outside.

And that was it. No further memories were forthcoming.

Jess drove to Barrowman's Point and parked the car. The day was calm, not a ripple on the sea, reflecting the blue of a sky without a cloud to intercept the sun's bright gaze. The setting was predominantly blue and green in contrast to the grey of the rainy day when Mr Winton had shown her around. But autumn was already encroaching and the Virginia creeper was beginning to give a blush to the old house. Sitting in the orchard, she absorbed the smells of earth, decaying vegetation and fruit; she walked round the front, gazed out to sea, but there were still no more memories of that week with Lydia. She needed to go inside the house again so there was nothing else for it, she would have to brave Mr Winton for another viewing.

'Mr Winton's on holiday, so Karen will show you around.' The young receptionist had no idea that she was imparting music to a potential customer's ears. She smiled. 'Two thirty tomorrow alright?'

She was back in the gloomy hall at *Sea Music*. 'Now would you like to have a wander round on your own or would you prefer me to accompany you?' Karen was tall and dark with a warm smile and they were on first name terms immediately.

As she wandered from room to room, she noticed that the feeling of well-being that had accompanied her on her previous viewing of the ground floor had been replaced by feelings of loneliness and emptiness and that, as she ascended the staircase, having decided to leave the cellar until the last, those feelings grew stronger. Since the memories had begun to return, she had a good idea which rooms had been her bedroom, Lydia's bedroom and Lydia's studio and when she stood in these rooms, she was disappointed at being unable to capture any further recollections. Once more the anxiety of searching and the frustration and fear that resulted from not finding, were strong.

Returning to the kitchen with a sense of trepidation, she opened the cellar door and turned on the light. In the refurbishment, the steep steps had been replaced by safer, more gradual ones. She stood looking down feeling none of the sense of alarm she had felt on her first visit, descended and looked around again feeling nothing. But far from reassuring her, this left her more curious than ever about her previous feeling of dread.

'Are you alright Jess?' Karen's voice came from the kitchen. 'Any questions you would like to ask? Or shall I leave you alone for another while?'

Might as well go, she thought. *I could stay here all day and still remember nothing.* 'Just coming.'

After exploration of the beach where, John had told her, she had spent many happy hours with him, Anna and Lydia and where, no doubt, she had also had happy times with Lydia on that last visit, she drove back to Manchester. She would stop trying so hard to remember and get on with her life. Perhaps, if she stopped trying the past would emerge when the time was right.

Part Two

Chapter Six

1975

Lydia Allan smiled as she put the phone down. Whatever Dave Collier had done to her, he was proving to be an excellent father. When he was at home, he rang on the days he wasn't seeing Simon and, currently on a walking holiday in Cumbria, he rang every day to enquire about him and to say how much he missed him. As she lifted her sleeping son and put him in his pram, she thought she just might increase the amount of time she let Dave spend with him.

After several days of cold, blustery weather, the wind had dropped, the sun shone and, as Lydia wheeled Simon through the park, vibrant with daffodils and crocuses, she was in a buoyant mood. Reaching the High Road, she headed for the greengrocer's, unaware that she was being tailed by a woman.

Parking the pram beside two others, she put on the brake and peeped at her son, still sound asleep, arms above his head, tiny hands curled. Sometimes the love and gratitude she felt for this child was overwhelming and she wanted to lift him up and take him into the shop with her. But that wasn't practical and reluctantly she turned away.

As she entered the shop, the woman followed. Lydia began to browse the vegetables while her stalker noted with satisfaction that there was a long queue. *She won't be out of here in a hurry. It's now or never.*

Leaving the shop, she undid the brake and, walking briskly, wheeled Lydia's pram round the corner on to a deserted demolition site. Lifting the baby from the pram, she put him in a car and sped away.

Approaching the M1, the driver stopped briefly to pull off dark glasses, a blonde wig, green raincoat and floral scarf; to remove false number plates. Glancing at the baby, still asleep on the back seat, Dave Collier laughed out loud. *I've done it! I've finally done it!*

Minnie Collier looked out at the darkening sweep of the North Yorkshire Moors where the steadily moaning wind had risen to a howl, dramatic dark clouds loomed and large drops of rain had just begun to bespatter the window pane. She stood for a few minutes absorbed; she had lived here for most of her life but she never tired of the ever-changing weather patterns. Then she drew the curtains, turned on the television and had just settled in her armchair before a roaring fire when she heard a car draw up. Her heart began to thump; she rarely had unannounced visitors and never at this time of the evening. Parting the curtains, she saw a man lift a bundle out of the car, then turn towards the house. Dave! And the bundle looked like a baby. No, surely she was seeing things. Mystified, she opened the front door before he had a chance to knock.

'Dave, what are you doing here? And is that a baby? What's going on?'

'Well Mam, let's see to this little chappie first. He needs changing and he hasn't had a proper feed.'

Dave thrust the baby into Minnie's arms before returning to the car to pick up several bags. Minnie turned off the television and while Dave changed the baby, she set about making up a feed with the formula milk he had brought.

Soon Simon, in Minnie's arms, was sucking hungrily on his bottle. Dave smiled. 'He was ready for that. He had his last bottle propped up on a cushion on the back seat; the milk was cold and he fell asleep before he'd finished it.' He leaned across, resting his hand on Minnie's shoulder.

'Well Mam, let me tell you, it's been one of the most nerve-racking days of my life, and also one of the best, but before I tell you about it, I think it's time for a big hug. His nibs there has been the centre of attention so far.'

He rose and kneeling by his mother's chair, enfolded her in his arms, giving her a kiss on the cheek. He then proceeded to tell her the version of events he wanted her to believe: he had wanted a baby for some time, but his girlfriend Lydia had never wanted children so when she got pregnant, she decided to have an abortion. By this time they were on the verge of splitting up and he assured her that, when the baby was born, he would be happy to bring it up. She had agreed but had later changed her mind, said she wanted the child after all and she didn't want him to have anything to do with it.

'I couldn't believe it Mam. I'd bought all the baby clothes, pram and cot. I'd hired a child minder for when I was working. I tried to persuade her to reconsider, or to have me back so we could bring up the child together. I still loved her Mam. But she was having none of it. Didn't want me in on the act at all. Then she announced I could have a couple of hours a week with Simon. Well I thought, you bitch – excuse the language Mam – if you think I'm going to agree to two hours a week with my son. I was livid, as you can imagine, but then I decided to change tack. Play your cards right Dave, I said to myself, stop hassling Lydia, be the perfect father and things might just go your way. But it didn't make any difference.'

Minnie looked at him through narrowed eyes.

'So this is why you rang to offer a reconciliation with me, why you came to see me a few weeks ago. I might have known there'd be a devious plan behind it.'

'No Mam, honest. I'd wanted things to be all right between me and you for some time but I was nervous about ringing you. After all I was the one who caused the rift.'

'Well why didn't you tell me I was going to be a grandma Dave? You know how I feel about my two grandchildren being so far away, in America. I'd have been delighted to have a grandchild in London, still a long journey, but not impossible.'

Dave leaned forward and patted her on the knee.

'Sorry about that Mam but you and me, well we weren't speaking when it happened and even if we had been, as I said, first of all Lydia was set on an abortion and even when I persuaded her to let me bring the child up, I had a feeling she might change her mind and not want me around. I wouldn't have wanted to get your hopes up for nothing.'

'And Simon's eight weeks, you say. Why did you leave it this long to do what you've done?'

'I kept hoping she'd change and let me have more time with him, even take me back, but no way. Then I had to plan things so that neither Lydia nor anyone else would suspect me.'

Minnie continued to listen to his tale, but she was sceptical. Yes some of it would be true, but she was sure he was changing things to put himself in the right and she was still convinced he had made his peace with her so that he could use her in his unscrupulous plan. But, in spite of everything she loved him and she was delighted by their reunion after her years of grieving for him. She felt a pang for the mother also grieving for her lost child, but as she lifted her grandson against her shoulder to wind him, stroked his soft cheek and smelt his distinctive baby smell, she knew she had bonded with this child and, despite her fears and misgivings, she would comply with anything Dave asked of her; she would not let anything or anyone take him away from her.

Dave had brought everything she would need for the child, except a pram.

'You won't need a pram yet. Simon needs to be kept in for a few months and then, when the hue and cry has died down, I'll think up some story for anyone who may be interested.'

'What about the shopping Dave?'

'Don't worry, I intend coming up most weekends and I'll bring whatever you need for Simon. You can do your shopping on Saturday as usual and if you want to see friends here, I'll take Simon out for a drive. Oh, and by the way, we can't keep calling him Simon. He'll be getting a new birth certificate and we must change his name.'

Minnie's mouth fell open and her eyes widened.

'What do you mean, a new birth certificate? How can you get that?'

Dave tapped the side of his nose and winked. 'Don't worry Mam.' He hugged her, 'You sure you want to do this?'

'Oh yes. I couldn't bear it if anyone took my grandchild away, but I'm worried sick about you. You will be careful Dave?'

He laughed. 'No need to worry Mam, no one's going to catch Dave Collier.'

Same old Dave, she thought, *cocky as ever.*

Minnie wanted to call the child George after Dave's late father, but Dave said he'd been thinking about names on the way there and had come up with Alexander. 'It's a good, strong, manly name. We can call him Alex for short.'

And so Simon Edward became Alexander David George.

—ɯ—

After her initial hysteria, followed by twenty-four hours of sedation, Lydia awoke to the renewed awareness that her child was gone. She was in part hopeful that the police would find him but she also had a terrible fear that she would never see him again. The tears came once more, quietly now and she thought they would never stop but she refused further sedation.

Dave came to visit, seemingly as distraught as she was. He held her hand.

'I came as soon as I could love. I phoned you yesterday morning as usual and when I got no reply I tried again in the afternoon and then the evening. I was getting really worried so I phoned Anna and John and they broke the news to me. They had been trying to get a message to me but as you know, I wasn't staying in one place...' His voice faltered. 'I can't believe this has happened.'

'Oh Dave I'm so sorry, it's all my fault. I should never have left him outside the shop.'

'Now Lydia, the last thing you must do is blame yourself. What else could you have done? You could hardly have taken a big pram into a small shop like that. Everybody does it. I'll bet it wasn't the only pram parked there.'

'No but that doesn't make it right...' she broke off and began to cry again, holding her face in her hands.

Dave put his arms round her.

'We must be positive love. I'm quite confident the police will find Simon. These cases are often quickly resolved. It'll more than likely be some woman who's lost a baby recently. A few enquiries at doctors' surgeries and hospitals and they'll soon track her down.'

Lydia reached for a tissue and blew her nose, then she leaned back and closed her eyes.

'I'll let you get some rest now Lydia. I'll come back later on, if that's okay.' He kissed her cheek.

Lydia came out of hospital to a house, full of reminders of her son. Her sister Anna wanted her to come and stay for a while with her and John, but she refused knowing that that would only postpone the moment when she had to face up to getting on with her everyday life, without her child. The police had no real leads. There were the usual timewasters, but no reliable eye witnesses.

For more than a week before Simon's disappearance, Lydia had been gradually weaning him off the breast. Now, her breasts were distended and painful and, in spite of being prescribed a milk suppressant, she developed a throbbing abscess which she had to have lanced. She was almost glad to have this physical pain as a distraction from the mental agony which was infinitely worse.

As the days went on and the police brought no news, Lydia felt intense anger: anger with Dave for being away enjoying himself when his son was taken, anger with the police for their failure to find Simon, anger with the abductor, but mostly anger with herself for being so careless as to leave her precious baby unattended on the busy High Road. She slept little and when she did, Simon was there to haunt her, never crying, always happy, smiling and gurgling as she bathed him, dressed him, fed him, played with him. Then she would awaken once more to the dreadful realisation of her loss.

Dave called frequently and sometimes she vented her anger on him and sent him away. Then she would be remorseful, for he looked wretched and she told herself he must be grieving as much as she was. She would call him then and apologise. He was never angry with her, but was an endless source of support.

Bless him, she thought in her better moments, *I wish I could support him the way he's supporting me.* She remembered how she'd once been so much in love with him, had thought him the most extraordinary man and how good their relationship had been for a time.

Chapter Seven

1973

Lydia walked into the room to the sound of Stevie Wonder proclaiming *You are the sunshine of my life*. Through a fog of cigarette smoke, she could see people dancing, standing around chatting, couples embracing on large floor cushions, though the night was yet young. She threaded her way to the kitchen and put her bottle of red wine on the worktop with the other bottles of wine, beer and spirits, poured herself a glass, then stood wishing that she could disappear. It had been a mistake to come. Jane, the hostess and the only person she knew here, was nowhere to be seen. Normally, she'd just get on with it, have a few drinks, strike up a conversation with whoever was nearby, join in the dancing, but it had been a harrowing year: her mother Kate had died from cancer. At just fifty-eight, she'd been vibrant and seemingly healthy until tiredness had taken its toll and her illness was diagnosed just three months before her death in August.

Lydia had been given compassionate leave from her job as an art teacher to look after her and had succeeded in keeping her at home in accordance with Kate's wishes. Anna did what she could but with a toddler to look after, that didn't amount to much more than making the occasional visit.

Lydia had returned to her job in the autumn term, but her enthusiasm had waned, she wasn't sleeping, she felt tired and low all the time and was reluctant to join in the social events that she had once loved. If it hadn't been a special birthday for Jane – her thirtieth – she would have refused the invitation.

Pouring herself a second glass of wine, she realised she was already feeling a bit tipsy, for she hadn't eaten. She had little appetite these days and as others helped themselves to the party food, she had no interest in it. *I must slow down, force myself to eat something.* Putting down her glass, she turned towards the food and bumped into a man. 'Sorry,' she started, then gasped in dismay as the contents of his beer glass went all over the front of her new pale blue mini dress.

'Oh I am so sorry…'

'It's all right, it was an accident.' But she was near to tears.

'No, it's not all right. It was stupid and clumsy of me, but I will pay to have the dress cleaned, I promise…'

Lydia rushed from the room and nearly had another collision, with Jane. 'Lydia. What's the matter?'

'Sorry Jane, I need to get out of here. I shouldn't have come.'

Outside, she hailed a taxi, sat back and took slow, deep breaths to ease her panic. *I can't go on like this, what must Jane think of me? And that man? Whoever he was. I'll make an appointment at the doctor's first thing on Monday.*

'Hello, Lydia? How are you today? I've been worried about you.'

'Oh hi Jane. I'm so sorry about last night. I never even wished you a happy birthday. I did leave your present though, on the hall table.'

'Yes, I got it. Thanks so much. What gorgeous earrings. But how are you?'

'Well, as you know I've not been feeling good for some time. It was a mistake to go to the party. I'm no good in crowds anymore and when I bumped into that man and he spilled his drink and ruined my dress... well, it was the last straw and I had to get out. Sorry again, but I'm making an appointment at the doctor's tomorrow. I think I'm on the verge of a nervous breakdown.'

'I suppose it won't do any harm to have a chat with the doctor. Anyway, *that man* is called Dave Collier and he's one of the nicest men I've ever met – courteous, caring, funny. He's very contrite about your dress and he wants me to ask you if he can get it cleaned for you or buy you another. Am I allowed to give him your phone number?'

'God no. I couldn't do with a complete stranger ringing me up and as for the dress, I loved it, but it was cheap – C&A's bargain basement.'

Jane laughed. 'Well it's your loss. He really is a lovely man and...'

'I believe you, now can we change the subject?'

—⁂—

'Do you mind if I join you?' It was almost two weeks later and Lydia was drinking coffee in a café on the High Road. Her doctor had put her on a course of tranquillisers and she was feeling more relaxed. She looked up at the man – quite tall, athletic-looking, longish, dark, wavy hair, pale blue eyes, thin face, not what she would consider handsome – but before she had time to reply, he continued, 'Jane's party? The other week? I ruined your dress.' As recognition dawned, she motioned him to sit down.

Several coffees later, Lydia had to agree with Jane's opinion of him and she heard herself accepting an invitation to the theatre.

Over the next few weeks, Lydia's life changed considerably and for the better. By Christmas, Dave had moved in to her terraced house in south London, though he had kept on his flat, saying he needed his own space every now and again. Lydia accepted this as something he needed to do and in truth, she was sometimes glad to have a bit of time to herself as well. She thought it made for a healthy relationship, not to be falling over one another all the time. She had thrown away her medication and Anna was shocked.

'Don't you think it was a bit premature to throw away the pills? And it could be dangerous. You're supposed to wean yourself off them gradually under your doctor's supervision.'

It was after dinner on Christmas Day. Dave and Lydia were spending the day with Anna and John. The men were in the kitchen doing the washing-up and Anna and Lydia were playing with two-year-old Jessica.

'Oh don't fuss Anna. I know when I'm better. Dave's the best thing that's ever happened to me and I'll be eternally grateful to Jane for inviting me to that party, even though I loathed it at the time.'

Anna said nothing. She knew of old that arguing with her sister would only put her back up and she was pleased that she was so happy with Dave. In many ways he seemed ideal, but she had misgivings about him though she couldn't put her finger on the reason for them.

'Dave, I think I might be pregnant.'

Dave looked up from his newspaper. 'Say that again, I think I'm hearing things.'

'I said I think I might be pregnant.'

Bloody hell, that's all I need – a screaming brat keeping me up at night, curbing my freedom. She's on the pill as well. I thought we were safe.

He forced a smile to spread across his face. 'That's great news. When will you know for sure?'

'Well I missed last month's period and this one's late. If it doesn't arrive I'll be seeing the doctor.'

Dave crossed the room and took her in his arms.

'Oh Lydia, I'll be so disappointed if you're not. I know we've not discussed children, but it's what I've wanted since meeting you.' He held her at arm's length frowning, 'You do feel the same?'

'Oh yes Dave. Before we met, I'd not even thought about children, but now, more than anything, I want this to be so.' She put her head on his shoulder and he stroked her hair.

Dave needed time to think this through. His fondness for Lydia was something he had never felt for any other women. He enjoyed coming home to her and they were good together. She was easy-going and undemanding and he knew that not many women would accept without a murmur that he needed to keep on his flat and have some time on his own there every now and again. He didn't want the responsibility of a child and he wanted no restrictions on his lifestyle, but he did want Lydia and it was obvious that she was delighted at the prospect of a child. Well it wasn't confirmed yet and he could only hope that she was wrong.

He was therefore, extremely surprised at his reaction when Lydia came back from the doctor and told him that their baby was due in January: pride mingled with a sense of achievement and narcissism. He Dave Collier had created another human being, an extension of himself, a legacy. He would live on in this child. He fervently hoped it would be a boy.

A few weeks later, Dave went to spend a night at his flat. Some of his business colleagues were coming round for a meeting and they would have a few drinks and make an evening of it, he said.

The following morning, as Lydia was leaving for work, she couldn't find her car keys. After searching high and low, she decided to ring Dave to see if he'd taken them by mistake. He never went to work before she did. To her surprise, the phone was answered by a woman. *Wrong number.* She muttered an apology, put the phone down and redialled carefully. The same voice answered. Lydia repeated the number in a query.

'That's right,' said the voice.

'And who am I speaking to?'

Dave came on the line. 'Hello?'

'Dave, it's me, Lydia, who was that?'

'Oh, eh, just the cleaner. What's up Lydia?'

She explained about the keys, then, 'I didn't know you had a cleaner.'

'I didn't think it was important enough to mention it to you and no I don't have your keys.'

Lydia felt very uneasy. On searching again, she found her keys down the side of the sofa, but her misgivings about the woman would not go away.

When Dave came home, he asked if she'd found her keys; neither of them mentioned the woman, but Lydia's suspicions would not dissipate.

She found herself doing things that were out of character: searching Dave's pockets, looking through papers in his desk. She found nothing, but the next time he said he wanted to spend time at the flat, she went round there half an hour before he was due home from work and parked in a side street where she had a view of the front entrance. An hour went by, then two. *What am I doing here? A pregnant woman sitting in a side street, waiting for someone who might be in there already, or who might not turn up for hours. I'm hungry and I'm tired and I must be mad. I'm going home.*

She had just started the engine when she saw Dave's car slow down at the barrier to the car park and there was no mistaking a woman by his side. Lydia tried to be calm. It could be perfectly innocent. The woman could be a secretary or something else to do with work. She could indeed be the cleaner. She would wait and test the water before coming to any mad conclusions. But she tossed and turned all night, finally dropping off at around five a.m.

'Lydia, I'm home. Where are you darling? Come here and give me a cuddle.'

She went easily into his arms. 'Did you have a nice time at the flat? Or was it mostly work?'

'Oh no, not this time. I had the place to myself entirely. Didn't see another soul the whole time, not even the cleaner. Bliss.'

Lydia was unsure how to react. Her first instinct was to blurt out her fears, but she was cautious by nature and above all, she wanted to trust Dave. Besides, maybe the woman lived in the flats and he was giving her a lift. She decided to say nothing for now, but she had to know.

Dave had never given her a key to his apartment. He'd made it very clear that it was his domain and Lydia had been tolerant of this. Now she needed proof that there was nothing going on and she longed to go round there and do some detective work. She tried to think of an excuse, but she knew it was futile. It was Dave's territory and that was that.

Her opportunity came unexpectedly on a Saturday afternoon about a month later when Dave announced that he was taking up running. This was no surprise to her: he was fanatical about his fitness and swam and worked out at the gym most days.

'Bye love, see you later, probably about an hour.'

'Okay, don't overdo it on your first run.'

'I'll be fine, fit as a fiddle.'

Lydia was both excited and anxious. She could see that Dave had left his keys on the desk. Going to the window, she watched him jog down the road, then she reached for the keys and headed for the key cutters, on the High Road.

Apprehensively, Lydia turned the key in the lock. She had chosen her time carefully: a Sunday afternoon. Dave was away on a business trip, not due back until Monday evening. There was unlikely to be a cleaner around on a Sunday.

The door opened directly into the living room, bright in the July sunshine, which streamed through a French window, leading to a balcony. Beyond the room was a small kitchen. Everywhere was tidy and spotless. The cleaner, whoever she was, did a good job.

Lydia scanned the main bedroom, but it was on the bathroom shelves that she found the first clues to a female presence: a jar of expensive night cream, alongside a couple of bottles of perfume. In the cabinet she found a box of tampons. She felt weak suddenly, but continued her search for further proof and found condoms in a bedside cupboard. She removed an envelope addressed to Dave, which she opened and began to read.

As Dave drove home on Monday evening, he felt pleased with himself. He had as usual combined a very successful business trip with pleasure. He hadn't taken Pattie with him this time and had picked up a young thing called Suzie in a bar. Pattie was getting far too possessive of late, didn't like it when he saw other women. Who did she think she was? She meant no more to him than any of the others did and he was looking forward to telling her soon that their brief liaison was over. He was also looking forward to getting home to Lydia. Now there was a woman who wasn't at all possessive; not many women would let him have his own space in his flat whenever he wanted, though he was careful not to make that too often. He pictured Lydia now with her straight, shoulder length, chestnut hair, her large deep blue eyes; sexier than ever now as she glowed in her pregnancy, her bump just beginning to show.

Dave turned his key in the lock, 'I'm home my love, come and give Davey a kiss, I've missed you.'

Lydia came into the hall, but she didn't approach him, just stood by the living room door.

'What's up love, you alright?' Then he noticed several cases in the hallway and his mood plummeted. Something was terribly wrong. He looked enquiringly at Lydia.

'I want you out of here Dave, as of now.' Her tone was calm, her face expressionless.

'What? What the heck are you on about?'

'I'll tell you what I'm on about Dave – your other woman, women even. I've been round to your flat and seen the evidence for myself – perfume, tampons, condoms – need I go on?'

Dave felt like he'd been kicked in the solar plexus and all he could mutter was, 'But how? How did you get in?'

'Never mind how Dave, I've got nothing more to say to you. Just take your bags and go. Now.'

Dave thought quickly. 'Lydia, those things have been there since my last girlfriend, before I met you…'

'Oh yeah? And this too I suppose? She proffered the letter. Dave didn't need to read it; he recognised Pattie's writing and knew exactly what it said. It was dated a week ago.

My darling Dave,

I've been trying to ring you, but you're never there. I'm sorry you have to go away this weekend and disappointed that you are not taking me with you.

The last time we went away was wonderful, and as for the other night! I still think about it!

I hope we can meet again soon and I promise you it will be better than ever!

Lots of love,

Pattie

Dave's mood changed. He knew this was something he wouldn't be able to explain away and defeated, he felt his hackles rise.

'You bitch. How dare you break into my flat and go through my things…'

'I didn't break in, I had a key cut…'

'You what?' Red-faced, Dave started towards Lydia, put his hands on her shoulders and began to shake her.

'How did you get your hands on my keys?'

'You're hurting me Dave, stop it and I'll tell you.'

Dave gave a final shake and let his arms fall to his sides.

'You left your keys when you went running.'

'But what made you want to go round there?'

'Never mind that now Dave, I just want you out of here. Now go or I'll call the police.'

Dave began to pick up the cases and put them outside, turning as he left.

'You haven't heard the last of this Lydia, remember you're carrying my child and you can't just cut me off like this…'

Lydia hurriedly shut the door.

Dave lit a cigarette and poured himself a large whisky, downed it in one and poured another. He paced up and down the living room. *Women! Fucking bitches all of them. I would never have thought it of Lydia. The audacity of the woman. Actually getting a key cut and coming round here to snoop. And as for that other whore Pattie. Writing to me like that, how dare she? Well that's it. From now on it's one-night stands only, I'll never trust the slags again.*

Draining his glass, he threw it across the room, then instantly regretted his action as the glass hit the wall and tiny shards cascaded over the carpet. At that moment he wished he really did have a cleaner.

Chapter Eight

As Lydia said goodbye to her colleagues and got into her car, she breathed a sigh of relief. It was the last day of term and her last day of teaching. Her dissatisfaction with her job since returning there the previous September had led to her taking the plunge and not just going for maternity leave, but resigning her post. She was determined to pursue a career as a freelance artist and that was something she could do at home, even while bringing up a child. She wasn't wealthy but her mother had left her and Anna comfortably off and they now owned *Sea Music,* the family home on the Northumberland coast. They had decided not to sell their old and much loved home but to keep it for holidays.

It was a couple of weeks since she'd thrown Dave out and she still felt a mixture of seething anger, worthlessness, *what have I done to cause him to stray?* And intense emptiness. But she'd never for a moment regretted her decision.

Now, however, she couldn't bear the thought of returning to her empty house and she turned the car in the direction of Anna's, hoping she was at home.

Anna was making the most of the sunshine, doing a bit of gardening while Jess splashed about in a paddling pool.

'Hi there, what a nice surprise. Cup of tea?'

'Cold drink if you have one.' Lydia kissed her sister and went over to the pool where Jess squealed with excitement at the sight of her aunt. Anna went indoors and returned with a glass of homemade lemonade.

'So how was your last day at work?'

'It was lovely. They knew I didn't want a big send-off, but they all brought in food to share at lunchtime and I got loads of cards and presents from the kids as well as my colleagues. I'll show them to you later; they're in the car.' She sighed. 'It's going to take some getting used to, even though it's what I want. I won't miss teaching, but I will miss the staff and many of the students.'

'And how are you keeping?'

'Physically, I feel fine. No nausea for four days, touch wood,' she tapped the side of her chair, 'but I'm very cut up about what's happened with Dave. I still can't believe the way he's behaved. How can you be so wrong about someone?'

'Yes, he's a real Jekyll and Hyde character.' Anna didn't add that she'd always had doubts about him.

Lydia finished her drink. 'That was good.'

'Like some more?'

'No thanks, maybe later. Anyway, getting back to Dave, I guess in retrospect, I did rather rush into things with him. I only met him in October and by Christmas we were living together. And you know, I knew very little about him really.'

'Yes, come to think of it, you've never told me much about his family. Isn't he estranged from his mother or something?'

'Yes he is but he never wanted to talk about his childhood. All he told me was that his dad's dead and he has one brother in America. He said he fell out with his mother and he didn't want to talk about it. I don't even know where she lives though I guess it's up north somewhere. When Dave was angry, I could hear his northern accent coming through. I'm not good at accents, but I'd say Lancashire or Yorkshire.'

Jess was climbing out of the pool and Anna picked up a towel. 'Had enough love? Come here, let's get you dry.'

'Let me do it Anna.' Lydia took the towel from her sister and held it open. The little girl ran into her arms. 'You're such a gorgeous girl, aren't you? Well you'll soon have a little cousin to play with.'

Anna bent to pick some weeds from a flowerbed. 'Anyway, it's just as well you didn't marry him. When I heard about the baby, I hoped you would. Now I'm so glad you didn't.'

'Yes, it would have complicated things. The irony is that I felt so secure, I could see no need for marriage.'

When Lydia arrived home, there was a bouquet of a dozen red roses at her door. The card read,

I love you Lydia and I'm sorry.
I've been a fool. Please let me come and explain.
All my love,
Dave

Lydia tore up the card, but she couldn't bear to waste the flowers, so she put them in a vase and went to bed in tears.

Dave Collier was drowning his sorrows in a bar in Soho. It was three weeks since Lydia had kicked him out, one week since he had sent the roses and not a word from her. Well what did he expect? The letter from that stupid bitch Pattie had been proof of his infidelity. He could easily have explained away the perfume and tampons, even the condoms, said they were relics of a previous relationship that he should have got rid of.

He was still furious with Lydia for having the cheek to get a key cut, but what had made her suspicious in the first place? Was it that time when Pattie answered the phone? Well if it was, she'd never given any indication of it. She'd carried on as normal, even encouraged him to spend time at the flat. Devious cow. He did miss her, but he knew that the main reason he wanted to get back with her was because she was carrying his child, his son, he hoped. She was carrying his property. How dare she think she could just cut him off like that and bring up his child on her own, or worse still, the thought struck him, with another man? He'd see her dead first. Why didn't he go round there now? Kick the fucking door in. He was certain she would have changed the locks. But no, that would put him in a worse position than ever. He called for another drink, at the same time eyeing up the two girls at the next table, one blonde, one dark. Now which one did he fancy?

—∽—

'Hi Lydia, it's me, Jane. Are you alright?'

'I'm okay.'

'You don't sound it and it's weeks since I heard from you. Have you been away?'

Lydia sighed. She knew she would have to tell Jane sooner or later.

'Sorry I've not been in touch. Can you come round? Or can we meet somewhere? I have rather a lot to tell you.'

'I'll be there in an hour.' Jane put the phone down.

Lydia finished her tale and picked up her cup of coffee, which had gone cold. She put it down after one sip. Jane who had listened without interruption, blurted out:

'I would never in a million years have thought it of Dave Collier. One of the nicest men I've ever met: kind, soft-spoken, courteous, charming. In fact if I didn't love Ted so much, I could have gone for him myself. And to think I encouraged you in the relationship. I'm so sorry Lydia that things have turned out so badly.'

'It's not your fault. You were taken in by him as much as I was. And that's the worst part, to think I was such a bad judge of character.'

'No you weren't and neither was I; he had a real dual personality and he only ever showed his good side to us. Ted and all my other friends who knew him thought he was wonderful.'

'In spite of everything, I do miss him Jane.'

'You're not thinking of taking him back, are you?'

'Definitely not, but he has a right to be involved with his child. He was so excited about the baby.'

'I think he'd make a rotten father.'

'We don't know that for sure. Now let's have another coffee and talk about something else'.

Lydia was getting into her car when Dave appeared and put his hand on her arm.

'We need to talk Lydia.' She recoiled. It was the first time she had set eyes on him since that July evening when she'd asked him to leave.

'Leave me alone Dave, I have nothing to say to you.'

'I didn't want to come round like this, but when I ring you put the phone down, you've ignored my notes. I'm truly sorry for what I did and I would like another chance. I love you Lydia and what about our child? He needs a father.'

Lydia noted the use of the male pronoun, but she said nothing, just got in her car and drove off.

When she'd found out about Dave's infidelity she was so hurt and angry that she'd decided to allow him no access to his child; if he came round pestering her, she'd move rather than let him see the baby. But in recent weeks, she wondered if she was doing the right thing. As she'd said to Jane, whatever Dave had done to her had nothing to do with his paternal rights and the child also had the right to know his or her father.

When she arrived at Anna's, she found her putting the finishing touches to a cake. It was Jess's third birthday and Lydia was joining them for a party with a couple of other mothers and toddlers. John was keeping Jess out of the way.

'Shall I take Jess to the park until it's time for the guests to arrive? Give John a chance to put up the balloons.'

As they returned from the park, John was in the garden and the little girl ran towards him. 'Give me a swing Daddy.' She screeched with delight as John lifted her and spun her round. As Lydia watched them she wondered yet again if she was doing the right thing by Dave and their child and after much soul-searching and several sleepless nights, she reached for the phone and dialled Dave's number.

Dave was both incredulous and delighted when Lydia phoned to say she was ready to talk, 'for our baby's sake.' He carefully prepared his script, even rehearsed it in front of the mirror, with complementary facial expressions: contrition, regret, self-deprecation, eternal love. *You'd have made a fine actor Dave*, he said to himself. He would blame Pattie, say she just refused to let go and he was weak.

But it hadn't gone the way he wanted. The curtain had come down before it had opened. Lydia started by saying she wanted no explanation for his infidelity. This wasn't about them, they were history. She was merely concerned about their child's welfare. In the early days, he could come to the house a couple of times a week and spend time with the baby. Any talk would centre on the child, not their relationship.

'Please give me another chance Lydia,' he pleaded, 'how can I have a proper relationship with my child in those circumstances?'

'As the baby gets older you will be able to spend more time with him or her, eventually having them to stay at your place.'

Dave's hand itched to reach out and punch her in the face, but he managed to keep hold of his temper, knowing it was in his interest to do so.

'Please Lydia, let me prove myself to you. Just give me a trial and I promise I'll never let you down again. You'll see.'

But she was resolute and now he paced his living room, fists clenched, muttering obscenities. He'd consulted a solicitor and he knew he had no rights in the matter. He was entirely at Lydia's beck and call. It was all so bloody unfair that women should have the upper hand in this and he wished now that they'd married. When he and Lydia were together, they'd been happy. He'd never treated her badly – alright a few affairs but so what? A man had his needs and although his sex life with Lydia had been good, he'd always had an eye for the ladies, couldn't resist a pretty face, a good figure. If the bitch hadn't been so meddlesome, they'd still be together and happy. Well he would contact her again, try and make her see sense.

Then, for the first time it occurred to him that maybe a different approach would be beneficial. The following day he went round the shops, then lifted the phone.

'Lydia, Dave here. Don't worry I'm not going to hassle you. I just wanted to let you know, I've been thinking about us and I can understand your point of view. I'm ringing because I've been window shopping and I've seen the most gorgeous pram and cot; I'd like to buy them for you, but only if you like them, of course.'

What is this about? Is he trying to bribe me?

'Let me have some time to think about it Dave.'

She consulted Anna. 'What do you think?'

'I'd go for it. Why shouldn't he pay his share? As long as you stick by your principles.'

'Hi Dave, ringing to say I'd like to take you up on your offer. When do you want to meet?'

'Saturday, two o'clock alright? You know Benson's on the High Road?'

Lydia loved the pram: a navy and white coach-built, the cot was white with coloured motifs and Dave threw in a carry cot as well. She felt beholden, but when she suggested they go for a coffee, he refused.

'No, I've taken up enough of your time. I'll get on home.'

The months passed. Dave rang occasionally. Was she well? Was there anything he could do? He sent parcels of nappies and clothes; their relationship was never mentioned. *Maybe he has changed. I don't want him back, but I think he will be a good father.*

On the last day of January, Dave called round to see Lydia. After the months of restraint, he was hoping that she'd be asking him back, not as a lover, but as the father of her child. The 'lover' business would come in time, he was sure of it. He'd rung her first and she'd agreed to his visit. They were having a cup of tea and he had come to the realisation from the way she was talking that she was of exactly the same mind as before, when she suddenly gripped her abdomen and groaned quietly, the colour draining from her face.

'Oh my God Dave, I think this is it!' As the pain subsided she lay back in the armchair, breathing deeply. Dave was genuinely concerned. 'Anything I can do love?'

'I think you'd better ring the hospital...oh, here we go again...'

She stood up, putting her hands to the small of her back, as Dave moved towards the phone in the hall.

'They said not to take you in, you could be hours yet.'

'This baby won't be hours; I think it's on its way now. I can't stop bearing down.'

'Let's get you into the bedroom, you'll be more comfortable.'

Lydia lay back on the bed, then raised herself on her elbows.

'I can feel something Dave. I think it's the head!'

She dropped back again with a moan.

'For God's sake Dave, help me.'

Dave was unfazed by what was happening. He'd done farm work and had assisted at the delivery of many animals. Pulling off Lydia's pants and knickers, he could see that she was right; a head of dark hair was visible between her legs. As Lydia bore down again, he gently eased the head out, then came a shoulder, a second shoulder and the rest of the body slid out easily. A boy! His son! As the baby gave a lusty yell, Dave found himself laughing and crying at the same time.

Lydia spent two days in hospital. She had no post-natal problems; the baby was healthy and weighed eight and a half pounds. She was grateful to Dave and his ego swelled as he was praised by her and by the staff. He felt sure that he would now be allowed a more active role in the care of his child, but he was wrong; Lydia was adamant.

It was then that the plan began to germinate in his mind. He would continue as he had in the last months of the pregnancy, abiding by Lydia's rules, never arguing. He would be a loving father to Simon in the short time he had with him. But he would watch and wait, familiarise himself with Lydia's routine, bide his time until the moment was right for the abduction.

Abduction? That was the wrong word. Simon was his and Lydia was denying him his paternal rights. She had no right to take control of his property. Well he'd show her. He'd watch her with the baby and think, *yes you enjoy your time with my son, for you won't have him for much longer.*

He knew that in order to carry his plan through, he must make peace with his mother. She was his only hope, for he knew of nowhere else he could take the child. He was confident that when he contacted her she would welcome the reconciliation with open arms as the quarrel had been his doing. He would not however tell her of his scheme as he knew she would never agree with it. Better to present her with the child as a *fait accompli.*

He had tailed Lydia on the High Road in the guise of the blonde woman and had chosen the greengrocer's for the snatch as it was only a few yards away from the demolition site which was usually deserted.

He was so amenable these days that he didn't think Lydia would ever suspect him, but to make sure, a week before the proposed event, he told her he was off on a walking holiday in the North and while he was supposedly away, he rang every day to enquire about Simon.

Chapter Nine

On a cloudless day in early August, Minnie decided to walk the last half mile into Raybridge. Parking her car on the grass verge, she lifted out the pram, set it up and placed the sleeping Alexander in it. This was her first outing with her grandson. She and Dave had agreed to wait until Alex was six months before coming out into the open and now that time had come and the day before, Dave had turned up with the folding pram.

As she wheeled her grandson towards the village, she recalled her reaction when, some months before, Dave had produced a falsified birth certificate stating that the baby had been born on the twelfth of February 1975, twelve days after his real birthday, in Birmingham. He was named as the father; the mother a fictitious Monica White.

'I know we agreed you should be named as Alex's father, Dave but seeing your name there I'm wondering if it's such a good idea.'

Dave had put his hands on her shoulders and bent down, looking straight into her eyes.

'Stop worrying Mam. I have never been suspected by the police, Lydia or anyone else. The police asked me a few questions about my whereabouts at the time and they were satisfied with my answers; there was no further investigation into it and because Lydia and I were not married, not even together at the time, my name wasn't mentioned in any of the news reports. Besides, the police have given up on the case.'

Minnie had said no more, but she was not mollified.

Now, as the first houses of the village came into view, she felt a mixture of pride and apprehension. First she must call on her friend Chrissie. She and Chrissie had been close since they were children and had always shared confidences. Minnie had some explaining to do.

Chrissie's front door was, as always, open and as usual, she knocked on the vestibule door before opening it and calling, 'Hello! It's me, Minnie. Can I bring this in?'

Chrissie stuck her head round the kitchen door. 'Bring what in?' Then she saw the pram. 'What's going on?'

As Minnie entered the kitchen, Chrissie shooed her huge grey cat Jasper off his comfortable seat by the range. He looked balefully at Minnie, eyed the pram as if he contemplated jumping in there, put his head in the air and left the room.

While Chrissie made tea, Minnie told her the story she and Dave had concocted: when Dave and his girlfriend had separated, she didn't know she was pregnant. The first he knew of his son was a couple of weeks ago when Monica had contacted him to say she was terminally ill and would he have the child. Dave was sceptical at first. How did he know the child was his? But when he saw him, he had no doubt. Even at that young age, there was no denying he was a miniature Dave. So he agreed, though he knew that his job would make full-time child care impossible and he'd turned to Minnie.

'You'll see what I mean about the likeness Chrissie, when he's awake.' Minnie accepted a cup of tea and took a sip.

'Believe me, I got the shock of my life when he phoned to tell me he had a child and an even bigger shock when he asked me to have him but I was also thrilled; well you know how I feel about Amanda and Jake being so far away. I'd have told you sooner but you were away in York visiting Marian.'

She leaned forward and lowered her voice, 'Oh and by the way, I'll be telling people in the village that Monica was his estranged wife, not his girlfriend. You know what prudes and gossips they are round here.'

Chrissie nodded, then put down her cup and went to the pram. She'd already had a peep, but now she pulled back the covers and took a long look at the sleeping child.

'Oh he is bonny and I can see the likeness to Dave. And he's called Alexander? That's a fine name. How old is he?'

'He's six months.'

Minnie rose now and joined her friend. She was right, he was bonny; more than that, he was perfect. Though he had not been weighed since he'd come to live with her, it was obvious that he was thriving. He was beautifully rounded with plump cheeks.

She knew that Dave was proud of the fact that his son was so like him. He would gaze adoringly at him and say with a smirk. 'He's my son through and through, not an ounce of Lydia in him.'

Minnie and Chrissie sat down again.

'Oh I'm sorry, Minnie, with all the excitement, I nearly forgot about the shortbread. Would you like a piece? Baked this morning.' She took a tin from a shelf, opened it and passed it to Minnie. As Minnie accepted a piece and commented on how good it was, Chrissie studied her friend who, she thought, had not been looking well for some months. She had always been thin but Chrissie was sure she had lost weight, her hair, grey with some dark still showing, had obviously not been permed for some time and there were dark circles under her eyes.

'But how will you cope looking after him? It can't be easy. I wouldn't like to start again. Marian's kids were handful enough last week.'

'Well I've only had him for a few days and I must say I did wonder how I would cope with a baby at the age of sixty-one but so far he feeds well and sleeps well at night. He rarely cries and he's full of smiles and chuckles. He's great at this age and I'm not thinking about what it will be like when he's older. Anyway, Dave will be coming up at weekends. That will give me a break.'

Just then Alex began to stir. 'Time for his feed.' Minnie didn't wait for him to wake properly before lifting him to show him off to Chrissie.

Dave had lived up to his promise. He'd turned up nearly every weekend bringing whatever was needed for Alex. There had been no hitches in the past four months. Minnie was at the village shops as usual on a Saturday. She'd had no unexpected callers and, on the few occasions she'd had friends to visit when Alex was out with Dave, she'd been scrupulous about hiding the baby paraphernalia.

But, in spite of Alex's equability and of her delight in him, the past four months had not been easy. Minnie had been constantly on the alert. Every time she heard a car, every time the phone rang, she expected it to be someone telling her that the game was up. As a consequence, she had headaches almost daily and frequent acute indigestion. But it was always at night that the magnitude of what she had done in colluding with her son, came to haunt her and she would toss and turn, racked with guilt. She thought often of Alex's mother and of what she must be going through. She would ask herself what else she could have done; she couldn't very well have turned her own son in to the police. If he'd told her in advance, she wouldn't have had any part in it – or would she? After all she'd wanted to be involved with a grandchild for so long. She had many photos of her American grandchildren, but they were a poor substitute for seeing them, spending time with them.

—ᴍᴥ—

It was now five months since Simon's disappearance and Lydia, who'd always been slim, had lost a considerable amount of weight and looked gaunt and pale. On Anna's suggestion, she had seen a doctor, but had refused a course of tranquillisers.

'They don't take away the pain Anna, they just suppress it. Do you remember when I was on something similar after Mum died? They did help the sadness and panic I felt at the time, but I also felt woozy and lethargic. Heaven knows I feel lethargic enough as it is.'

It was true. In the early days, she had often had bouts of striding about, crying out loud, tearing her hair and ranting at anyone within earshot. On those occasions, Dave was the only one who could calm her. Now she spent most days sitting about the house in her dressing gown, staring into space. She had no interest in housework, cooking, reading, her art work or any other activity. She thought about her baby constantly, sometimes picturing him well-cared for in a loving home; at other times imagining him dead, or worse still, continuously ill-treated. She would go into the nursery she had prepared with so much love and stare down at the empty carry cot; then she would open drawers and hold tiny vests, sleep suits and other garments to her face and the tears would flow unrestrainedly.

One day, holding one of Simon's blankets, she stood at the nursery window looking at life going on as usual: cars going up and down the road, mothers walking children to school, pushing prams, people at the bus stop, cyclists. What were they doing, going about their business as usual? How could they go on as if nothing had happened? Didn't they know she had lost her child? She hated them all!

She looked at her car in the street below and seriously contemplated ending it all. What if she went out in the middle of the night when there was no one around and put a hose to the exhaust? It was supposed to be a quick and painless death.

Startled out of her morbid musing by the telephone, she hesitated before going downstairs to answer it. It was Anna.

'Just ringing to see if you'd like to come out for a run with me and Jess.'

'Oh I don't know. I'm not so good today.'

'All the more reason for coming out with us. And it's such a lovely day. I'm thinking of driving down to the coast and you know how Jess loves spending time with you.'

At this Lydia brightened. The little girl had just turned four and regardless of her own loss, Lydia still loved to spend time with her. It was the only thing that gave her any real pleasure. She agreed to the outing and a day on the beach with two of the people she loved most put all thoughts of ending it out of her head.

Nevertheless, she decided to take the precaution of disposing with the things that had helped to put her into such a melancholy state of mind. On the drive home, while Jess, exhausted by the sea air and activity, slept soundly, she asked Anna if she would come soon and help her to pack up Simon's things.

'I want it all gone – carry cot, cot, pram, clothes, everything. I'll get a local charity to come and collect it.'

Anna reached over and held her hand. 'Are you sure Lydia?'

'Absolutely. As you know I've kept them, hoping against

hope that Simon would be returned to me. But he won't be. I just know. They're just constant reminders.'

'But what about Dave? He might want to keep something of his son's.'

Lydia hadn't considered what Dave might want, so when she got home she rang and asked him.

'No love, the memories are painful enough and I can't even bear to look at the photos I took...' He broke off and there was silence.

'Dave, are you still there?'

A stifled sob. 'Sorry Lydia, you caught me at a bad time.' They cried quietly together.

Afterwards Dave smirked to himself as he poured a large Scotch. Once again he congratulated himself on his performance and thought how he had missed his vocation. What a fine actor he would have made. Far from being upset, he was in his element, enjoying his position of power. He had control of his son, got his revenge on Lydia, foiled the police; his mother was on his side.

In her distress, Lydia had turned to him more and more and he relished this. His revenge was all the sweeter, knowing he was the cause of her anguish and paradoxically her main source of comfort. Certainly, she was not looking her best these days – he chuckled to himself at the euphemism – but he still found her attractive, all the more so in fact because of her vulnerability. If they were to get back together, that would be his ultimate triumph.

When he called round the following day to offer help, he found that Lydia and Anna were already busy clearing out Simon's room. Another opportunity for his acting. He put on his most concerned expression.

'You shouldn't be doing this Lydia, let me help Anna.'

'But Dave, it will be just as difficult for you as it is for me. Although believe it or not I'm beginning to find it almost therapeutic.'

The three worked quietly together. Dave broke the silence. 'I think I need a breath of fresh air. Shall I put the kettle on when I go down?'

'Oh yes please, tea for me,' said Anna.

'Coffee please,' said Lydia.

'He's finding this really hard,' Lydia whispered to Anna as Dave retreated. 'I'll go and have a word with him.'

She found Dave in the garden smoking and pointed to his cigarette. 'Can I have one?' Dave jerked his head back, eyes opened wide.

'Am I hearing things? You hate smoking.'

'I just feel I need a prop of some sort. And who knows? I might like it.'

Lydia accepted a cigarette and held it to the flame of Dave's lighter. Inhaling, she began to cough and splutter.

'Oh my God, this will be the death of me, but who cares? I don't care about anything anymore.'

She took another inhalation and only coughed once. Dave put his arm round her.

'I care Lydia. I know I've behaved badly in the past, but I've always cared about you, I can even explain what happened if you'd just give me a chance.'

Lydia held up a hand.

'Please Dave, I don't want to talk about that...'

'Okay, okay, but listen. I've been thinking. Why don't we go away on holiday? Somewhere completely new, away from all our memories. Just you and me. Somewhere where no one knows what happened; where we're just two ordinary people.'

After one more puff on her cigarette, Lydia looked at it with disgust and crushed it out. She sighed.

'Do you really think that would change things? Make us feel better? Simon and the thoughts of what's happened will be with me wherever I go.'

'And with me. I just thought a break, a change of scene would do us good. And in case you're worried there'd be no strings attached. We would go away as friends, with separate rooms of course and I promise I won't mention what happened in the past.'

'Give me time to think about it Dave.'

She asked Anna's opinion.

'I think it would do you the world of good to get away from here for a while: sunshine, sea air. I can understand your reservations about going with Dave, but you must admit, he's been wonderful over the past months and he needs a holiday as much as you do.'

'Yes you're right. He has been brilliant and I've not been supportive to him. I've thought only of myself. This is something he really wants, so I will go along with it and, as you say it might do me good.'

Chapter Ten

Dave and Lydia were sitting outside a tapas bar in the village of Salobreña in Southern Spain. In late September the weather was still well into the eighties and they had chosen a shady spot. Dave was sipping a cold beer and Lydia had iced water. It was the third day of their holiday. Dave leaned forward, 'You are enjoying yourself Lydia?'

'Oh yes Dave. I feel so much more relaxed since we came here. I still think about what happened of course but I'm not dwelling on it as much. How about you?'

'Yes I feel the same. It's certainly helped to have a complete change of scene.'

He took another sip of beer and lit a cigarette. 'I've been thinking. What do you say to hiring a car for a few days? I thought it would be nice to get out and see something of the countryside. We could drive through the Alpujarras, see the Sierra Nevada...'

'Oh yes and visit Granada and the Alhambra Palace. It's supposed to be a fantastic place.'

'You think it's a good idea then?'

'Absolutely, to tell you the truth I'm getting a bit fed up with lying on the beach. It's been great but like you, I feel the need to move about a bit.'

Lydia was enjoying Dave's company. He was the perfect companion, showing only the attributes that had first attracted her: wit, sense of humour, courtesy. Ever solicitous, he was there when she needed him but didn't encroach when she wanted time on her own. She had no difficulty remembering why she had fallen in love with him.

On the last night of the holiday, Lydia experienced a sudden and acute sadness as she did her packing. She had mixed feelings about going home. She was looking forward to seeing her family and friends, but dreading the return to the house which held so many happy memories of Simon; where in spite of clearing out his things, she still felt his presence in every room. And she would miss Dave. Yes he would still be around, but it wouldn't be the same. In the past ten days, she felt she had got to know and like him all over again.

Lydia woke with a start. She'd been dreaming about Simon for the first time in weeks. He was about six or seven months old and she was carrying him when he turned and startled her by speaking. 'When can I come home Mummy, I want to come home.' Then he wriggled in her arms and disappeared and she was left holding a blanket. Sitting up, she turned on the light and looked at her watch: two-twenty. Surely the dream was an omen; a sign that her baby was alive and needed her. As the tears began, she asked herself how she could go on in this way. When she got back, she would get in touch with the police again. They had said there was nothing more they could do, but surely there must be something. She felt a pressing need to talk to Dave and, getting up, she pulled on a top and a pair of shorts, tiptoed along the corridor in her bare feet. She knocked gently on his door. Silence. She knocked again and quietly called his name. 'It's me, Lydia.'

'Just a minute.' Dave opened the door and peered out, heavy-eyed, then stood aside to admit her.

'Oh Dave, I've had the most awful dream about Simon. I can't bear to be on my own.'

Dave put his arms protectively around her. 'Don't worry Lydia, Dave's here. Now come and sit down and tell me about the dream.' He led her towards the bed.

—m—

Anna was shocked when she heard that Lydia had renewed her relationship with Dave.

'I know what happened to Simon brought you closer again and he has been a tremendous support to you, but are you sure you've done the right thing? You always said you could never trust him again after what he did.' Anna passed her sister a cup of coffee and looked through the window at Jess who was happily chasing leaves on that breezy autumn day.

'Well, I've not entered lightly into it. He was so lovely when we were away that I began to wonder if I should have him back, but I hadn't really seriously considered it and then it… happened.' She told Anna about her dream.

'But can you trust him now? What's changed?'

'Well he told me about Pattie – the woman he had the affair with. He had finished with her a few months before he met me, but she kept ringing him up and writing to him. He ignored that and then she started coming round when he was at the flat and wouldn't leave him alone. He still found her attractive and he was weak, but he'd finished the affair just before I went round snooping. If I'd left well alone things would never have gone wrong between us. He swears he'll never let me down again and I believe him.'

Anna couldn't credit what she was hearing. Was her sister so lonely and desperate after her loss that the cheating Dave Collier was better than no one? To hide her feelings, she got up from the table and opened the back door. 'Jess, come in now. Mummy's got some milk and biscuits for you.'

The little girl came bounding in, face flushed, all smiles for Lydia who lifted her on to her knee.

'Hello Jess. How's my best girl today?'

Anna poured milk into her cup and opened a packet of biscuits. 'Is Dave going to move into yours again then?'

'For the time being yes, but to tell you the truth I can't bear that house since Simon's gone. I'd like to make a fresh start. I suppose I could move into Dave's but it's a bit small for two people and Dave likes his time to himself, so do I.'

Anna poured more coffee for them both. *Yes, we know why he likes his space. Oh I'm getting cynical, maybe I should give him the benefit of the doubt.* 'I do hope it works out for you Lydia.'

Dave was triumphant. He was at the zenith of his revenge: Lydia had come back to him. She was even more dependent on him. On return from their holiday, she had still been insistent on challenging the police about their inertia.

'No love, you mustn't go; I'll go and have it out with them.'

He had no intention of going, but he reported back that the police had had few leads to begin with and there was nothing new.

'It's difficult Lydia but what can they do. I believe they've done all they can. I know you had that dream and it was awful but I've got a gut feeling that Simon's alright. As I said before, I think he's with some poor woman who lost her child and that he's loved and well cared for. Small compensation for us I know but better than feeling that something terrible has happened to him.'

They discussed their living arrangements. Lydia was adamant that she needed to get out of her house. Dave suggested that she put it on the market and that they start to look for another property. They could live at his place in the interim.

'I know it's small and you want a garden, but surely it'll be fine for the time being.'

Lydia agreed, unknowingly accommodating Dave in the next stage of his plan which was to let her move in with him and then when the time was right, to finish the relationship. Now that he had achieved his aim, he no longer wanted her. There were so many other women and he didn't want his freedom restricted. Shortly after he had taken Simon, he had had a private vasectomy, certain that he would never want another child.

They cleared out the house, getting rid of some things and putting the furniture and most of the other stuff into storage. A For Sale sign appeared in the front garden. Lydia was excited, more animated than Dave had seen her in months. 'Well Dave, where shall we live? London is our oyster.' There was no question of them leaving the city because of Dave's work and because Lydia did not want to leave her family and friends.

They spent a lot of time exploring areas north and south of the river.

Three a.m. and Minnie paced the floor with Alex. Nearly ten months old, he already had four teeth which had not given him any bother, but now, cutting his latest teeth he cried for hours every night. Minnie would carry him around, rock him, sing to him, but nothing distracted him for long. Rubbing his gums with a teething jelly would pacify him for a while, but just as she was drifting back to sleep he would again set up a yell.

Since she had told people about her grandson, the indigestion had disappeared and the headaches had lessened to one or two a week, but now she was worn out from lack of sleep and during the day, finding it a struggle to keep up with a lively, crawling baby.

She was angry with Dave. He was due the following day but it was more than six weeks since he'd been up. Well she would give him a piece of her mind when she saw him. What had happened to his promise to come up most weeks if not every week? Shortly after his last visit, he'd rung to say he was off to Spain for a week. Lydia was harassing him, he said, wanting to get back with him and he felt the need for a break so he was going off on his own. Then shortly after his return, he rang to say he was changing his phone number and for the time being, he didn't want her to have it. Lydia was often round at his place these days, he said and he didn't want her to know he was back in touch with Minnie.

'I don't want her to know where you live or anything about you. I have to be so careful for both our sakes.'

Minnie was puzzled, 'How come she's suddenly round at your place so often? You're not back with her, are you?'

Dave gave a scornful laugh. 'Oh course not Mam. She can't stand being in her own house anymore. Too many painful memories. She's put it on the market and I've said she can come round to mine when things get really difficult but she's not living here. Don't worry, my supporting her won't go on for much longer and I promise I'll ring you every day.'

'Why won't you give me your work number?'

Dave sighed. 'As I've told you before Mam, it's too risky. You never know who might hear something or even be listening in on an extension. As I said before, I will ring every day, I promise.'

And true to his word he did but that was not enough. She

needed to see him; needed his support; needed him to take Alex off her hands for one or two nights a week or even a fortnight, so that she could get some rest.

When she broached the matter during his phone calls, he always cut her short. 'Things have been difficult at work Mam and Lydia has been very needy. I'll explain when I see you.'

As Dave drove towards Yorkshire, he rehearsed what he was going to say to his mother: Lydia was taking up so much of his time and as if that wasn't enough, there were a lot of problems at work and he'd had to work long hours to sort them out. His weekends had been taken up with this. *That's it Dave, play the sympathy card.*

And indeed when he arrived with his explanation Minnie was so relieved to see him and so sympathetic to his plight that she couldn't bring herself to take him to task. He stayed for two nights and she slept well, not hearing Alex cry once.

'Are you saying he didn't cry again last night?' She looked askance at her son as she placed a plate of bacon and eggs in front of him. 'You must tell me your secret.'

'Sheer coincidence Mam. I just happened to take over when he was totally exhausted.' *But the few drops of whiskey in the bottle did help.* He chuckled to himself.

Chapter Eleven

In spite of the sleepless nights and her subsequent extreme tiredness, Minnie still blessed the day Dave had turned up out of the blue with her much loved grandson. But she was fearful. There was the fear that their crime would be discovered but that was as nothing compared to the fear that Dave would one day arrive on her doorstep and take Alex away. What if he got a new girlfriend, maybe wanted to get married, or even if that didn't happen, she was concerned that when the boy was older, he would want to take him to live with him. She hoped she would still be able to see him, though you never knew with Dave, but it wouldn't be the same.

She thought back to when her sons were little. Dave, so like her with his dark hair and blue eyes; Tom, like his dad with his blond hair and grey eyes.

Her husband George, a farm labourer, had joined the army soon after war was declared. He had come back on leave in 1941 and Dave was the result of their reunion, born in March 1942.

The war came to an end and George returned. He had been held prisoner since shortly after she had last seen him and she hardly recognised him: he had lost both weight and muscle tone, his six foot frame was stooped, his blond hair mostly grey and thinning. At forty-two he could have been taken for early to mid-fifties.

Tom was born in April 1946 when Dave had just turned four and she thought he would be pleased to have a little brother but

one day when she turned her back to prepare some vegetables,
Tom suddenly set up a roar. One minute he was sound asleep
in his crib, Dave playing with his cars on the kitchen floor, the
next minute, he sounded as if he was in pain. Then, as she
changed his nappy, she found an angry mark on his little thigh.
She looked from him to the innocent-looking child quietly
playing on the floor and knew that the baby had been pinched
by his brother and that from now on she had to be vigilant.

Sometimes, when she fed Tom, Dave would try to clamber
on to her knee, pushing at the baby as he did so. By the time
Tom was walking, Dave had started school but when he was at
home, he was always in control, snatching his brother's toys and
refusing to let him join in his games. Living in such a lonely
spot, they rarely had other children to play with and her heart
went out to Tom when she saw him spurned once again by
Dave. He would hang about the kitchen bored and lonely. She
remonstrated with Dave and things changed for a while but their
games nearly always ended in fights, with tears from Tom.

When Tom started school, things appeared to improve
between the brothers. In his first term, she walked with them
to Raybridge, fearing that Dave would bully his brother on the
way. Then she noticed a change in Dave. He was much calmer
and when Tom cried in the mornings, he took him under his
wing with soothing words. Minnie was amazed and she breathed
a sigh of relief.

On his release from the army, George had returned to his
job as a farm labourer and he spent as much time as he could
with Dave, playing football and rough and tumble games. They
roamed the moors together and George taught him to fish in
the many streams. Dave soon proved his skill with a catapult and
brought home rabbits, wood pigeons and other birds and these,
together with the fish and Minnie's home grown vegetables

provided a very reasonable diet at a time when rationing was still in force.

George had also been delighted with the birth of his second son and he spent as much time as he could dandling him on his knee and singing to him. He included Dave in these activities as much as possible and he never seemed to notice the looks of resentment, almost of hatred, he often gave his brother. Minnie noticed and she was fearful.

George would have said that he treated the boys equally, but Dave noticed subtle differences. His father made allowances for Tom because of his age, saying things like, 'He can't go any faster Dave, he's only little', 'Be patient Dave, he needs time to grasp that' or 'I think we'll go home now; Tom's getting tired'.

One day in the summer holidays the boys were climbing over a barbed wire fence when Dave reached out and pushed Tom. It was an unpremeditated reaction to the resentful thoughts he was having about him. Tom got caught in the wire as he fell and his left leg was scored, the wire digging in deeply near his ankle. Dave was shocked when he saw the pouring blood and worried that Tom would tell on him so, as he extricated him from the wire, he was at pains to explain it was an accident, 'I didn't mean to push you Tom, honest I didn't. I was trying to help and my hand slipped. You won't say it was my fault will you?'

Tom was too upset to reply.

As they entered the kitchen, Minnie threw up her hands in horror, 'Oh my God, look at you!'

Over the racket of Tom's bawling, Dave told his version of events, hoping desperately that his brother had believed him but as George lifted Tom and set him on the table, he yelled through his tears, 'It was his fault; he pushed me.'

'Liar! It was an accident.' Red in the face, Dave clenched his fists.

'Now, now, we'll talk about what happened later. Let's get this wound seen to first.' Minnie poured disinfectant into a bowl of water and produced some cotton wool.

George turned to Dave. 'Climbing over barbed wire indeed. What a stupid thing to do. Apart from anything else, barbed wire means "Keep Out".'

'Dave you're supposed to look after your little brother, not let him do dangerous things,' Minnie said, as she washed the cuts. 'The scratches aren't deep but I think this cut near the ankle needs stitching George. Do you think you could fetch Doctor Richmond?'

As George went to get his bicycle, he turned to Dave.

'Do you realise how serious this could have been? You can do without your supper tonight. Go to your room. And if I find you did push him, you'll be in deep trouble.'

Dave stomped upstairs and slammed the bedroom door. Sitting on his bed, he let the tears come. *I hate you Tom you sneak and tell-tale and I hate being the oldest. Why do I have to look after that stupid baby all the time? And he was the one who wanted to go into that field. It isn't fair, it just isn't fair.* He stamped his feet, then picked up a penknife and stuck it in his pillow, making a deep incision. He wanted to tear it to shreds but as feathers began to fly out, he had a sudden panic about what he had done. *Oh my God, I'm going to be in worse trouble than ever now.* He hastily turned it over, put the knife down and awaited the wrath of his father when Tom convinced him he'd been pushed.

When Doctor Richmond had been and gone, George came into the bedroom.

'Your brother swears you pushed him. So what do you have to say for yourself?' Arms folded across his chest, he stood looking down at his son.

'I didn't Dad, I swear. I just sort of fell against him, honest.'

'Why would he lie about it? He really looks up to you Dave and I think he's more upset about you pushing him than he is about the injury.'

Dave began to cry again. 'Honest Dad I didn't, I didn't.'

George rolled his eyes. 'Oh quit snivelling, a great lad like you. Now as punishment, you're to stay in your room for the rest of this week which means of course, you'll miss the pictures on Saturday.'

'Bu…but what about my paper round?'

'You needn't worry about that; I'll tell Ted Morton you've got a bug.' As he left the room, George's parting shot was, 'And be thankful that I don't take my belt or razor strap to you like a lot of fathers would.'

Dave was both devastated and furious. To be kept in his room for the remainder of the week – Thursday to Saturday – was bad enough, but to miss the film. The boys rarely got to the cinema as the nearest one was in the town fifteen miles away and he'd been looking forward to this one: *Shane*, starring one of his favourite actors, Alan Ladd.

I'll get even with you Tom, see if I don't. He began to plot his revenge.

Downstairs, Minnie sat by her injured son, stroking his head as he fell asleep, wondering which one to believe. She didn't want either of her sons to be liars; she remembered Dave's early jealously of his brother but surely that was firmly in the past. Dave had been protective of Tom for ages but why would Tom lie about the brother he clearly worshipped?

'I believe it was an accident,' she said to George later, 'Dave must have fallen against him, like he said and Tom thought he'd pushed him.'

'No, I don't think so Minnie. I know you think the sun shines out of that lad's backside but I've noticed things when

I've been out with them. I'd say there was still a lot of jealously there.'

George and Minnie had given Dave a bicycle for his eleventh birthday in March. Both boys had learned to ride on their father's bike but Dave had been clamouring for ages for one of his own, saying he could get a paper round if he had a bike. A new one was out of the question, but George found a very reasonably priced second-hand one in excellent condition. He brought it home when the boys were in bed and left it in the shed. No fuss was made of birthdays. Minnie would bake a cake and they would have something special for tea but they didn't usually get presents or cards.

On this occasion, just before tea, Dave was sent out to get a bucket of coal. Entering the shed in the gloom of early evening, he was amazed to see the bike. At first he thought it was George's but no, this one was bright red and looked new. Surely it couldn't be for him? Opening the door wider, he was able to make out a label tied to the handlebars: *Happy Birthday Dave*. It was his happiest birthday ever and, true to his word, he did get a paper round at Morton's in the village.

Dave took good care of his bike and at night, always put it in the shed where there was only room for one. Pleased with the care his son lavished on his present, George was happy to keep his own bike outside, covered with tarpaulin.

One morning, a couple of weeks after the barbed wire incident, Dave got up early to do his paper round; George had already gone to work and Minnie and Tom were sound asleep. Taking his bike from the shed, Dave rode off in the opposite direction to Raybridge. After a short distance, he dismounted, lifted his bike over a stile and went through a wooded area towards a stream. Standing on the stream embankment, he lifted the bike and, using all his strength, dashed it into the water. Then he climbed down and repeated the action, making sure that the wheels were buckled, before wedging it between some large rocks. Satisfied with his work, but near to tears at the destruction of his beloved bike, he ran home as fast as he could and burst into the house, shouting for his mother.

'Mam, Mam, my bike's not there, someone's stolen it.'

'What? What's going on?' Half asleep, Minnie appeared at the top of the stairs in her nightie.

Dave's tears were genuine. 'It's my bike Mam. It's not in the shed. Someone's taken it.'

'I wondered about getting a padlock for the shed,' George said when he came home, 'but it's so quiet in these parts and burglaries are almost unheard of.' He patted Dave on the shoulder. 'Cheer up son, we'll see about getting you another one. Maybe sooner than you think.'

Two days later when the brothers went off to fish, Dave made sure they followed the route he had taken for his act of destruction. 'I'll race you to the stream,' he shouted as they ran through the wood. Then he let out a wail. 'I don't believe it; it's my bike, look Tom it's my bike in the water.'

Scrambling down he tugged at it but it was well and truly lodged. 'Well don't just stand there gawping you ninny, give us a hand with this.'

Together the boys dislodged the bike and brought it up the embankment. Dave examined it. 'It's completely knackered. But who would steal a bike and then do this to it? It doesn't make sense.' He scratched his head, then turned slowly to his brother, his eyes narrowed. 'Wait a minute, it's the sort of thing would be done for revenge…and I have no enemies…apart from you.' Loudly he spat the last word, bringing his face close to Tom's so that the little boy started back and almost fell.

'Me? I'm not your enemy Dave.' His face puckered and there were tears in his voice.

'Oh no? Well who got me into trouble the other week for something I didn't do? Stuck in the bedroom all week and missed the Alan Ladd film. I bet you were all cocky sitting there with your toffees.' He pushed him then and this time he did fall over. 'You did this, didn't you? Didn't you? Own up, own up.'

'No Dave, I didn't, I swear I would never do a thing like that…' Tom was crying now and his words were cut short as the blows started to fall. After a final punch, Dave shouted, 'I'm going home to tell.' And he ran off.

Once again Minnie was worried about her sons. Once again, she abhorred the thought that either one was a liar but it looked very much like one wasn't telling the truth. She was puzzled as to why someone would steal a bike and then destroy it. It certainly looked like an act of vengeance but she found it hard to believe that her little seven-year-old was capable of such a thing. She knew that Dave was his hero, or at least had been before he pushed him on to the barbed wire. Had he lost his respect for Dave? Was this his revenge for the inflicted wound? *No*, she told herself, *it was much more likely to be Dave's revenge on him.* She rebuked herself for thinking that but, she asked herself, what else could she think?

George agreed with her. He'd asked around and there had been no other thefts in the area. Dave was adamant that he had no enemies. He was very popular at school, he said and he got on well with people he met in the village. He could only think of one person who would have done it.

As it couldn't be proven either way, George felt he had no option but to let both boys go without punishment. Dave would not get another bike unless he paid for it himself and surely this was punishment enough. As for Tom, his punishment had been Dave's wrath and subsequent beating and, if he was innocent, Dave's duplicity.

Dave kept his job at the newsagent's, walking the three miles into the village and going straight to school afterwards. He had been saving most of his earnings and in a few more months, he bought another second-hand bike. Minnie and George were proud of his enterprise. Things had settled down between the brothers but Minnie noticed that Tom had grown quieter and there was a sadness about him. Her heart ached for him.

Although he took pains not to show it, Dave was furious that Tom had gone unpunished and he thought long and hard about how he could get even but he was in no hurry to act. This time there must be no suspicions cast on him so he was willing to bide his time until the unpleasant incidents of this summer had faded and firstly he must make his peace with Tom. One Saturday when they were alone in the front room and Minnie was in the kitchen baking, Dave put down the comic he was reading and looked across at Tom who was engrossed in a jigsaw.

'Look Tom, I didn't push you that day. I know you've never believed me but I'm telling the truth. It was an accident. And as for the bike, I didn't do that to get you into trouble. Do you really think I'd do that to my own bike? I don't know who did it but I'm sorry I accused you and I'm sorry I beat you up. Please let's be friends.'

Tom didn't know what to think. Could he have been wrong all along? He remembered the hard shove as he crossed the fence and it definitely didn't feel like an accident. As for the bike, he still harboured doubts but he was desperate to be on good terms with Dave, so he said quietly, 'Okay then.'

Dave punched him gently on the shoulder, 'That's the stuff, no hard feelings from now on?' Tom smiled, 'No hard feelings.' He felt a lightness he had not felt for a long time.

An unseasonably warm day for April. Dave had gone cycling with a couple of mates from the village, Tom had gone off to play on his own as he often did, George was working and Minnie was enjoying the peace and quiet as she prepared some vegetables for the evening meal. She glanced at the clock. George should be home soon and Dave had said he'd be back in time for tea. She wondered where Tom was. He'd been gone a while. Still he was very good at amusing himself and she expected he'd be back soon. For several months, things had seemed better between him and Dave and she was relieved about that. As she put the potatoes on the range, she thought how good it was to see them both so much brighter and happier.

A terrible roar intruded on her thoughts and she ran to the window and looked out to see her younger son crossing the yard, bedraggled and dripping wet. He was limping and blood was pouring down his face. Horrified, Minnie opened the back door where Tom almost fell into her arms. 'Oh Tom, my darling, what's happened to you?' Tom could hardly speak for crying but she gleaned that the rope swing had broken and he had fallen into the stream. On examination she found a deep cut on his forehead, some scratches on his arms and legs, bruises on his body and a swollen ankle. Just then George arrived and, for the second time in eight months, was sent off to get Doctor Richmond.

The evening meal forgotten, Minnie removed Tom's wet clothes and fetching some warm water, proceeded to wash away the blood and dirt, speaking soothingly all the time to the boy, who at last fell silent.

Next to arrive was Dave who gaped, putting his hand to his mouth. 'What's happened to him?' Minnie explained that he'd been on the rope swing and had fallen in the stream.

'I didn't fall off the swing Mam, the rope broke.'

Dave frowned. 'Broke? It must have been frayed. I never noticed the last time I was down there but that was a while ago as you know.' He turned to his mother. 'Dad not home yet?'

'I've sent him to get the doctor. This cut needs stitching and I think his ankle might be sprained.'

The doctor arrived. 'I see you've been in the wars again young man. Yes definitely a few stitches required.' He opened his bag and Tom cringed as he remembered the last time he'd had stitches.

George and Minnie were thankful that his injuries were comparatively slight and that he had managed to get himself out of the water, in spite of the sprained ankle.

As Dave busied himself making a pot of tea, he was jubilant. *So it's happened. I knew it was only a matter of time.* He chuckled inwardly.

A couple of years earlier, the boys had made the swing by suspending a rope from a tree on the stream bank – a different part of the stream from where the bicycle had been found – and the last time he'd been down there, Dave had noticed how frayed it was. He was about to tell Tom that they needed a new rope when he suddenly had his idea: Tom hadn't noticed the fraying; he was often unobservant about practical things; in a dream world of his own, so Dave said nothing. It was the ideal situation for his plan of revenge. Sooner or later the rope would break. He didn't have to do anything, just be patient. He hadn't been near the swing since that day and now his patience had paid off, with impunity. He didn't wish for more serious injury for his brother. It was enough to see him squirm as Doctor Richmond stitched his wound and to see him unable to run about and play, because of his sprained ankle, as the days grew warmer and longer. True he had to have time off school, but he knew that that would only add to Tom's misery, as he loved school. He never asked himself how he would feel if Tom had been more seriously injured – or killed.

Minnie's uneasiness about her older son returned. She had noticed an air of smugness about him after Tom's accident and she mentioned it to George.

'You're imagining things love. Dave had nothing to do with it; he's not been down there for ages and you know what Tom's like, he wouldn't have noticed if the rope had been replaced by a cobweb. Just be thankful that his injuries weren't any worse.'

Minnie wanted to believe him but she still felt uneasy.

Both boys did well at school and got places at the grammar school. George and Minnie had high hopes for them going to university and getting worthwhile, well-paid jobs. But while Tom applied himself diligently to his studies, Dave had little interest in book-learning. Bright enough to get by with the minimum of study, he just scraped through his 'O' levels and begged to be allowed to leave school.

'But what do you want to do with your life?' George was

really concerned that his elder son would not end up like he had in unskilled, poorly-paid employment.

'I've been offered an apprenticeship. Bill Weaver at the garage wants to train me up as a motor mechanic. Maybe I'll have my own garage someday, but whatever, it's a good skill to have.'

Minnie and George were pleased and agreed to their son leaving school. George wishing that he had had the chance of learning such a skill when he was young.

Dave worked well for more than a year, although he became increasingly restless and felt more and more stifled by village life, with the nearest town fifteen miles away and public transport non-existent in the evenings. He was fed up with the heavy, greasy, dirty work in the garage and he wanted to get away and be his own boss.

He saved as much money as he could, doing farm-labouring jobs in his spare time. One day he handed Bill his notice and told his parents he was off to London, knowing what their reaction would be: George stared at him as if he had just announced he had burned the garage down and it was a few moments before he spoke.

'You what? Have you gone mad? You've left a good apprenticeship to go to London? And what sort of job do you think you'll get there?' He banged his fist on the kitchen table so hard that their teacups jumped and spilled some of their contents. Minnie wrung her hands.

'Oh Dave don't do anything hasty. Think of all the hard work you've put in and the good job you'll get when you finish.'

'It's already done Mam. Like I said, I've handed my notice in and I know I can make a go of it in London. I might not get much of a job at first but in no time I'll be earning good money in my own business. Mark my words.'

Minnie, though amazed at his self-assurance, was no less fearful.

'Dave, you haven't thought this through and I'm sure Bill would have you back. He's a decent bloke.'

But Dave had made up his mind and, although he was only sixteen and his parents could have refused to give their permission, they knew that that would not be a good idea. Knowing Dave he would go anyway and may not even let them know where he was living.

Dave arrived at King's Cross on a mellow September afternoon in 1958. He had been in touch with an employment agency and they had secured a job for him: porter in a residential hotel in Earl's Court. It wasn't what he wanted to do, but it was live-in, he had his own room and his food was provided. It was low-waged but with no bills to pay, he was determined to save most of it towards his longed-for business, though he still had no idea what that would be.

He started work at seven-thirty, had a few hours off in the afternoon, then worked again till eight in the evening. He was free on alternate weekends. He used his free time to walk the length and breadth of the city, familiarising himself with it and pondering possible business ideas. Walking round Soho, he was tempted by the many pubs and clubs, but he didn't succumb. He needed every penny for his proposed venture; time enough for pleasure later.

On his wanderings, he was especially interested in the many markets selling everything from fruit and vegetables, new and second-hand clothes and furniture, to antiques. This seemed a good business to go into. Stalls were cheap, but he needed to think carefully about what would sell well. Rationing had come to an end and, after the austere war years, women were eager to buy fashionable clothes.

As he approached eighteen, Dave was concerned about being called up to do his National Service. He couldn't bear the thought of the discipline of the armed forces and he wanted to be his own boss as soon as possible; not defer it for two years. Talking to some lads about it, he made the happy discovery that a forged doctor's certificate could be had for a sum of money; careful as he was with his money, he had no qualms about handing some over for this purpose.

Soon afterwards he decided to go for a stall selling women's fashions and, finding a reasonably-priced supplier, he set up his stall and found that women flocked to it. He was pleased with his success, but one day as he was packing up, he was approached by a bearded man in his mid-forties.

'Hello mate. How's the stall going?'

'What's it to you?'

'Just interested. Used to have a stall here myself, before the war, selling similar goods. You got a good supplier?'

'Yeah.'

'Bet he's not as good as my mate. He could sell you stuff for half what you're paying now and the quality's as good, if not better.'

'Is that so?' Dave was sceptical.

'Want to come to the warehouse, see for yourself?'

Dave thought, *well why not? Can't do any harm.*

When he entered the warehouse and was told the price of the goods he had no doubt that they weren't legal but he didn't care. At wholesale prices like these, he could knock a bit off his stall prices; more goods would sell and he'd be coining it.

Dave was right: his business thrived and his savings

mounted. Then he expanded into shoes, men's clothing and soft furnishings. He had three stalls, making it necessary to employ staff. But his heart was not in clothing and furnishings. During his apprenticeship with Bill Weaver he had come to love cars, even though he grew tired of working on them and with his finances soaring, he had recently become the proud owner of a second-hand Ford Zephyr. Two-tone blue and sleek, it was his pride and joy and he spent many hours cleaning and polishing it. Not many people had cars at that time, but Dave knew they were a coveted possession and that with the comparative affluence of the day, the number of owners was on the increase. A second-hand car dealership seemed like a promising enterprise and one that he would enjoy in a way that he had never enjoyed his market stalls, lucrative as they were. And so he sold his stalls at a tidy profit and opened his first car venture.

Dave had already proved himself a good, if not always honest, businessman and his car dealership, Collier Motors, thrived and moved from a bomb site in east London to bright new premises south of the river. When he met Lydia in 1973, he owned a second showroom and had a very healthy bank balance.

The rift with Minnie had happened three years previously. His father, always a heavy smoker, had developed emphysema and had been deteriorating for a couple of years. Tom had fulfilled his parents' dream and got a place at university, where he studied physics. Shortly after graduating, he'd applied for and got a job in America.

Minnie missed both her sons, for although Dave was in London, he was so busy building up his business that he rarely visited. *Surely he'll come home more often now that his dad's ill,* she thought as she made the phone call to tell him the news. Dave did come up that weekend, but afterwards his visits were as infrequent as ever and his phone calls only slightly less so. Tom, meanwhile made the long-distance call from America a couple of times a week.

'Can you not come up more often Dave? It would do your father the world of good; he loves seeing you and hearing about the car business and life in London.'

Silently Dave mimicked his mother's reproachful voice and made a face at the telephone. 'I'll try Mam, but it's not easy; the business takes up most of my time.'

But things didn't change. Even at the end when Minnie rang to say that George was in a coma it was, 'Not much point in me coming up then Mam. It won't make any difference to him; he won't even know I'm there.' Minnie was shocked. Surely even Dave couldn't be so unfeeling?

'I can't believe I'm hearing this Dave. We don't know for sure that your dad wouldn't know you were there but apart from that, do you not want to see him one last time before he goes?' She swallowed hard to try and hold back her tears.

Dave did come to his father's funeral. Tom had arrived the previous day. He greeted Dave coolly, having heard from his mother about his apparent lack of feeling. 'So you managed to get away. I thought you might have been too busy making money to come.'

'Oh so she's been moaning about me has she? Well let me tell you, it's none of your business what I do. At least I didn't go running off to the States…' He stopped as Minnie entered the room. 'You two catching up on old times?' Dave and Tom said nothing but Dave seethed inwardly. *So you've been criticising me to my brother, have you? You see more of me than you'll ever see of him. Who helped you out when you wanted a bathroom put in; when you wanted a phone installed; when you needed driving lessons and a car to take Dad to his hospital appointments and later to visit him? I was earning good money when he was having a good time at college, too poor to help you with anything. Well he always was the favourite.*

Dave had planned on staying until the day after the funeral; now he felt he couldn't bear to be in the company of his mother and especially his brother for longer than was necessary. When the funeral meal was over, he excused himself, saying he had to make a phone call.

He took Minnie aside. 'Look Mam, I'm sorry about this. I've just checked in with work and something's come up. It's urgent and they need me back there as soon as possible.'

Minnie sighed. 'Oh surely not Dave. Not on the day of your father's funeral. I was hoping you'd be here till tomorrow at least. Can't someone else deal with it?'

'I only wish that was the case. I'll come back with you and get my things, then I'll be off.' Minnie said nothing, but as soon as they were back in the house she burst into tears. 'I don't know how you can be so unfeeling Dave. I don't believe there's any situation at your work that couldn't wait for another day or two. Your father's gone and I need some support. Have you not thought about that?' She flopped down on the sofa, head in hands.

'You'll have him, won't you? For another few days.' He nodded towards Tom. 'Your blue-eyed boy. Surely that's enough for you.' He stomped upstairs and came down with his holdall. Tom was comforting Minnie. Without another word, Dave went out, slamming the door.

As he was putting his bag in the boot, Tom came running out. 'You bastard! How could you do this to her on the day of Dad's funeral.' But Dave was already starting the engine and sped off without a backward glance.

A few days later Minnie rang to apologise. 'Sorry about the other day Dave. I should have been more understanding about your work. I don't know much about running a business and I suppose you had no choice but to go back when you did…'

Dave interrupted, 'Missing blue-eyed boy are you? That why you're ringing me? Look Mam, I have nothing more to say to you. I've done my best to help you and Dad out financially. I can't help it if my business takes up so much of my time. You've never understood that, but you'd never have got your bathroom, your phone, your car and other things without my help. What's he ever done for you? Taken himself half way across the world, that's what.' He was shouting now and Minnie was crying.

'He is not my blue-eyed boy, I've always treated you equally and so has your father.'

'Oh yeah? What about the things I got blamed for? You even thought I destroyed my own bicycle to get him in trouble. You couldn't prove it was me but you believed it, I know you did. And before you say anything else, I don't want you to ring me again, in fact I'm going to change my number. You can go crying to Tom in future.' He slammed the phone down.

Chapter Twelve

Lydia dreaded Christmas that year. It would have been Simon's first and she still blamed herself for his disappearance. She found herself wandering round toy shops and the children's department in book shops, thinking about what she would have bought him, inadvertently punishing herself.

Nevertheless, she was determined to make it as normal as possible. She and Dave were invited to spend it with Anna, John and Jess and Lydia insisted on staying over on Christmas Eve as she wanted to be there when Jess opened her presents in the morning.

'I don't think that's a good idea Lydia. What would have been Simon's first Christmas and you want to watch another child open her presents. It'll be like rubbing salt into the wound.'

'Jess is not just another child; she's my niece and she means the world to me – all the more so after what's happened.'

'Well you go then love. I'll come over on Christmas Day.' Dave had turned towards the window and was staring out at the expanse of parkland below.

'Oh I'm sorry darling. I've been very thoughtless.' She went and put her arms round him; turned him to face her, seeing tears on his cheeks. 'I wasn't saying I wouldn't find it difficult, more than difficult. I just feel I have to put myself through these things, otherwise I'll never heal. I'll stay here with you if you want me to.'

He wiped away the tears with the palms of his hands. 'No you must go if that's how you feel. We all have different ways of coping and in general, I'm better off on my own at times like this.'

On Christmas morning, a sleepy Jess was carried downstairs by John; Lydia and Anna coming behind.

'You sure you're okay?' Anna searched her sister's face.

'Yes I'm fine. I can't wait to see Jess's excitement.' But inside she was apprehensive. Jess stood gazing at the mound of presents under the tree with a mixed expression of bewilderment and joy and had to be prompted by her parents to start tearing at the paper. As the gifts emerged, she whooped with delight as she held each one up for the adults to see.

Lydia was caught up in the euphoria of the moment, but as she watched Jess play with a teddy bear, almost identical to the one that had been in Simon's pram when he disappeared, the little girl began to metamorphose into a plump, eleven-month-old baby.

Where are you now Simon, my beautiful baby. Are you also delighting at presents in a loving home? Or are you...

Suddenly the room was suffocating and her breath was laboured. Luckily Jessica had finished opening her presents.

'Shall I make some tea and get some juice for Jess?' Without waiting for an answer she left the room and in the kitchen, she opened the back door and stood taking deep breaths of the early morning air before turning to put the kettle on. Strangely, though she could feel the tears behind her eyes she couldn't bring them forth and, thus suspended, they combined with the lump in her throat to bring on a crushing headache which remained for several hours.

'That was one of the most harrowing days of my life,' she said to Dave on the way home.

'I thought you coped very well. In fact I couldn't believe how well.'

'Oh I went through all the motions: laughing, joking, complimenting them on the food, playing with Jess, but inside I've been in turmoil and I couldn't wait to get away.' She told him about what had happened in the morning.

Dave leaned over and put his hand on hers. 'I still think you shouldn't have stayed over, but to tell you the truth it was just as difficult for me. I guess there's no easy way and I was going through the motions there as well. I couldn't wait to get away either.'

Lydia gave him a sidelong look and smiled. 'You know, we'd have made a fine pair of actors.'

Dave squeezed her hand. *If you only knew.*

Minnie had failed to understand why Dave couldn't spend Christmas with her and his son. He had tried to explain. 'Lydia's in a bad way. It would, after all, have been the baby's first Christmas and remember she still thinks I'm also grieving for his loss. She's begged me to spend time with her and I have to go along with it. I can't risk her ever suspecting anything.'

Minnie looked up from changing the baby's nappy and put a hand on her hip. 'Well if she means more to you than your son...'

'Well that's ridiculous and you know it! Of course I want to spend Christmas with Alex but I feel I need to play along with Lydia for the moment...'

'Hah, a long moment. You've been pandering to her ever since you brought Alex here, nearly nine months ago.'

Dave rolled his eyes. 'Can you still not see it Mam? Do I

need to spell it out again? She's got to see me as the grieving father, this good bloke who supports her even though he's going through hell himself. I can't risk her or anyone else having suspicions about me.'

Minnie lifted Alex and put him in his high chair. 'Okay, okay, I know what you're saying. I'm just disappointed that you're not going to be here for Christmas. This is my fifth Christmas without your father and it's a lonely time of year for a widow with one son in America and the other one who wasn't speaking to her until recently. I usually go to Chrissie's but it's not the same as family at Christmas. Well at least this year I'll have Alex.'

'I tell you what Mam. I'll come up one day before Christmas and we'll have a proper celebration: tree, presents, turkey, the lot. And don't worry, this thing with Lydia won't go on much longer, I promise you and then I'll be able to spend a lot more time here.'

Reassuring words, but as Minnie began to feed Alex her troubled thoughts persisted. *Yes until you find another woman and then will you take my darling away from me?*

On the day before Simon's first birthday, Lydia recalled in detail the events of that day, the thirty-first of January: the sudden onset of labour, how Dave was conveniently there, the quick delivery, her first look at her son, her cuddling him in the ambulance on the way to hospital. Her euphoria.

The more she thought about it, the more her distress grew until she felt she couldn't bear it any longer and she couldn't contemplate living through the day itself. Once more she considered ending it all and once more she was saved by a phone call.

'Lydia? It's Pam, Anna's next door neighbour. Anna's just been taken into hospital with appendicitis. She's asked me to ring you and ask if you can come and look after Jess. I'm with her at the moment but I need to go to work soon.'

Lydia hurried to her car, her mind now focused on Anna and Jess and all thoughts of her own troubles gone. She spent Simon's birthday caring for and playing with Jess who asked repeatedly where her mummy was but seemed happy to spend time with Lydia. It wasn't until she went to bed that Lydia gave in to a bout of weeping; her deep sadness and sense of loss was alleviated somewhat by her gratitude that she'd been available to help Anna, to save Jess from distress and to save them, Dave and John from the trauma of knowing she had taken her own life.

It was in early February that Lydia began to notice a change in Dave. He was unusually quiet and withdrawn, wasn't as affectionate and when she tried to initiate love-making, he was invariably tired. She didn't suspect him of infidelity. They were living at his flat so he no longer had his own space to go to and anyway, he was nearly always at home in the evenings. One evening she asked him if he was worrying about anything. He sighed.

'I'm okay Lydia, just a bit tired, that's all.'

'Everything okay with the business?'

'Oh yes, no problems there. I guess it's the aftermath of Simon's birthday.' He stood up abruptly and reached for his jacket, taking out his cigarettes and lighting one.

'You seem to have done remarkably well over that time.' She was shocked by the sneer in his voice.

'I was distracted by Anna's appendicitis and looking after Jess, but that doesn't mean I wasn't upset. When I got Pam's phone call I'd been reliving every moment of the day Simon was born and I was almost in despair. You know the saying, *every cloud's got a silver lining*? Well I would never tell Anna but it was certainly true on that occasion. But I cried myself to sleep at Anna's that night.'

She knew she would never tell him about her contemplation of suicide.

'I could have done with you here that night. There was no need for you to stay. John was there. You could have come home after he'd visited Anna.' He flicked ash into the ash tray. 'You sweet on your sister's husband or something?'

'I can't believe you said that Dave. It's ludicrous and you know it. I needed to be there for the morning. As you know he goes to work early.'

By this time Dave had poured himself a Scotch. He took a sip, glaring at her over the glass, then put it down and banged his fist on the coffee table.

'I couldn't believe you weren't coming home to me on that night of all nights and if you couldn't see that I needed you here, then I wasn't going to ask.' He drained his glass and got up to pour another. Lydia rubbed her hands over her face. 'God I'm so sorry Dave. But I know you usually want to be alone when you're upset and you did assure me that that night was no different.'

'Well maybe you should have been more sensitive to my mood.' He drained his drink again. 'Anyway, I'm going for a walk. Don't wait up.' He went to the cupboard to get his coat and went out slamming the door.

St. Valentine's Day was coming up and Lydia was determined to make it a day for Dave to remember. Things had not improved between them. Simon's birthday had not been mentioned since and there had been no more harsh words but Dave was still distant and it was weeks since they'd made love. St. Valentine's was a Saturday, making it impossible for her to organise a surprise meal at home, so she booked an expensive restaurant in the West End. She anticipated getting a card and maybe flowers on the day, and even wondered if he had organised a surprise meal or outing for her but there was no post that day.

'I hope you're free to go out for a meal this evening.' She leaned across the breakfast table and touched his cheek.

'A meal? What's the occasion?'

'Dave, how could you forget? It's Valentine's Day.'

'Oh that? So you think that merits a meal out in the circumstances?' His lip curled.

'The circumstances? You mean Simon and what's happened? What has that got to do with us celebrating our love? You do love me, don't you Dave?'

He leaned across the table and took her hand in his. 'Of course I do and I'm sorry I forgot the date. It's all been getting to me more and more since Simon's birthday.'

She felt a modicum of guilt then. If anything, things were getting harder for her too but she felt she must try and make things right between her and Dave. She came round the table and sat on his knee. 'Dave, oh Dave, it's not getting any easier for me either but I want it to be alright between us, otherwise what's the point in anything?'

The restaurant was one of the best London had to offer. Tables adorned with red roses and candles in honour of the occasion, were set in booths, making it possible to believe that you had the place to yourself.

Lydia had bought a new dress for the occasion: silk and clingy, aquamarine to compliment her chestnut hair which was shoulder-length and centre-parted. She knew she looked good. The food was as might have been expected at the price, but Dave pushed his starter away after two mouthfuls.

'I can't do this Lydia. I can't do normality and I don't know how you can. You're his mother, for God's sake. How can you sit and eat as if nothing's happened? I love you but I need time on my own. I thought we could make this work but it's just getting harder and harder.' He stood up and threw his napkin down, 'I've got to go, see you later.' He stormed off.

Lydia was dumbfounded and wanted to run after him but she had enough presence of mind to seek out the waiter and pay the bill before she left. Outside there was no sign of Dave. They'd come by taxi so as they could have a drink, so she hailed a cab. The flat was empty and she sat up till after one waiting for him, then spent a sleepless night tossing and turning and imagining what he may be up to: everything from being with another woman to ending his life.

She finally drifted off around five to be awoken at seven-fifteen by Dave standing by the bedside, gently shaking her.

'Wake up love, we need to talk.'

Her eyelids felt as if they'd been stuck with glue. 'Talk? Now? Can't it wait?'

He hunkered by the bedside, 'No love, it's now or never.'

Ridiculously, the lyrics of the Elvis song came to her mind and she almost sang them, then sanity prevailed. 'Just let me go to the loo Dave, then I'll be ready to talk.' As she washed her hands she wondered what could be so urgent as to warrant talking at that time of the morning.

Dave was sitting on the bed and as she sat next to him she took her hand in his.

'Lydia, I do love you but I'm finding our relationship very difficult at the moment. The truth is I've put my grieving on the back burner most of the time in order to support you and things have just gone from bad to worse for me.' Lydia started to protest and he held up his hand. 'Let me finish. The fact is, I need time on my own to grieve and I suggest we have a trial separation.' He squeezed her hand. 'I feel like a shit for springing this on you, but I've been thinking about it all night and there was no easy way to tell you.'

'Where have you been all night?'

Dave released her hand and stood up. Walking to the window, he parted the curtains and looked out.

'When I left the restaurant, I went for a drink, then I spent the night walking and thinking. I've walked for miles.'

'Where will you go?'

'I'm going to ring my mate Ken, in Highgate. See if he'll put me up for a while but before that I'd like to go abroad for a week or so – Italy maybe, or the South of France.'

'Oh Dave.' She came and put her arms round his neck, laid her head on his chest. 'I do love you, you know and I'm sorry I've been selfish over the months. I've been so caught up in my own grief. But I thought things were better between us since we got back together…well until recently, that is.'

Gently he held her wrists and moved her arms away. 'Yes I know love and I'm truly sorry to do this to you but it may all work out for the best. Now I'm going to make some breakfast. What would you like?'

Lydia shook her head, sure that she would choke if she attempted to eat. 'Just tea for me thanks.'

After further discussion, they agreed on a four-week separation and the following morning Dave left, saying he had managed a last minute booking to Rome. Ken had agreed to him staying with him on his return. He kissed Lydia on the cheek, 'And remember, no contact unless it's a matter of life and death. We must use this time to examine our lives and our relationship, then we'll review things.'

Dave's flight to Rome was no last minute booking. The tickets had been booked two weeks earlier for him and a woman called Wendy who was his new secretary. Until now their trysts had taken place during hours snatched from work and he was looking forward to spending a whole week with her in a luxury hotel.

Then he would go and spend some time with Minnie and Alex. He had been neglectful, hadn't even been able to visit Alex on his birthday, so he looked forward to telling Minnie that his preoccupation with Lydia was more or less at an end and that he would make things up to her and his son.

Chapter Thirteen

Lydia missed Dave terribly but she was also angry with him. He was the one who had suggested they resume their relationship and now, less than six months later, they were having a trial separation at his instigation. She knew she didn't want to lose him but at the same time she told herself that that was a real possibility and she must brace herself and build up her inner resources against it happening. After all she'd managed without him before and surely she could do so again. She was sure that she wouldn't lose him completely. Their relationship may change but she could not imagine a time when they wouldn't be friends after all they'd been through together and with the first anniversary of Simon's disappearance looming.

'I've decided I'm not going to sit around moping in the hope that Dave will want to carry on our relationship,' she said to Anna as they fed the ducks in the park with Jess. 'I'm going to get stuck into my art again. As you know I've not touched a brush since Simon was taken.'

Anna looked at her in wonder and relief. 'Oh I'm so glad Lydia. That's the most positive thing I've heard you say in ages.' She threw the bread bag in the bin and they turned towards the play area, Jessica running ahead. 'Wait for us Jess.'

'I'm not saying it will be easy. I'll have to force myself but I gave up teaching to go freelance and I'm determined to make a go of it.'

Anna lifted Jessica on to a swing. 'I've just had an idea.

Remember my friend Carrie Martin? She's recently opened a coffee shop in Dulwich. *Indigo* it's called and I know one of her plans was to have exhibitions there: paintings, pottery, jewellery and so on. She's got a gallery behind the shop. She might well agree to you exhibiting some of your work.'

Lydia pushed Jess on the swing. 'Push me higher Lydia. Higher.'

'But I haven't done any new work for ages.'

'Doesn't have to be new does it? You've got plenty of stuff she could use. Shall I ask her? In fact why don't we both go along tomorrow, I've not been yet. John and I were invited to the opening but it was just after I came out of hospital.'

Cautiously Lydia agreed. She was pleased now that she hadn't put her paintings and art materials into storage but had decided to keep them in the spare room at Dave's against a time when her enthusiasm for the subject would return.

On seeing samples of Lydia's work, Carrie was impressed and agreed to an exhibition. The cafe had opened with a display of pottery which was a great success and was due to continue for another few weeks. That would give Lydia time to prepare.

She sorted through her work selecting pictures that she thought would have popular appeal, many of which she had forgotten she had ever done. Quite a few needed framing and she did that herself, getting out her tools, measuring and buying the materials. It was time-consuming but she had little else to occupy her and for the first time since Simon's disappearance, she found herself totally absorbed in a task. She was excited at the prospect of the exhibition and amazed at how prolific she had once been. As she worked, she felt a serenity she had not known for nearly a year. Nothing could fill the emptiness left by Simon but she no longer felt needy and dependent on Dave.

She still wanted him in her life but if he wanted to end the relationship, then so be it.

At last the four weeks of separation came to an end and the day before their meeting, Dave rang to ask her not to cook anything for him as he would already have eaten. The next day, in spite of her bravado, she felt nervous and she had little appetite. She made a cheese sandwich, nibbled at it and threw most of it away. She jumped when she heard Dave's key in the lock. She had dressed casually, but with care, her hair up in a ponytail. Glancing in the mirror, she saw that she looked tense and strained, so she forced a smile to her face, determined that the new Lydia would be bright and positive.

'Dave.' She wanted to run into his arms, but hesitated, waiting for him to make the first move.

'Hello Lydia.' He put his hands on her shoulders and kissed her cheek.

'Can I get you a drink?'

'Nothing for me thanks, let's just sit down and talk.'

He sat in an armchair and took out his cigarettes. Lydia sat on the sofa, wondering what was coming. Dave drew deeply on his cigarette and sat back, exhaling through his nose.

'I'll get straight to the point Lydia. Before we separated, I thought I was still in love with you. As you know I was finding our relationship difficult but I really thought a trial separation would make me realise how much I missed you and how important you were to me. I'm afraid it's had the opposite effect. I care about you of course but that old spark has gone. I'm sorry.' He shrugged, 'Anyway maybe you're feeling the same way?'

She leaned forward, cupping her chin in her hands.

'No Dave, on the contrary, I've missed you very much and I couldn't wait to see you again. But I've not been sitting around in misery. I'm having an art exhibition, in a few weeks' time and I've been extremely busy preparing for that.'

'Oh? Where?'

'At a newly-opened gallery in Dulwich.'

He smiled for the first time. 'Well that's good news. I'm really pleased for you.' He sounded genuine.

'So you weren't also planning on ending the relationship then? I thought you might be.'

Lydia shook her head, 'No Dave, I wasn't, but I have acquired a new inner strength in the last four weeks. I no longer have that sense of dependency on you. If you came back, you'd notice the difference, but if you're determined to end it then there's nothing I can do.' She spread her hands.

'Well that's good, for I am determined.' He jumped up. 'I've got to go, no use prolonging things. You can stay here until you get sorted with somewhere to live. Ken says I'm welcome to stay with him for a while. Any movement on your house?'

'A couple more viewings but no takers, I'm afraid.' Dave was pulling on his coat as he moved towards the door. Lydia stood up. 'You will come to the opening of my exhibition?'

'Sorry love. I wish you well of course, but it would be a mistake to come.'

She tugged at his arm. 'But Dave, surely we'll still be friends?'

'Maybe in time Lydia. It's too soon for that. If your feelings for me haven't changed, don't you think it would be very hard for you?' He touched her face. 'Yes I'm sure we'll be friends in time and once again I'm sorry.' And he was gone.

She had been half expecting this but she couldn't believe how abrupt he had been. So that was it then, they weren't even to meet as friends at the moment. But he was right, she still loved him and it would be a mistake to think she could see him as a friend at present. Lydia felt no emotion, just a dull flatness and she sat in an almost catatonic state for what seemed like hours. It was when she took herself off to bed that the tears came.

Dave was fuming as he drove to Ken's. He had considered going to Wendy's but no, he decided, he'd had enough of women for one evening. Lydia's calm and resigned reaction had been unexpected to say the least. He had hoped for a tearful scene with pleading. What on earth had got into her in the past four weeks? Maybe the separation had been a mistake: he should just have told her they were finished and walked out. It was the last instalment of his revenge drama and it was marred by her acceptance.

He thumped the steering wheel so hard he swerved, narrowly missing an oncoming van whose driver leant on the horn. Dave gave him the finger. In spite of his disappointment at Lydia's reaction, he was still pleased that he had achieved his revenge and that his days of supporting her were over. He had no intention of letting her stay at his flat for long. He would tell her that he was no longer getting on with Ken and needed his place back. He knew this would upset her because much as she loved her family, she didn't want to live with them.

The morning after their meeting, Lydia awoke with a feeling of intense sadness, but she was determined there would be no more tears. She had no option but to accept the status quo and she was going to be strong. Looking in the bathroom mirror, she noted that her eyes were still puffed up from weeping, her face pale. *Right,* she said to herself, *it's time you took life in your own hands. You're not thirty yet and you're beginning to look haggard.*

She didn't want to continue living at the flat with its many reminders of Dave. She would go and nag the estate agent. It was nearly five months since her house had gone on the market. She and Dave had seen a few properties they were interested in; she would see if they were still available and if so, have another look at them. Meanwhile, she knew she would be welcome at Anna's.

But before she had time to go to the agent's, there was a phone call about another viewing, resulting in an offer which she accepted. She was disappointed to find that the houses she and Dave had seen as possibilities had been sold. Her search would start again.

She rang Dave and told him about the offer and that she was moving in with Anna. 'Okay Lydia if that's what you want but remember I'm happy for you to stay at mine at the moment.' He sounded sincere but inwardly he was incensed and when he put the phone down he kicked the leg of the side table several times, leaving a mark. Luckily the table was old and scuffed so he wouldn't have to explain the mark to Ken. *The bitch, so she's going to Anna's after all. She's got the better of me again.*

The thought that she was probably leaving because she still loved him and couldn't bear the reminders of him went some way to consoling him.

It so happened that the anniversary of Simon's abduction fell on the opening of Lydia's exhibition. Carrie provided wine and cheese for a gathering of friends and acquaintances and, although she felt wretched, Lydia had no option but to put on a brave face and carry on. She was surprised and delighted to put

Sold stickers on several of the paintings and on the way home she turned to Anna, 'That was a brilliant idea Anna. Thank you so much for suggesting it.'

Anna smiled. 'The first exhibition of many I hope. You did well to sell so many paintings already. But tell me, how are you feeling?'

Lydia sighed. 'About the anniversary you mean? Pretty awful! And I know when I go home, I'm going to relive every moment of that terrible day.'

Anna squeezed her knee. 'Then why don't you come back with me tonight? Talk to me about it.'

The sale of Lydia's house was finalised in June and she still had not found anywhere she wanted to live. She had laid out her art materials on a trestle table in Anna's spare room, but in spite of her good intentions, she found she couldn't get down to doing anything. There were too many distractions: talking with Anna, playing with Jess. The house was small and, much as she loved her family she felt she needed space and time on her own. She thought about the family home in Northumberland. In the three years since their mother's death, Anna had been there a few times with John and Jess. Lydia had only been once with Dave, early on in their relationship. She'd wanted to show him the family home she was so proud of and the beautiful surrounding area. But it had brought back painful memories of her mother's last illness and she'd not been back since. After the abduction, Anna had several times suggested that she go there for a break but she had no heart for it. Now she wondered if going there could be the solution. It wouldn't speed the finding of a home in London, but she needed a change of scene.

Suddenly the idea seemed very attractive.

Anna was pleased. 'I've been suggesting that for some time. I do hope you'll feel you can work there.'

'Oh yes, I think so, that's partly why I want to go, but also, I've been thinking, if there is an afterlife Mum will be wondering why I've left it so long.'

Anna hugged her sister. 'No she'll know why and she'll understand, but she'll also be delighted to see you there.'

Chapter Fourteen

As she drove north, Lydia was excited at the prospect of seeing her old home for the first time in more than two years and she remembered when they'd gone to live there. That was back in 1954 when she was seven and Anna was ten. Their mother was from Northumberland but she'd gone to teach in Edinburgh, met their father Eddie and married him in the spring of 1939. Eddie's family owned a large department store in Edinburgh and he was involved in the business. Anna was born in June 1944 and Lydia in May 1947.

Having survived his years in the army during the war, their father died of a heart attack in 1948 when the girls were four and one. He left them well provided for and there was no need for Kate to return to teaching. After Eddie's death, they spent most summers at their mother's childhood home. They loved the area and especially the house which had been in Kate's family for generations. They were fascinated by its name, *Sea Music* which, their mother explained, had been given to it by her great grandfather when he'd bought it back in 1820.

In 1953 Eddie's widowed father died and, as Eddie had been his only child, he left the department store to Kate who had no interest in the business and put it on the market. She told Anna and Lydia that she had also decided to sell their house and move back to Northumberland.

The girls were shocked. Anna groaned. 'Oh no Mum, I can't

bear the thought of leaving all my friends and starting at a new school.' Lydia folded her arms and pouted. 'Neither can I.'

Kate sighed. 'I know you think it will be difficult, but you'll soon make new friends. You're very popular girls.'

'The other children will make fun of our Scottish accents. They always do when we go on holiday.' Anna's lip trembled.

'But that's just it, you've got friends there already and some of them will be at the same schools. And as for making fun of your accents, I've heard you mimicking theirs as well.' Kate laughed.

The girls were sullen and sulky for a few days but they knew there was nothing they could do. Their mother's mind was made up.

And so their life in Edinburgh came to an end and after tearful farewells and promises to write regularly, they moved to *Sea Music.*

That summer they worked hard at practising the local accent. When they went to school in September, they found that far from being ignored or bullied, they were feted as 'The new girls from Edinburgh' and there were rivalries over who would be their friends.

After relatively untroubled teenage years, Anna, on leaving school decided she wanted to spend time in the capital and she was accepted on a nursing course in London; three years later, Lydia followed her there to study art. Kate missed her daughters but shortly after her return to Northumberland she had taken up a teaching post and as well as still having some old friends in the area, she had made new friends and her life was busy and fulfilled.

—∭—

Lydia parked on the gravel drive and took a deep breath of sharp, salty air before hurrying to unload the car as a downpour began. When she'd left London the weather had been cloudy and cooler than of late and the further north she'd travelled the cloudier it had become.

She always used the back door and as she entered the kitchen, she felt a sudden chill and a shiver ran down her spine. Momentarily fearful, she laughed at her absurdity. *If there is a ghost here it's only Mum and there isn't one, it's just that the temperature's dropped.* The place smelt musty, so in spite of the chill, she went round opening windows and stood peering through the driving rain at the sea: dark grey and angry looking. *Don't think I'll be venturing out this evening.*

Kate had not installed central heating, so Lydia went in search of coal to light a fire and turned on the immersion heater. A hot bath was probably the only thing that would warm her properly.

As the days went by, the temperature rose, but it remained overcast much of the time and it was windy. Lydia decided she would see the first week as a holiday before knuckling down to her work and she made the most of the better days walking on the cliff tops and beaches, collecting shells and pebbles. She paddled but the sea temperature didn't rise sufficiently to entice her to swim.

As usual she thought constantly of Simon. He would be seventeen months now. At eight weeks old he had had a sparse amount of dark, downy hair. His eye colour still hadn't changed from the grey-blue of new-born's and she wondered if they were pale blue like Dave's, deep blue like hers or perhaps brown like Anna's and Jess's. Some people had said he resembled his father, while others had thought he looked like her.

She pictured him running towards the sea, squealing at the

cold water as it lapped over his feet; digging in the sand, laughing. Some part of her still believed that he was safe and well. When the darker thoughts intruded she would push them away with difficulty. Certainly there was something soothing about being in this natural environment after the hustle and bustle of London and she would lie in bed at night revelling in the complete darkness and listening to the music of the sea.

She'd not heard from Dave since their last meeting and at first she had found that difficult and it had taken her all her time to resist the urge to call him. Now she was both surprised and relieved to find that her urgent need for his friendship had disappeared and she was glad he was not in her life anymore. She rang Anna and asked that if, on the off chance he should ring, she would not disclose her whereabouts. She admitted to herself that it was unlikely, given that it was he who'd ended the relationship but she wanted to be sure.

After a week Lydia set up her easel in a sandy cove. It was a calm day with nothing more than ripples disturbing the surface of the North Sea. It wasn't what she wanted; she wanted to paint great storms, tempestuous seas, dark clouds, forked lightning, but it was a start. Here she was sitting at her easel for the first time in, how long? She couldn't remember.

Having already primed her canvas, Lydia began a leisurely mixing of colours for the tranquil scene when all at once her pace changed and she found herself almost frantically creating the strongest of colours. Her brush flew over her palette, then over the canvas as if controlled by some unseen force. Not that she thought that at the time: she was conscious only of the urge to paint.

When she stopped, it was as if she was looking at the painting for the first time and she was amazed at what she saw. An impressionistic picture; turbulent seas with mountainous waves rising up to the sky in places. A picture full of energy and vitality, alive with movement and colour: both sea and sky a mixture of crimson, pale ochre, cyclamen, jade and ultramarine. And right in the middle was a small sailing boat, amazingly still upright, bravely battling its way through the storm on the crest of the waves.

Lydia was shocked for two reasons: it wasn't her usual style of painting and there was, it seemed to her, an intense anger, almost a madness about it.

As she gathered her materials and walked back to *Sea Music* she was extremely worried. Had the events of the past year and a half taken their toll to the extent that she was now bordering on mental illness? Should she ring Anna and tell her what had happened, ask her opinion? She decided against that. Anna had had enough of a traumatic time supporting her.

She phoned Jane.

'No Lydia, I don't think you're going mad. I would say the painting was a good outlet for the anger you must have. I know you felt angry for a time but then you seemed to suppress it. And I guess that, much as you've been very brave about Dave, you must have anger towards him as well.'

'I suppose you're right; I've been so busy putting on a brave face that I've not let my true feelings out. I could fucking kill him, if you want to know.'

'That's more like it. I'll kill him for you if I ever run in to him, the bastard.'

Lydia laughed. 'It's great to talk to you Jane. You'll have to come up and see me when I've had a bit of time on my own.'

'Will do but you just carry on painting and see what happens. It's great you've started again and I'm looking forward to seeing your seascape.'

155

When Lydia looked at the painting again the following morning, she was pleasantly surprised. *It's rather good*, she thought. Yes, it was an angry picture, but there was the little sailing boat valiantly making its way. She decided to call it *Survival*.

But she was no longer wanted to paint the sea or the beautiful Northumbrian countryside. She had a strong urge to paint abstracts, not a style she was usually drawn to. She turned one of the bedrooms into her studio and after less than two weeks of living at *Sea Music*, she found that her inertia had disappeared and been replaced by an almost feverish desire to paint. She was up early every morning, in her studio as soon as she'd had breakfast. By mid-afternoon she would force herself to take a break and go for a walk, to make the most of the summer, before returning to a simple meal and further painting until the light began to fade.

In August she had visitors. Jane came for a long weekend and later, Anna, John and Jess came for a week. Pleased as she was to see them it was with great reluctance that she dragged herself away from her work to spend time with them.

Anna looked at the paintings in amazement. 'You have been prolific. And abstracts. Not your usual thing but they're very good, I must say.' She studied the paintings closely. 'May I ask what they represent? Or am I supposed to know that by looking at them?'

Lydia came and stood beside her. 'They're feelings Anna but can you guess which they are?'

Anna stood back a pace and scrutinised them further.

'Mm, that one with all the reds and oranges is surely anger and the one with mostly blues could be sadness I suppose. I don't know about the others.'

'You're right about anger; the blue one is pain, specifically the pain of loss, which incorporates sadness of course; the grey is depression and inertia; the yellow is fear, anxiety, insecurity.'

Anna's eyes widened. 'Oh? I always think of yellow as such a happy and optimistic colour.'

'Yes, so did I until I did this. I was more than surprised at the emotions it brought up in me.'

Anna put an arm round her sister. 'Sounds like these paintings contain all the things you've been feeling since Simon disappeared.'

'Exactly. Since coming here I've felt compelled to work through all those feelings by painting. Believe me, it hasn't been easy. There were times when I felt like tearing my hair out, but I can't stop.'

'And do you feel any better for it?'

'Yes actually, yes I do and the painting I'm working on at the moment is more positive.' She turned to her easel where an unfinished picture rested: predominantly green, violet and pink. 'I still have the compulsion to paint but I'm taking my time with this one. The frantic urge I had with the others is no longer there and when I work on this, I feel calm and peaceful. As always I feel great love for Simon, but I really believe now he is well-cared for and happy.'

Anna examined the picture more closely. 'Well I must say, it would seem as if *Sea Music* is working some magic on you. I'm so glad you came.'

'Yes, so am I. And I was wondering if you'd mind if I stay on here for a while? As you know I only planned to come for a couple of months, but now I'm not sure when I want to go back.'

Anna frowned. 'God Lydia, you don't have to ask my permission. It's your house as much as mine and I'm more than happy to see the effect it's having on you.'

'Yes but we did talk about letting it out. You're missing out on a bit of income from it…'

Anna interrupted, 'I've been thinking about that and I don't know about you, but I couldn't bear to let it out to strangers. No, stay as long as you like; as long as I can come here for holidays, I'm happy.'

Chapter Fifteen

While Lydia was busy with her painting by the North Sea in Northumberland, Dave had taken a cottage for himself, Minnie and Alex by that same sea in North Yorkshire.

Since finishing with Lydia in March, he had stayed at his mother's most weekends, much to Minnie's delight. She still feared that he would take Alex to live with him at some stage but, she told herself, if that were to happen, it would not be in the near future. Dave's work would not allow him time to care for a baby, so it would not be until after Alex started school; unless he married or got seriously involved with another woman. She questioned him then about his relationships: was there anyone new on the scene since Lydia? Anyone he was serious about? He said that he never wanted to get seriously involved again; he had been hurt too much by Lydia's actions and Minnie was somewhat reassured by this.

It was true. Not that he had been hurt by Lydia but, as he saw it, she'd done her utmost to disempower and humiliate him, even emasculate him. He still seethed when he thought about it but then he would look at his son and remember that he was the one who had won out in the end, leaving her to a life of loss and grief. He wondered sometimes how he had ever become involved with her. He, Dave Collier who took pride in being seen with a succession of attractive women; pride in using women and then casting them aside. After the first split with

Lydia, he had vowed that he would never again become ensnared and he had kept his vow.

Now, on a cool and sunless day, he sat behind a windbreaker on the beach, building sand castles with his nineteen-month-old son and wishing he was on a sun lounger by the blue and sparkling Mediterranean. He had done his best to induce Minnie to try the delights of southern Spain but she was not to be persuaded. No one could convince her that flying as a means of transport for any creature apart from birds and bats, was anything short of madness, foreign food would be sure to upset her delicate digestive system and why go all that way when they had perfectly good seaside resorts practically on their doorstep.

'Fancy a cuppa Dave?' Minnie laid down her knitting and produced a vacuum flask from her bag. *Tea indeed. A stiff drink would be nice.*

'No thanks Mam, maybe later. Me and Alex are just off to get some water to put in the moat.' He took his son's hand and they ran towards the sea.

'Be careful Dave and don't let him go in the water, it's far too cold today.'

'He's only going for a paddle,' Dave shouted back as he rolled his eyes and gritted his teeth. What on earth had possessed him to book the cottage for a fortnight? They'd only been here four days and he'd had enough. He was bored: playing with a baby was all right in small doses, not all day, every day and Minnie was really getting on his nerves with her constant nagging. Well he would endure the rest of this week and then make up some excuse about work.

—◊—

Lydia had completed her *Emotions* paintings and she was still surprised at their style, so unlike her usual, they might almost have been done by another artist. On one hand she felt they weren't of her and on the other that she had poured her very soul into them and she marvelled at the strange dichotomy. But she was pleased with her achievement and she set about looking for a place to exhibit her work. She was delighted to have sold all those she had exhibited at Carrie's cafe in Dulwich and it had boosted her confidence.

One picture she would not part with: the one she'd named *Survival.*

She decided that she must seriously start thinking about earning some money. She had been living on her mother's legacy, but the money wouldn't last forever and she needed to make sure she didn't begin to erode the proceeds from the sale of her house. Selling paintings was all very well but she needed a regular income.

Her initial idea on giving up teaching had been to illustrate children's books and she still liked that idea so she went to the library to look up lists of agents and publishers, then sat at her mother's old typewriter composing letters of introduction.

Meantime she found a home for her *Emotions* series in a small gallery and set about framing them and producing a statement of her work. On the evening before the opening, Jane rang to ask if she remembered Dan Wilson from the English department at their school.

'Well of course I remember him Jane, he and I were good mates. Why?' She suddenly had the awful thought that something bad had happened to him, so she was relieved when Jane went on in a cheerful tone.

'Well he's written a book – a children's book. It's been accepted for publication and he would like to talk to you about illustrating it. He asked me for your phone number, but I thought I'd better ask you first.'

'Wow, that's amazing. As you know that's what I want to do. Yes of course give him my number.'

'Will do and the best of luck for the exhibition. Sorry again I can't make it but we're up to our eyes at work.'

Dan rang the following evening and a few days later some chapters arrived in the post. Lydia was fascinated by the story: *Tom and the Pterodactyl* about an eight-year-old boy who lived with a strict aunt and uncle while his parents were abroad on business. He was schooled at home and was not allowed to mix with other children. He longed for friends and for a pet and one day he came across a pterodactyl in the woods. Having survived when all the other pterosaurs had become extinct, it was, like Tom, very lonely.

After his initial fear, Tom had become close to him and together they had had the most amazing adventures, encountering many friends and enemies: human, animal and supernatural.

Lydia immediately thought about Simon. She imagined him having great adventures with animal and human friends, not because he had to escape a strict and unloving home, but because his home was full of magic and love. She sent Dan some sample sketches which he was happy with and she began work in earnest. She had a picture in her head of what Simon may look like at eight: sturdy and strong with Dave's dark hair. She wondered again about his eyes – pale blue? Deep blue? No. She decided to give him the brown of her sister and Jess.

As she continued to work on the illustrations, she poured all her love, hopes and fears for her child into them.

—⟶∿⟶—

Lydia went back to London for Christmas; the first time she'd been back in six months. She had led a solitary existence in that time and although it was enjoyable at first to be back with her family and to visit friends, she soon found herself longing for the peace of *Sea Music,* its eponymous sounds and the dark velvet sky, alive with stars. *Am I becoming a recluse?* She decided she still needed her friends and family and she loved talking to them on the phone, but there was a limit to the time she wanted to spend with others and she couldn't bear crowds anymore.

She had hoped this second Christmas without Simon would be a little easier, but in truth it was just as difficult. At five Jessica was more delightful than ever and as always playing with her and reading to her, brought her some ease.

As they wrapped presents on Christmas Eve, Anna asked if she had any thoughts of returning to London for good. Lydia finished tying a ribbon and set the parcel under the tree. 'No, not at the moment anyway. I want to get these illustrations finished and then I'll think about it. But the house really has had an amazingly positive effect on my work and I'm reluctant to let that go.'

'Well you could come back and see if it makes any difference. Once you're in the flow of things you might be surprised.'

'True enough.' Lydia said nothing more, but she wondered about where she would work. She needed her own place, but she didn't want to buy until she was sure that London was where she wanted to be. *Maybe I could rent a studio while I make up my mind?* But as she left the noise and busy-ness of the capital behind and arrived at the tranquillity of *Sea Music* late on New Year's Day, she knew that her mind was already made up.

—m—

Dave hadn't enjoyed Christmas. He had no excuse now for not spending it with Minnie and Alex but he cut the time as short as possible, arriving on Christmas Eve and departing on the 27th, claiming that he had to be back for work, though in fact the business was closed until after the New Year.

He enjoyed Alex opening his presents and although at nearly two, the boy was becoming more interesting, he was precocious at language and he got on Dave's nerves with his constant chatter. And when he wasn't talking, Minnie was.

Waving goodbye to his mother and son, he breathed a sigh of relief and turned the radio up to full blast. He knew he cared about Alex but he bored easily with toddler's games and he longed for the day when he could take him to football matches and talk to him properly; the day when he could take him to live with him, not in London, of course, that would be too risky. He'd had no contact with Lydia or her sister since March and he wondered where in the city Lydia had bought her new house. Trouble was, he loved London and no other city in Britain appealed to him. Maybe he would sell the business and go abroad, open a little bar in Spain.

The truth was, ever since cutting ties with Lydia, Dave was at a loose end. He had no focus anymore. For more than two years, he had plotted and schemed. The abduction, though scary, had also been exciting. Since he had taken Alex, their relationship had been on his terms. He'd revelled in the whole pretence of supporting Lydia while playing the grieving father; there had been a few blips at the end when she had asserted herself, but all in all he had been the one who had called the shots. And his *tour de force* had been wooing her back only to dash away her hopes again.

Shortly after he'd told her it was over, he'd become aware of a feeling of flatness, of futility. There was no excitement in his life anymore, his only interest in women was sexual, his business was thriving and that was great but there was no challenge in it. He needed something else in his life but he knew not what.

Chapter Sixteen

Lydia laid down her pencil and sat back from the drawing board, lifting her arms above her head in a leisurely stretch. She got up and stood looking out of the window at a blustery day, more like March than July. Rain was driving against the window and the turbulent sea and ragged sky together formed a palette of greys. She looked at her watch. Time to prepare lunch. She was thankful that she had invited Luke here, having no inclination to go out in this weather. She had made a Bolognese sauce earlier. She would re-heat it and cook spaghetti when Luke arrived.

As she set about making a salad, she thought about her friendship with Luke. They had met when he'd come to do some decorating in the spring. *Sea Music* had not been decorated since her mother's time and while she'd been there, Lydia had had no thought of changing things. That is until March when she'd been in the house for nearly two years. She'd again had a harrowing time around Simon's birthday in January, resulting in a period of apathy about her work.

Tom and the Pterodactyl had been a huge success, both from a literary and an artistic point of view. Dan had not written anything since but she was now much in demand for her illustrations and she was busy with another book. If she didn't get on with it, she told herself, she would lose her commission. But as the third anniversary of Simon's abduction approached, she was near to despair as she once again re-lived her last weeks with him.

I've got to stop this. Re-living the past is not going to bring Simon back and it is only compounding my grief. I'm never going to get over losing Simon but I've got to try and make things easier for myself. Being here at Sea Music has helped but I need to make changes.

She wasn't quite sure what changes she needed to make. But one morning she got up and looked at the faded wallpaper and curtains, the chipped woodwork, the threadbare carpets on the stairs and in the main sitting room and decided that the house needed revamping. And if that gave her the impetus to make changes in herself and continue her work, it would be an added bonus.

She consulted Anna who was in agreement that the house needed redecorating and that some carpets needed replacing. They discussed colour schemes and Anna was happy for Lydia to make the final decision on paints and soft furnishings. She had long ago turned their mother's bedroom into her studio and removed the carpet; the floor boards were spattered with paint. She would have them sanded and sealed. She asked her neighbours for advice on painters and decorators and Luke Matthews and his partner Mike Willis came highly recommended by all.

Pleased as she was at the prospect of fresh new rooms, Lydia had dreaded the disruption, but the men worked quietly and unobtrusively with the least possible amount of disturbance and at the end of each day, they did a thorough clear up.

Apart from making them cups of tea, Lydia had no contact with them and at times, she almost forgot they were there. Until they started work on her studio and she went in with tea and biscuits, to find Luke staring intently at *Survival* which leant against the wall.

'Oh I forgot to remove that. I must put it with the others.' She hesitated. 'What do you think of it?' she was surprised to hear herself ask. Luke accepted the tea and a biscuit before answering.

'I think,' he said slowly without taking his eyes off it, 'it's stunning, quite amazing.' He turned to look at her and she noticed for the first time his dark brown eyes, fringed with thick lashes.

She felt embarrassed suddenly. 'Do you really think so?' He turned back to the painting.

'Yes, it's very powerful. Some very strong emotions went into the painting of that, I'd say. Actually I'm envious, I wish I could paint like that.'

'Do you paint? I mean apart from house painting.' Lydia gave a little laugh and immediately felt silly.

Luke smiled for the first time, his normally serious face lighting up. 'I dabble – watercolours, oils, just a bit of a hobby, but I enjoy it.' He drained his cup and she took it from him. 'Well I'd love to see your work sometime.'

He shrugged. 'I wouldn't call it work and I think I'd be too embarrassed to show it to a real artist…'

'He's really good,' Mike cut in, 'but he's always putting himself down.' He turned to Luke, 'Aren't you mate?'

Luke threw a cloth at him. 'Shut up and get on with your work!'

Lydia laughed as she left the room.

Forgetting all about the conservation, she was surprised when, at the end of the day the work was completed, Luke produced a large carrier bag.

'I wondered if you'd take a look at this.' He cleared his throat. 'I never thought I'd do this, but I was thinking about what you said the other day and I thought why not? Why not get a professional opinion?'

He took a tissue-wrapped parcel from the bag, unwrapped

it and handed Lydia a water colour. It was a tranquil scene: a seascape at sunrise. Lydia studied it, surprised by what she saw, though she chided herself for that later.

'I think this is really good Luke, you've really captured the essence.'

Luke's eyes widened. 'You really think so? You're not just saying that because I've put you on the spot?'

'Absolutely not. I would never do that. No I think you have real talent if this picture is anything to go by and I'd like to see some others.'

A few days later she'd gone round to his house to view his work and that was the start of their friendship. Luke told her that he had been passionate about drawing and painting since he was a young child and it was his ambition to be an artist.

'But my dad thought it was a 'sissy' job with no prospects. "If you want to paint son then be an honest-to-goodness painter and decorator like me," he said and he forced me into becoming an apprentice with the firm he worked for. I enjoy my job, but I've always regretted not standing up to him.'

In the four months since, they'd met regularly for coffee or meals in restaurants or at one or other of their homes. They went for walks and Luke asked her advice on his work. She didn't think he needed much advice: he was a natural and she encouraged him to exhibit in the local gallery where she had exhibited hers but he was lacking in confidence. She learned that he was thirty-three and unattached since the breakdown of a serious relationship nearly two years before.

In turn she told him about her relationship with Dave and the loss of their baby. He was appalled, said he couldn't think of much worse happening. There was a growing attraction between them but it had remained unspoken until four weeks ago. They'd had dinner at his place and, as she was leaving, they hugged as usual but the quick peck on the lips turned into a lingering kiss. Lost in the kiss for a moment, Lydia pulled away.

'I'm not sure about this Luke. It's not that I don't find you attractive, I do but I don't know if I'm ready. After my relationship with Dave, I find it hard to be trusting and I do still get very low at times. I expect I'll grieve for Simon forever.' To her horror she found herself weeping.

Luke held her, saying he understood her reluctance. He'd felt the same after his last relationship had broken down and that it was only now, having got to know her that he could contemplate getting close to someone again.

'I love you Lydia and I would never do anything to hurt you. I'm prepared to wait if you think you might change your mind at some time but above all, I don't want to lose your friendship.'

Lydia felt her resolve weakening as she leaned back to look him in the eye, gently putting a hand on his face. 'I won't stop seeing you. I value our friendship too much.'

They had carried on as before and the incident hadn't been mentioned since.

Now as they ate lunch, Lydia thought as she did frequently, how appealing this man was. He wasn't tall, probably about her own height, 5'7", of stocky build, longish dark hair, often as now, pulled back in a ponytail, and those beautiful eyes. She felt the strong pull of attraction and she fervently hoped that one day soon she could move on in the relationship aspect of her life as she had in the area of her art.

'That was delicious as usual.' Luke laid down his cutlery and pushed his plate away. Lydia got up from the table. 'Like some fruit? I've got strawberries, raspberries, apples.'

'Not for me, I'll just have coffee if that's okay.'

'You should eat more fruit,' she chided as she reached for the cafetière.

Lydia poured the coffee and sat down. 'Well I'll miss you Luke.'

After lunch he was driving to Newcastle to meet up with a friend and they were taking the ferry to Amsterdam for a two-week cycling tour of Holland and Germany.

He put his hand on hers. 'I'll miss you too Lydia. But when is your niece coming? She'll keep you busy.'

'Anna and John are dropping her off next Saturday and I am looking forward to having her here I must say.'

'So how long is she staying?'

'Well they say they'll be away ten days but I wouldn't be surprised if they come back a bit earlier. They've not been away anywhere without Jess since she was born. They're bound to miss her.'

Jess was excited at the prospect of spending time with Lydia at *Sea Music*. She loved the house and the sandy beach below the cliffs. And she loved Lydia and had missed her since she had moved away from London.

As they drove up the motorway, she chattered about paddling, swimming and making sandcastles. Anna and John exchanged glances. They were a bit anxious about leaving her for the first time for more than a few hours.

They needn't have worried. She settled in well. She and Lydia spent time at the beach and went for walks but she was also good at occupying herself so Lydia was able to continue with her illustrations. As always, the child was fascinated by the house: the sheer size and number of rooms compared with their rather cramped semi in London. She especially liked the warmth of the big kitchen with its large range and the coal fires that Lydia lit in the snug back room on chilly evenings. There were no open fires in her London home. She loved her bedroom with its view of the sea. She was enchanted by the name and she loved going to sleep at night to the sea's lullaby.

On the Saturday after her arrival, Lydia decided to have an outing to Newcastle; she needed some art materials and she would buy some more crayons and paints for Jess. They would have lunch and go to the cinema. She'd looked in the paper and Disney's *Snow White* was on. They were early for the film and as they sat waiting for the lights to dim, Lydia watched idly as a grey-haired woman came in holding a little boy by the hand. There was something so familiar about the child that Lydia sat upright in her seat and stared. He reminded her strongly of someone. She stifled a gasp as realisation dawned: she was looking at a miniature Dave Collier. Same dark wavy hair, same facial shape and expression.

The pair proceeded up the aisle and moved towards a seat two rows in front of Lydia and Jess. Lydia felt the adrenaline coursing through her body and her hands were shaking. She gripped the back of the seat in front in an attempt to steady them and was relieved when the lights dimmed but she found it impossible to concentrate on the film. Her eyes kept going towards the silhouette of the child. He looked about three or four years old with a sturdy little body. Simon would be three and a half now. Could it possibly be that she had found him at last? Her eyes strayed to the woman. Was she masquerading as Simon's mother? No she was too old for that surely – middle to late sixties. Was she then his supposed grandmother? Had someone younger abducted him and did she perhaps know nothing about it?

At last the film came to an end and the lights went on again. Lydia was pleased that Jess had so obviously enjoyed it but she kept a close watch on the woman and child as they made their way out. *What now? I can't very well confront this woman with an accusation. Even if it is Simon, she may not have had anything to do with the abduction. And anyway I can prove nothing and I may be totally wrong about the whole thing.* Nevertheless she was compelled to follow and she was relieved to see the pair turn into the car park where she had left her car. Suddenly the boy shrieked 'Daddy' and letting go of the woman's hand raced in the direction of a man who was smiling and holding out his arms. Lydia felt the blood drain from her face, she felt light-headed and sounds seemed to come from afar. She held Jessica's hand tightly as if for support, for the man was none other than Dave Collier.

'You're hurting my hand.'

Lydia had momentarily forgotten about Jess. 'Oh I'm sorry love.' She relinquished her grasp. They had reached the car and she bundled Jess in and closed the door after muttering, 'I'll be back in a minute.' She raced across to where Dave had just put the child in a car and was holding the door for the woman.

'Hello Dave,' her voice quivered. He looked round, took a couple of steps back and stumbled. 'Lydia? Lydia, what are you doing here?'

'I could ask you the same thing but more to the point, who is that child?'

'Well…eh…he's my son.'

She felt herself grow light-headed once more. 'Simon? But I don't understand.'

'Simon?' He raised his eyebrows, laughed, 'Of course not. His name's Alex. You thought you were the one and only then, didn't you? Well, as you found out, you weren't: this boy was born a couple of weeks after Simon.'

'I don't believe you. I'm going to get the police on to this.'

'Do what you fuckin' like.' He got in the car, slammed the door and sped off.

Lydia was trembling as she returned to her car; her hands were shaking again and she felt in no fit state to drive. She sat taking deep breaths. 'What's wrong Lydia?' Jess was staring fixedly at her.

'I'm alright sweetheart. Just got a bit of a headache. I think we should go and have something to eat before we go home. How about some chips?'

'Oh yes please.' Chips were a rare treat for the little girl.

As they sat in the cafe, Lydia tried to appear as normal as she could for Jess's sake and she concentrated hard on her chatter, though her mind was anything but quiet.

—m—

Dave had booked a holiday cottage for Minnie and Alex in a resort just north of Newcastle on Tyne. He didn't take holidays with them anymore but had joined them for the weekend. Minnie started to question him as soon as he got in the car.

'That was her, wasn't it? That was Lydia, the mother.' She lowered her voice as she said this and her eyes darted towards Alex. 'Do you think she believed you? What if she goes to the police?'

'Don't worry Mam, she can't prove a thing. And she hasn't a clue where you live.'

'Maybe not but she knows where you live. Maybe she's following us back to the cottage.' She looked fearfully out of the back window.

'I don't think so Mam.' He leaned over and turned the radio up high. His signal to Minnie to shut up.

Dave was quite unnerved by his unexpected meeting with Lydia. What on earth was she doing in Newcastle? He knew her family home was just up the coast. Did it mean she was staying there? She'd really put him on the spot, appearing out of the blue like that and he felt he'd been pretty smart, admitting that Alex was his son by another woman. But did she believe him? Would she really go to the police? Well what if she did? They couldn't prove a thing – or could they? They might discover the birth certificate was a forgery and they could soon find out that Alex's supposed mother had never existed. For the first time in years, Dave Collier was frightened and he needed a plan.

Driving back to *Sea Music* Lydia was relieved when Jess fell asleep. Now she could think about the events of the afternoon. Her head teemed with questions. She was convinced that the child was her son. But was that because she wanted him to be? Was it possible that Dave Collier had abducted his own child? She remembered how upset he had been when she had offered him limited access to the child but she also remembered how he had seemed to accept that eventually and how supportive he'd been after Simon went missing, in spite of his own very obvious grief. She didn't think she could have survived without him. Was she being ridiculous about the whole thing? Dave Collier was certainly capable of fathering two children at around the same time. Any illusions she'd had about him had long since been eroded. She wondered where the boy lived and who the older woman was. She didn't even know if Dave was still at the same address. He may not even still live in London. He could be contacted at his business, but what if he'd sold the business? If she did go to the police, surely they would be able to trace him.

It was a fine evening and when they got home, Jess went to play in the garden. Lydia was still undecided about what she should do. She needed to think rationally about this. Why would

Dave kidnap his own son? To get some sort of twisted revenge on her? Why was she hesitating about ringing the police? Was it because she thought they wouldn't take her seriously, think she was just a hysterical woman, overreacting because she had lost her child? She desperately needed to talk to someone about what had happened, get some advice. Luke, Anna and John. Why were they all away when she needed them? She rang Polly, a close friend from school who still lived locally. No reply. She tried Jane's number, keeping her fingers crossed but once again she was disappointed.

Lydia decided to go to her studio and do some painting; that always helped to both calm her and to clarify her thoughts. She went out to see if Jess was alright and found her in the orchard playing some make-believe game.

'You alright out here?' Jess nodded. 'I'll be in my studio painting if you need me.'

Part Three

Chapter Seventeen

2002

Minnie Collier kissed and hugged her grandson Alex, watched him get into his car and waved until he was out of sight. It was a gloomy February afternoon with a chill and penetrating drizzle and she shivered as she closed the door and returned to her seat by the fire. Her old tabby cat Ruby jumped on her knee and distractedly, she began to stroke her.

She was tired, bone tired, but more than that she was weary of life. Well, she thought, what did she expect? It was the day after her eighty-eighth birthday, the damp weather was playing havoc with her arthritis, all her close friends had passed on, one of her sons was in America, the other in Spain, her much cherished grandson lived in London. He had come up for her birthday and he did come to see her as often as he could but he was a busy man so that wasn't as often as she would have liked. Realising that her eyes were wet with tears, she pulled a hanky from her sleeve and dabbed at them impatiently. Reluctant as she was to disturb Ruby, she needed a cup of tea. The cat gave a discontented miaow as she settled her on a cushion and went through to the kitchen. As she brewed her tea, she gave herself a stern talking to.

Pull yourself together girl and stop feeling sorry for yourself. Here you are at the age of eighty-eight with your mind still intact, your health reasonable for your age. Yes the arthritis is painful but you can still get about and fend for yourself, you still live in your own home and you have a very loving grandson who comes to see you whenever he can. Many younger people would envy your circumstances.

Cup in hand, Minnie looked through the window. Darkness was descending rapidly and the moors were now almost totally obscured by the thickening mizzle. She recalled, as she often did, the night when Dave had turned up on the doorstep with Alex and it reminded her of something she had promised herself she would do before her demise – which she thought couldn't be that far off – something she kept postponing. Well she would procrastinate no longer. Switching on a lamp she opened a drawer in the sideboard and took out a writing pad and a pen. Then she sat at the table and began to compose a letter.

Minnie laid down her pen and read what she had written. She had made many changes but she was happy with the final draft and she would write it out properly tomorrow. This evening she was too tired. The fire had died down and she added a shovelful of coal before going into the kitchen to make some cheese on toast. Her mood of despondency had dissipated and she felt lighter for having written the letter. As she seated herself by the fire once more, Ruby in her lap, and looked round her cosy sitting room, she gave thanks, as she often did, that she had had the sense to keep on this cottage when she had gone to live in Spain. She still had a vivid recollection of the day Dave had told her he was moving there.

—✺—

When they had returned to the cottage after the altercation with Lydia, Dave had told her that Lydia and her sister had a house in Northumberland. He'd been there once with Lydia and he remembered exactly where it was.

'I'm wondering if she's staying there. I'm going to see if I can get the number from Directory Enquiries. Then I'll ring and apologise for my behaviour earlier, ask her if I can come up and explain about Alex. If I can't get the number or she doesn't agree, I'll go up anyway. I was always good at twisting her round my little finger so I'm sure I can convince her that what I say is true.'

Even though it isn't, Minnie thought, but she said, 'Oh you will be careful Dave. What if she's already told the police.'

There was no phone in the cottage, so Dave went out to a call box. He was perturbed when there was no reply. *Maybe she's not staying there after all; maybe she didn't go straight back; oh God I hope she's not sitting in a police station already!*

He felt a surge of relief when, on trying again, the phone was answered. He came back smiling and rubbing his hands.

'She's agreed. I'll drive up later. I have a few people to contact about work first. Don't wait up for me.'

'No Dave, I will wait up. I need to know what happens.'

Minnie was worried, very worried. She wondered if Dave was telling the truth about Lydia agreeing to see him. In the car park, she'd seemed convinced that Alex was her child and she had been very angry. Surely she would have rung the police by now.

Having bathed Alex and put him to bed, she tried to settle herself to watch one of her favourite television programmes, but she couldn't concentrate. Her mind kept wandering, wondering how Dave was getting on, hoping that things were going well. Surely he wouldn't be much longer? Her stomach churned with nerves and she got up to peer through the curtains once more.

Finally, after what seemed like hours, she heard his key in the lock. She hurried into the hall. 'Dave! At last! How did it go?'

Dave dropped into an armchair and put his head in his hands. Minnie felt the grip of fear.

'Dave?'

'It was terrible Mam; Lydia's dead.' He got up and began to move about. Minnie flopped on to the other armchair.

'Dead? Oh my God!' She put a hand over her mouth. 'How? What happened?'

Dave continued to move about the room as he told his story.

'As I approached the house I got a bit nervous. It occurred to me that she might have changed her mind and involved the cops and that they'd be waiting for me. Also, I'd forgotten to ask her if she was there on her own or with someone else. I didn't fancy having to plead my case in front of a boyfriend or family member. So I parked my car a couple of hundred yards down the road and approached the house cautiously. I was relieved when I saw only Lydia's car parked at the front. There were no lights at the front of the house, even though it was getting dark. I was about to knock on the front door when I remembered that Lydia spent a lot of time at the back and didn't always hear the knocker so I went round the back, saw a light in the kitchen and had a look through the window. The kitchen was empty. I knocked a couple of times and when there was no answer I walked round the house but there were no more lights. I knocked at the front door. I was convinced someone was in and I was getting more and more frustrated. But then I started to get worried. Lydia was expecting me, after all. I suddenly had an awful feeling something was wrong. Then I noticed that the kitchen window wasn't locked so I opened it and went in calling Lydia's name. The cellar door was open and the light on, so I

went towards it calling her name again. I looked down and...'
He sat down and put his head in his hands again.

'And?' Minnie prompted. Dave looked at her. He shook his
head. 'It was awful Mam. Lydia was lying in a heap at the foot
of the steps. Her head was twisted so that she was looking up at
me, staring. It was pretty obvious that she was dead, looked like
she'd broken her neck.

'Oh my God! It just goes to show what can happen, falling
down a few stairs. They say most accidents happen in the home.'

'You haven't seen those stairs Mam. They're really
treacherous, nearly vertical. I remember being wary of them that
time Lydia took me there. I'm surprised they never had them
altered. It's a miracle there wasn't an accident before now.'

'So what happened after that? You did phone for an ambulance?'

'Well I panicked a bit. I knew I had to get out of there and I
needed to cover my tracks so I closed and locked the window,
went out through the front door and got away as fast as I could.
My first thought was that if Lydia had been murdered and, if
she had already rung the police about me, then I would be the
prime suspect. And don't worry Mam, I made sure I didn't leave
any fingerprints.'

'Did you not think to put in an anonymous call for an
ambulance? If the woman is living there on her own, then
goodness knows when she will be found!' Minnie stood up,
hands on her hips.

Dave wiped a hand over his face, looked at her as if he was
explaining something to a small child. 'Mam, I needed to get
away. Her death had nothing to do with me. She was already
dead. What does it matter when she's found?'

Minnie sighed. They were clearly coming from different
places. 'Let's both try and calm down, think rationally about this.
I'll go and make a cup of tea.'

'It's not tea I need. It's a strong drink. Bring me that bottle of whisky I brought up with me. You could probably use a drink yourself Mam.'

But all Minnie wanted was a cup of strong, sweet tea and she went through to the kitchen to put the kettle on, returning with a steaming mug, a tumbler and the whisky bottle.

'I do think it was an accident Mam. There was no sign of a disturbance, at least in the kitchen. Mind you it could have been someone with a key. I know nothing about Lydia's life now. I suppose she could have been killed in a lover's quarrel or by someone else bearing a grudge. Oh I don't know.' He put down his cup and stood up again, ran his hands through his hair.

'Oh Mam, you have no idea of the thoughts that are running through my head. One minute I'm thinking what if she'd changed her mind about seeing me and had already rung the police, I could be getting a visit at my work on Monday. Then I think, what if she was so disturbed by seeing Alex, thinking he was Simon that she threw herself down the steps. It would be all my fault.'

To Minnie's horror, he began to cry. She had not seen him cry since he was a small boy. Moving to the arm of his chair she took him in her arms and he rested his head on her shoulder. 'Oh Mam, Lydia treated me badly, but she got her comeuppance when I took Si… Alex but I would never have wished this on her. Who could have done that to her?'

'Maybe it was an accident,' Minnie said as she wrapped her arms round him and let him weep.

Dave and Minnie talked for another hour or more while Alex slept the sleep of the innocent, oblivious to the events that were to change the course of his life.

'I need to get away from here Mam.' Extremely agitated,

Dave kept jumping up, pacing about, biting his nails, sitting again, until Minnie felt like screaming.

'I have friends in Spain, I could see about getting a flight tonight...no, no, I'll leave it till tomorrow. No one knows where I am exactly and maybe there'll be some news tomorrow about Lydia's death – that's if the body's been found by then of course.'

'Sounds like a good idea.' Minnie was relieved to hear that he wasn't going to run off in a panic, 'Why don't you make an anonymous call to the police so that we're sure there will be something on the news by tomorrow.'

Dave rolled his eyes and shook his head. 'Are you stupid altogether Mam? It must be seen to be an accident. How many times...'

'All right, all right. I wasn't thinking straight. Look I'm going to try and get some sleep.'

But sleep would not come to Minnie that night, tormented as she was by the fear that her son could be facing a murder charge. Her greatest fear however, was that Dave was not telling the truth. Was Lydia really already dead when he got there? Surely it was too much of a coincidence. Was it not more likely that Dave had tried to convince her that Alex wasn't her son and she wasn't having any of it?

Minnie had seen the conviction in her eyes when she'd confronted Dave in the car park and she firmly believed in a mother's instinct. She felt sure she would always know her own child no matter how long it was since she'd seen him, her own grandchild come to that.

She had also seen how angry Dave had been after the altercation and she knew how strong his hatred for Lydia was and how vindictive he could be. She thought back to the misdemeanours against Tom, both actual and suspected, his anger with her and Tom after his father's funeral, his estrangement from her.

She was tormented with guilt over Lydia. What a dreadful life the poor woman had had, losing her child like that; her life ending both prematurely and violently. Well at least her suffering was over now. Why, she asked herself, had she ever had any part to play in it? But she knew the answer to that.

Finally she dozed but before long Alex was bouncing on her bed. 'Grandma, Grandma wake up. It's a sunny day, can we go to the beach? Will Daddy come with us?'

Minnie groaned and turned over as the events of the night before came crawling up her abdomen and stomach, to lodge in the area of her heart. Oh that she could turn the clock back; not so far back though, that she didn't have this child. In spite of her misgivings, she knew she would never want that.

Having settled Alex with a colouring book and promises of sandcastles, ice cream and fairground rides, Minnie bathed and turned on the radio as she dressed. The local news was due soon. She wondered if Lydia's body had been found yet. When the news came on and there was no mention of the death, Minnie's anxiety rose, knowing that potentially, as Lydia appeared to live on her own, she could lie at the bottom of those precipitous steps for days, weeks even. Then on Monday morning, relief came when the death was reported briefly as an accident. Evidently there were *no suspicious circumstances*.

Dave had stayed over on Sunday night in the hope of hearing some news. Now, greatly relieved, he returned to London. Minnie and Alex were staying at the cottage until the following Saturday. Minnie wanted to go home. She didn't think she could enjoy the holiday after what had happened but Dave persuaded her to stay. She had often wondered since how she had managed that week, going through the motions of enjoyment with Alex for, underneath her laughter and feigned excitement, she was still consumed with the fear that her son was a murderer.

In her better moments, she remembered how Dave had seemed genuinely upset by Lydia's death. She hadn't seen him cry since he was a child. She knew however that Dave was also a very competent actor as she remembered how, after the abduction, he had spent a lot of time with Lydia pretending to grieve and at the same time consoling her. She knew he had done a terrible thing in taking Alex but surely he wasn't capable of murder, was he?

—⁂—

Dave came to stay the weekend after their return and Minnie was shocked to hear him lay out plans to open a bar in Spain.

'It's something I've been thinking about for some time. I was hoping to do it when Alex is a bit older but this whole business of Lydia's threats and then her death has unnerved me. It certainly looks like she hadn't been in touch with the police but, for some reason I don't feel safe here anymore. What if she told someone else? If things change and the death is treated as suspicious after all, I would definitely be a suspect.'

'But no one knows you were there that night and if she did tell someone else they would surely have gone to the police by now.'

'I know that Mam but it doesn't stop me worrying. What if they don't go to the police and start to blackmail me instead?' Dave sounded panic-stricken and Minnie thought he was letting his imagination run away with him, at the same time wondering why he was so frightened if he was innocent.

'So I've decided to go sooner rather than later. Once I'm in Spain, the law can't touch me. So,' he continued, 'I've decided to sell my businesses, my partner Bill wants to buy me out and I can stay with friends in Spain until I find my new business and somewhere to live.'

So this was it: Minnie's greatest fear of losing Alex was about to be realised. The day she had dreaded was about to happen much sooner than she thought.

'Does that mean you'll be taking Alex?' She heard the quiver in her voice, felt the tears gather behind her heart.

'Oh yes, not immediately of course, but as soon as I get sorted with some proper accommodation over there, I'll want him to join me.'

Would she ever see her grandson again? The tears began to escape and she remained silent and turned away, not wanting Dave to know she was crying. So absorbed was she in her thoughts of abandonment she didn't hear Dave ask her a question.

'Well you will won't you?'

Minnie pulled out a hanky and dabbed at her eyes and nose, took a deep breath.

'What? I will what?'

Dave gave an exasperated sigh. 'I said, you will come with us, won't you Mam?'

Minnie thought she was hearing things but she answered immediately. 'Yes, oh yes of course I'll come,' while her head teemed with all sorts of doubts. Several times Dave had urged her to take Alex on holiday abroad but she wouldn't hear of it. She'd never been further than Scotland, didn't like hot weather, worried about what foreign food would do to her already delicate digestive system, she would miss her friends and how could she make new ones when she couldn't speak the language? But she knew she would go to the ends of the earth to be with her precious grandson.

Minnie had no illusions about why Dave had asked her to go. She knew perfectly well that she was going along as a child minder and nothing more but that was fine. Something told her to hold on to the cottage which had been in George's family for generations. She could not imagine that she would ever come back to Yorkshire and leave Alex behind, however difficult she may find conditions in Spain, but at least she could come back for holidays and then when Alex was grown up, if she was still around, she would have her home to come back to.

—∽—

Dave had been in Spain for just over a year, when Minnie undertook the journey with four-and-a-half-year-old Alex in the early autumn of 1979. Bill had paid him a good price for his business and he had bought a bar and several apartments on the Costa del Sol. He had also bought a villa for himself and Alex and had had an annex specially constructed for Minnie in the grounds.

When she heard they were to fly, Minnie had been a seething mass of nerves. She'd begged Dave to let them travel overland but he'd pointed out, not unreasonably, that it was far too long and arduous a journey to be undertaken by a sixty-five-year-old woman with a young child in tow.

'Couldn't you come and take us over in the car?' she pleaded to no avail. Dave explained that, apart from anything else, he didn't want to be seen to be connected with her and Alex. 'You can't be too careful,' he warned.

Knowing it was a lost cause, Minnie had taken herself to the doctor, explained the situation and been given enough tranquillisers to help her over the journey and, though still fearful, she did feel somewhat calmer.

When she looked back on her Spanish days, she wondered how she had managed to survive for fourteen years in that country. From the start, it had more than lived up to her worst fears and expectations. She had been pleased with the villa and especially with her annex. One of her anxieties had been the thought of sharing living accommodation with her son. There was a swimming pool – not that she ever went swimming – and a mature and well-tended garden. But the temperatures were so high when she first arrived that she rarely used the garden. In fact she thought that the heat was literally going to kill her. She and Alex went for siestas in the afternoon but she still found it stifling at other times. There was often a breeze by the sea which was five minutes' walk away and, having done her housework in the early morning, she spent most of the day on the beach, under the shade of a parasol while Alex played in the water and sand but the days were long and tedious.

She largely cooked the meals she would have cooked at home but many of the ingredients she needed were unavailable and shopping was a trial as she had no knowledge of Spanish. There were few other British people living in the area in those days and she was lonely for Chrissie and her other friends. She rarely went near the bar: the British tourists who frequented it were a nightmare, drinking heavily and carousing, playing loud music.

But she knew she must put on a brave front for Dave. When they'd first arrived, she'd spent so much time complaining, that one day he'd turned to her and said, 'If you don't like it here Mam, you know what do. Go back to Yorkshire. It's a good job you kept your house on, isn't it? But remember Alex stays here with me!' She'd stopped grumbling and, as the autumn progressed and the temperatures became more bearable, she felt more at ease but she was very lonely. The following year as the heat rose again, she had suggested to Dave that she take Alex back to England for part of the summer and he had readily agreed.

Chapter Eighteen

Alex Collier settled himself on the plane, fastened his seat belt and tried to find a comfortable position for his long legs in the cramped space. Never at ease with flying, he gripped the arms of the seat tightly and squeezed his eyes shut as they sped along the runway. Only when they were airborne did he begin to breathe more easily as he watched the chequered fields shrink and the cows and sheep change into insects. Withdrawing a blue envelope from his pocket, he turned it over in his hand and read yet again the words written in his grandmother's shaky scrawl: *Alex. (Do not open until I have gone.)*

He recalled the day last week when Minnie had told him about it. How small and thin she had looked in the hospital bed. A little bird in a pink bed jacket: white head and beady blue eyes. She had lifted her head slightly and turned those once piercing eyes upon him.

'It's in the file box where I keep my bank details, receipts and personal papers.' And she'd reiterated the exhortation he was now reading on the envelope. Then, exhausted after such a long speech, her head had fallen back on the pillow and she had closed her eyes.

Minnie died six hours later, remaining conscious until she had greeted Tom and his wife Suzie who had come over from New York and Dave who'd arrived shortly after them, much to her surprise. She had thought he was not coming and she had resigned herself to that.

In the busy days following his bereavement, Alex had forgotten all about the letter but when the funeral was over and Tom and Suzie had returned to the States, Dave to Spain, Minnie's words had come back to him.

He must have read the letter at least a dozen times since then, and now he once again removed the blue writing paper. The letter was dated almost three months ago, 18th Feb. 2002, the day after her eighty-eighth birthday and the last time he had seen her before getting word that she was in hospital.

Dear Alex,

I am writing this on the day after my 88th birthday, for although I am in good health, I feel I will surely not go on for much longer. Who knows I might live to be 100, get greetings from the Queen! But that's alright as long as you read this and if you are reading it now, then I will have passed on. (To better things, I hope!)

For nearly 27 years you have been the most important person in my life. Not that I don't love my sons (even your father for all his ways!) and my other grandchildren but they are so far away and as you know, I rarely see them. You are special to me because I brought you up from when you were a tiny baby.

You will no doubt be shocked at what I am about to tell you and believe me, I've thought long and hard about whether or not to do so but I think you have a right to know the truth.

It is true that Dave is your father, but your mother was not Monica White as you have been told and as it says on your (fake) birth certificate. (She never existed.) Your mother was a woman called Lydia Allan. She wasn't married to your father and they separated before you were born. Dave was very angry with her because she wouldn't let him be fully involved with you. He did see you but it was very limited. So partly to punish her and partly because he thought she had no right to keep him from you, one day he took you from your pram outside a shop and he turned up at my house with you. It was the end of March 1975 and you were 8 weeks old. (You've always thought your birthday was the 12th Feb, but it was the 31st Jan.) I was appalled by what he had done but I fell in love with you immediately and I knew that I could never bear to be parted from you so I went along with his plan even though I knew it was wrong and I was terrified we would be found out. But Dave was crafty. He put on a great show of grief over 'losing' his son and he gave Lydia lots of support, so he was never suspected.

Well over the years, I can't begin to tell you the amount of guilt I felt about what had happened and the effect it must have had on your poor mother. Then one evening when you were 3 and we were on holiday near Newcastle, Lydia appeared out of nowhere, spotted you with Dave and suspected what had happened. She confronted Dave who lied, saying you were his child but by another woman. She didn't believe him and threatened him with the police. Your mother lived in London where you were born but Dave thought that if she was up in the Newcastle area, she might be staying at her family home up the coast. He said it was owned by her and her sister and they kept it for holidays and he drove up to try and convince her that he'd told the truth. (He said he'd rung her first and she'd agreed to their meeting.) Later that night, he came back to tell me that when he got there, no-one answered his knocking, though Lydia's car was there and he had a sense that something was wrong. He found that the kitchen window wasn't locked so he went in and he found Lydia dead at the foot of the cellar steps. Not surprisingly, he panicked and ran off. He was in a terrible state. He seemed truly sorry that Lydia was dead but he was also very frightened that the police would treat it as murder and that he would be a suspect even though he'd not had anything to do with her for a few years because even though she had agreed to see him he was worried she might have changed her mind and told the police.

The verdict was accidental death but Dave was unnerved by the whole thing and that was why we ended up living in Spain. (He had always planned to go when you were a bit older.)

So though you were always told you had no relations on your mother's side, you do have, if they're still around. I have kept the newspaper cuttings from that time. You will find them (if you haven't already done so) in a big brown envelope amongst my other documents.

Alex, I hope you can forgive me for what I did and maybe I will also need your forgiveness for telling you these things that you may not want to hear. Over the years since you became an adult, I have often been tempted to tell you but I was always frightened of how your father would react and if I'm honest, how you would react to me. I didn't want to lose you. I didn't and still don't want Dave to go to jail. You must do what you think best of course but be careful. I dread to think how he may react if you tell him especially as you two don't get on.

I hope you can forgive me Alex. I wish you a happy life.
Love always,
Your gran.

Alex recalled how he had read the letter three times before its meaning had finally sunk in. He had then searched for the brown envelope and found four press cuttings inside. Opening the first cutting from a local paper, he felt his legs buckle; he gripped the table edge tightly for support before collapsing into the nearest chair. A woman was staring at him from the paper's yellowed and fragile folds. She was looking straight at him and smiling warmly as if she were there in the room with him. So this was Lydia, his mother. It was a head and shoulders portrayal, black and white so he couldn't tell the colour of her hair or eyes. The hair looked dark, was centre parted and shoulder length. Alex stared at the face for a long time; he read the accompanying script. It was succinct, stating that thirty-one-year-old Miss Lydia Allan had been found dead at the foot of the cellar steps at her home, *Sea Music*, Barrowman's Point. There was no sign of a break-in or burglary and police were treating the death as an accident. The victim's sister Mrs Anna Cooper and brother-in-law Mr John Cooper were unavailable for comment. It went on to say that Lydia was a talented artist who had had many exhibitions locally and had illustrated a number of children's books, most notably the best seller *Tom and the Pterodactyl* by Dan Wilson.

The second report, from a national paper, was identical. There was no photograph.

The other two cuttings from the same papers, were short obituaries. Lydia Allan, born in Edinburgh in May 1947, moved to Northumberland in 1954, studied art in London and taught the subject for a few years before going freelance. A summary of her career as an artist, highlighted her talent as an illustrator of children's books, citing again *Tom and the Pterodactyl*. There was an account of the tragic abduction of her eight-week-old son Simon in 1975.

There was also a photograph of *Sea Music*. It was a friendly-looking edifice, staring out to sea from its cliff-top location, its stone walls covered with Virginia creeper, intimating nothing of the horror that had happened there.

Now that he had read Minnie's letter so many times he could almost recite it by heart, it didn't detract from the shocking truth. His whole life; his whole sense of who he was,

was based on a lie. Yes he was still Alex Collier, son of Dave Collier but who was the woman whose photograph still stood by his bedside back in his apartment in London? The woman he'd always believed to be his mother. He had never been told much about her. According to Dave she came from Birmingham and had been raised in care, had never known her parentage and had no known relatives. She and Dave had had a brief relationship and neither of them had had any idea she was pregnant when it came to an end. Then, more than a year later, she'd contacted him to tell him she was terminally ill and to ask if he would bring up their son. Dave wondered if the child was his but when he saw him, the likeness was so strong, even at that early age that he had no doubt and agreed to her request. However, because of his work, it would be difficult and, as he didn't want to employ a stranger, he turned to Minnie. In the photograph, the only one he'd ever seen of her, he saw a slim woman in her early twenties, wearing a green and white patterned trouser suit: wide flares, bomber jacket, platform shoes, her blonde hair long and voluminous, her eyes heavily made-up. Handsome, rather than beautiful, she was smiling flirtatiously at the photographer.

So if Monica White did not exist, who was the woman in the photo? And were the police right about Lydia's death being an accident? Was it a fateful coincidence that his father just happened to be there that evening? Lydia may have agreed to see him but, if she did not believe his story, she may have been about to expose him. Had he pushed her down the cellar steps to silence her? It was a horrifying thought, but one he couldn't dismiss. In many ways he was not surprised by the abduction. His father could certainly be callous, cruel and unforgiving, as he knew to his cost. But was he capable of murder? He had never known him to be physically violent but in the circumstances Minnie had described and fearful of being shopped to the police, it was surely possible.

As Alex tucked the letter back in his pocket, he remembered the rage that had bubbled up inside him when he had finally absorbed the meaning of Minnie's words. Rage at both his father and his grandmother for the tapestry of deceit they had woven around him. However, he couldn't stay angry with Minnie for long. Whoever his biological mother was, his gran had been the only mother he had ever known. And he had such fond memories of his childhood with her.

Alex's reverie was interrupted by the air stewardess leaning over to ask him to fold his table. So lost in thought had he been, that he hadn't heard the announcement that they would shortly be arriving in Malaga.

Chapter Nineteen

Alex picked up a hire car from the airport and drove west along the busy coast road; the turquoise Mediterranean sparkling on one side, the oppressive conglomerate of high-rise blocks on the other. Over the years, his father's business had expanded and Alex knew that many of the bars, restaurants, shops and holiday apartments amongst that urban hotchpotch belonged to him. After Minnie returned to England, he had sold the villa and bought a smaller one in the hills above Marbella.

In the years since Alex had left for university in 1993, the rift between him and his father had widened and he hadn't been back since shortly after his graduation nearly six years ago.

When the meaning of Minnie's words had finally impacted on him, his reaction had been to ring Dave straight away and throw accusations at him. Then a small voice of reason had taken over and he had stopped to think about what he must do. In spite of everything, he still loved his father and he didn't want to see him going to prison. He knew nothing about what had gone on between him and his mother and he felt his dad should be given a chance to explain himself. But what if he had murdered Lydia? His head teemed with questions and in the end he decided that the best course of action was to go and see Dave. When he had rung to say he was coming over, he had been surprised by Dave's reaction. He had sounded genuinely pleased to hear from him and pleased that he was coming to visit. He had even asked how his work as a freelance translator was going.

At Minnie's funeral he had been extremely cool with him. Alex informed him it wasn't really a social visit. He had a serious matter to discuss with him. 'Sounds ominous,' Dave said, 'but whatever, it will be good to see you.'

As he neared Dave's home, Alex felt a pang of guilt at what he was going to confront him with.

Parking his car in front of the house, he got out, stretched his legs and took a deep breath, filling his nostrils with the aroma of pine resin, wild marjoram, basil and other herbs he couldn't distinguish. He looked around. In six years the place hadn't changed. The garden was a collage of colour and the views over the Mediterranean, from its hillside position were stunning. *Now keep calm,* he instructed himself. *Don't jump in straight away; listen to Dave's side of the story before you make any judgements.*

Dave and Alex were sitting by the swimming pool, looking towards the sea where the sun was about to dip below the horizon and the sky's radiance of yellows and oranges was reflected on the calm water. The air was balmy, the myriad scents of the garden and the woods beyond, pungent in the evening air. Cicadas chirruped, an owl hooted.

So peaceful, thought Alex, nervous again at what he was about to unleash.

Covertly, Dave watched Alex as he ate his paella. He knew he loved his son. Why was it that they did not see eye to eye? Why was he so different from what he had wanted him to be? So like Lydia. Yes he had loved her too, in his own way. But neither had she lived up to his expectations. Minnie he had loved, yes she had got on his nerves a lot of the time but she had gone along with his plans, made it possible for him to take Alex away from Lydia.

'Did you enjoy that?' Dave asked as he refilled their glasses with Rioja.

'Yes it was very good.'

'I've become an excellent cook over the years, though I say it myself.' He turned to Alex.

'Sorry I didn't have much time to talk to you at Mam's funeral. I had some very pressing business here and had to come back sooner than I'd hoped.'

Alex wanted to say *your business interests always came before family* but he remained silent. There was no point in getting Dave's ire up before he had even dropped his bombshell.

He remembered his surprise when Dave had turned up at the funeral. He hadn't made the journey when Minnie was in hospital, so he hadn't expected him to come but there he was, carrying the coffin with him, his Uncle Tom and three of the undertakers. He'd seen the tears in his eyes and had known that he had genuinely cared about Minnie.

In the silence that fell between them, Alex studied his father. He had grown more handsome over the years and looked nowhere near his sixty years. He was still a fitness fanatic and, in his tight-fitting white T shirt and navy shorts, he could see that his body was still toned and muscular, tanned by constant exposure to the southern sun. Abundant as ever, his dark hair, interspersed with grey, was cut quite short.

Dave shifted in his chair. 'Anyway you said you wanted to talk to me about something?'

'Yes,' Alex took a sip of his drink, set the glass down and cleared his throat. He would get straight to the point.

'Who was my real mother, Dad?' Surprised at how calm his voice sounded.

Dave put his glass down and screwed up his face. 'Eh? What are you talking about?'

Alex leaned forward and gazed fixedly at him. 'You know perfectly well what I'm talking about. Monica White never existed. She was a figment of your imagination. Now I want to hear from you who my real mother was.'

Dave drained his glass and Alex could see that he had paled considerably under the tan.

'Are you crazy? You've got your birth certificate, you know who your mother was.' He raised his hands and spread his fingers wide.

Alex withdrew a folded paper from his pocket. He had made a photocopy of Minnie's letter, fearing that Dave might tear up the original. 'Then how do you explain this?'

He thrust it at Dave who picked it up, opened it and surveyed the writing. 'What's this? A letter from your gran?'

'Yes, now read what she has to say.'

Dave began to read. Alex watched his face carefully but it was impassive. Then he gave a snort of laughter. 'Very amusing, the ramblings of a senile old woman.'

'My gran was far from senile as you very well know.'

Dave laid the paper down on the table, smoothed it with his right hand and sat staring pensively at it for what felt like several minutes. Then he raised his head and looked at his son. 'Alex have you told anyone else about this?'

'No of course not,' he sounded peeved that Dave should think such a thing. 'At the moment this doesn't concern anyone but you and me. I needed to get your side of the story, from you, not just from gran's letter.'

'Well I reckon it's time to come clean but first let me get some whisky and I've got some cigarettes in the house somewhere. I hardly touch them these days.'

He returned carrying a full bottle of whisky and two tumblers. Alex put his hand over his glass. 'Not for me thanks.'

Dave lit a cigarette and inhaled deeply, drank some whisky and began his tale.

It was the same story he had told Minnie on the night he had brought Alex to her: Lydia hadn't wanted children and had wanted an abortion when she became pregnant. They were on the brink of ending the relationship and he had said he would be happy to bring up the child. She had agreed and then changed her mind after he had bought everything for the baby and hired a child minder for when he was working.

By this time, Dave was in tears. 'I was madly in love with your mother Alex. I wanted to get back with her so we could bring you up together but she wouldn't hear of it. Then she announced that when the ch…you, were born she would only let me spend a couple of hours a week with you. I couldn't believe she was being so cruel. After all, I'd never treated her badly and she was well aware of how much I loved her. It was senseless vindictiveness.'

He paused and wiped his face with a large handkerchief, blew his nose. 'Sorry Alex but you know, even after all these years and everything that's happened, it still hurts.' He lit another cigarette. 'Well I was also angry of course. I argued with her but there was no changing her mind. Then I decided to change tack, stop hassling her, behave in an exemplary way, thinking she would change her mind about my involvement, but no! No! No! No!' He had balled his hands into fists, his knuckles white.

He went on to tell Alex about Lydia going into labour when he was with her and how he had helped to bring him into the world. By this time, Alex was near to tears himself. What he was hearing certainly threw a different light on things.

Then having described how he had planned and executed the abduction, Dave sat back and folded his arms. 'So now that you know the truth Alex, can you really blame me for what I did? Surely you must agree that Lydia behaved abominably.'

'From what you've told me, she certainly didn't behave well but nothing gave you the right to steal her child...'

'My child.' Dave interrupted, thumping the table.

'Yes your child as well, but she was the one who was going to lose out. She was the one who must have grieved for years while you were still involved with me. And did no one suspect you? After all you had a grievance about access and you weren't together anymore.'

Dave gave a derisive laugh. 'No I was not a suspect, far from it. Don't forget, I had been playing the generous and caring card for some time, going along with Lydia's wishes on everything. I was supposedly away on a walking holiday when the abduction took place and I made sure I rang every day to ask about you. And, this was my best card of all, I put on a great show of grief when I heard the news but at the same time, I went out of my way to comfort and support your mother. Even her family were impressed. No Alex, Dave Collier isn't caught that easily. And Lydia deserved everything she got.' He gave rip to a litany of misogynistic expletives. Alex stood up abruptly, pushing the table so that the glasses fell over and one rolled over the edge and smashed on the patio.

'I can't believe I'm hearing this. How could you put up a show of grieving yourself and comforting her, pretending to be a paragon when all the time you were laughing up your sleeve at the poor woman? Of all the cold hearted, callous... you're despicable!

'And was her death an accident? What a coincidence that you found her dead when you feared she might rumble you and involve the police.'

As Dave started towards him, fists clenched and raised, Alex lifted a chair and held it between himself and the blow that he was sure was coming but at the last minute Dave let his arms drop by his sides. 'No I didn't kill Lydia; it was an accident. So you're going to go running to Old Bill now? Tell them your dad is a murderer and a kidnapper...'

'Yeah and a liar who had his son's birth certificate forged and told him stories about a woman who didn't exist. My God! When I think of how I kept that one photograph by my bed. How I used to talk to her when I was upset. Who was she anyway?'

But Dave had turned and was walking towards the house.

Dave went into his bedroom, locked the door in case Alex came looking for him and went out on to the balcony where he sat turning another glass of whisky round in his hands, the bottle on the table beside him. As he drank, he mulled over the evening's events. He had never, in his wildest imaginings, thought that Alex would find out the truth about his mother. What was Minnie thinking about? He would never have believed she would do such a thing. Stupid, guilt-ridden old hag. There was one thing about him, he never felt guilty about the abduction. Lydia had deserved it. Minnie had written the letter to appease her own conscience never giving a thought to the trouble it could cause. Even if she didn't care about him, it was a wonder she hadn't thought about the effect on her grandson.

He didn't doubt for one minute that Alex would go to the police. He had never seen his son so angry, so outraged. Should he go and try and reason with him now? Apologise for what he had done to him, try to convince him that he had nothing to do with Lydia's death? No, better to wait until they had both calmed down.

—m—

Dave woke feeling stiff and cold. His watch told him it was 02.40; the temperature had dropped considerably. For a moment his mind was blank. Then the events of the evening hit him like a blow to the solar plexus. He lifted the whisky bottle and shook it. It sounded almost empty; had he really drunk that much? Pouring what remained into his glass, he sipped and at that moment he felt his anger well up again, more intense than ever. Why was he, Dave Collier sitting here worrying about what would happen when the police were informed? He remembered how he'd wondered if Lydia had done just that. For, although her death had been reported as accidental, he had lived for days in fear of the heavy knock of the law on his door, all the time planning on how soon he could get away to Spain. He knew he would be safe in a country where the extradition law, in force since the last century, had recently been severed as the result of a political dispute, and where many criminals had subsequently taken refuge.

But things had changed: in November 2001, the British government had signed a new extradition treaty with Spain and he knew that extradition warrants had been issued on many criminals who had taken sanctuary on the Costa del Sol. Well there was no way Dave Collier was going to be one of them. He prided himself on his status in the local community. Ostensibly he had never put a foot wrong where the law was concerned, either in Spain or in Britain. His businesses were all above board, if not run completely honestly – all except one that is. For some years Dave and several other pillars of the community had had a very lucrative side-line, in drug smuggling. He couldn't bear to think of the consequences if that were discovered, any more than he could bear to think of the consequences if Alex went to the police.

Well he would make sure he didn't. Standing, he realised how wobbly he was and he put a hand on the table to steady himself, then he went into the bedroom and turned on a lamp. The gap between the back of the wardrobe and the wall was small. Dave was only just able to insert his thumb and index finger, lifting a key ring, holding two small keys, from its hook. All the drawers in the chest had locks but he only ever locked the bottom one. Unlocking it now, he felt under the winter bedding and located the case.

'Oh you beauty,' he said aloud when he lifted the lid and saw the shiny, black firearm, nestling inside. He lifted it out and fondled it then picked up the silencer. He could go along to Alex's room now, put a bullet in his head. End all this. He knew the ideal place to dispose of a body – a deep and narrow ravine up in the mountains.

Hurrying along the landing, he opened the door to Alex's bedroom, turned on the light and lifted the gun to aim at Alex's head. Then he dropped his arm: the bed was empty and still neatly made.

Dave felt his legs buckle and he slumped to the floor, feeling both relief and chagrin. What was he thinking of? How could he have done that to his son? Yes, Alex was a big disappointment to him but he loved him nevertheless, of that he had no doubt. Getting to his feet, he stumbled to his own room and, with shaking hands, returned the gun to its case and to its hiding place.

But where was Alex? Had he gone off somewhere? Surely he wasn't still in the garden at this hour, unless he had fallen asleep out there. Outside, he saw that Alex's car was missing. Did that mean he was at the police station now, recounting his tale? No, things were not so critical as to warrant going at this hour. Maybe he had decided to book into one of the hotels? It had not occurred to Dave that he would do that, even in the circumstances. Hopefully he would return in the morning. Things might look different to him in the light of day.

After his confrontation with Dave, Alex sat by the pool trying to calm himself. He was frightened because of the very violent feelings he felt towards his father; he had never before known that level of rage within himself. He knew it was not a good idea to stay at Dave's that night, as he had intended. He needed to get away.

He entered the house cautiously and went to his room to retrieve his bag. The last thing he wanted was another run-in with Dave, so he was relieved to find that silence prevailed. Then, too exhausted to drive to Malaga, he booked into a hotel in Marbella. He would try for a flight home first thing in the morning and then he would be on to the police at the earliest opportunity.

Alex tossed and turned for several hours, one minute furious with his father: the crime against him was bad enough but if he had killed Lydia, then that was worse, much worse; the next minute wondering if he could bear to involve the police and maybe see him spend years in prison. Even in his anger he knew he still cared about the man. By morning, he had decided he would allow himself a cooling off period.

Dave's hands were shaking so badly, he couldn't lift a cup of coffee to his lips without slopping it over the table and he knew that the tremble wasn't just, or even mostly, caused by the amount of whisky he had drunk the night before. He was seriously frightened. He had woken around ten o'clock and there was still no sign of Alex. He knew he had a mobile phone but he didn't know the number. There was nothing for it but to wait in the hope that he would return. The hours dragged and Dave could not sit still or apply himself to anything. He paced round the garden and patio. He rang a couple of people whom Alex might have gone to visit. No one had seen him or heard from him.

Just in case he had already returned to London, Dave rang his apartment. No answer. He left a message.

Alex, it's your dad. I can't tell you how sorry I am about everything. I was hoping you would come back so that we could talk more. I swear I didn't kill Lydia. Please ring me.

Chapter Twenty

On his arrival home, Alex was surprised when he picked up Dave's message. He had no intention of ringing him. He needed time to think.

He had just settled down with a cup of coffee when the phone rang. Wondering if it was Dave, he reached over and turned on the answer machine. Best to monitor his calls.

Dave was panic-stricken. Alex had not returned his call and he had rung several times since, still getting the answer machine. Did that mean he wasn't at home? Or was he just ignoring his calls? The best thing would be that he was he still in Spain and that there was still a chance that he would come back to talk things over. The worst thing would be that he had already involved the police. He could kick himself for not making sure he had his mobile number.

As the day wore on, Dave's agitation grew to the point where he felt like getting on a plane and turning up at Alex's door. Not that he would do anything so foolish. Several shots of whisky failed to calm him. Finally, after making yet another call to London, he decided to get in his car and go for a drive. He needed to think about his next move and he always had a clearer head when driving.

—◊—

Tired and overwrought, Alex was in no mood for cooking that evening so he went out and bought a pizza and as he ate, he was still wondering about whether or not to involve the police. Minnie's letter did not prove anything. It was a confession to her part in his abduction and an accusation against Dave. It also showed that Dave had been at *Sea Music* on the night Lydia died, raising the suspicion that he might have caused her death. The case would have to be reopened.

The phone rang. Alex rolled his eyes; it was probably Dave again. But when he played the message back, he was surprised to hear another voice.

Hi Alex, this is Fred Lee, your dad's friend. Can you ring me back ASAP? It's very important.

Alex wondered if it was a ploy of Dave's to get to speak to him. He thought about ignoring it but decided it could do no harm to call back. There was a suggestion of urgency in the voice. Fred answered immediately and it was not good news. Dave had been involved in a serious road accident and was in hospital in a coma. In spite of recent events, Alex felt his heart thump. He sat down in the nearest chair. 'So when did this happen?'

'About an hour ago, maybe more. He was on the mountain road going towards Ronda and a motorist coming behind, saw him take a bend too fast and his car go flying over the edge. I'm afraid that's all I can tell you at the moment.'

Alex rang the hospital but they were unable to tell him anything more. In different circumstances, he would have returned to Spain as soon as possible; now he felt no desire to see the man who had committed such atrocities against his own family. He wondered that such a thing had happened, so soon after his revelations and their quarrel. Had Dave deliberately driven his car over the edge? He would never before have believed Dave capable of suicide but in the present situation, it was not unthinkable.

Alex had lost his appetite for the pizza and threw what

remained in the bin. Then he made coffee and went out to sit on his balcony overlooking the common. It was a warm May evening, the air permeated with the heady smell of hawthorn blossom. Dog-walkers and runners were out in force, a few couples strolled hand in hand.

He thought about his life with Dave.

Having been brought up on the North Yorkshire moors until the age of four and a half, Alex had led a quiet existence. He rarely saw other children and as a result, had become very good at occupying himself. Minnie didn't have the energy for any kind of boisterous games but she took him for walks. She had a good knowledge of birds and other wildlife and of plants and under her guidance, he became conversant with them.

Minnie had been top of her class at school and one of her great regrets was being taken away from her studies at fourteen and put to work in the mill. She was an avid reader and she read regularly to Alex. By the time he went to Spain, he was able to read and write. Dave was impressed but gave Minnie little credit. Alex, he thought, was a bright boy, like his father.

Alex did have some happy early childhood memories of Dave teaching him to swim and taking him sailing, playing games of pirates and cowboys; making him laugh but as he got older, his memories were not so pleasant. He thought it had started with football. Dave was passionate about football and was a leading player on the local team. He looked forward to his son following in his boots, maybe even going professional. But Alex had poor co-ordination and couldn't get the hang of it at all. After several attempts Dave had finally given up and shouted in exasperation, 'What are you? A fuckin' girl?' It was the first time he had sworn at his son and the first of a long series of similar remarks that he used in an attempt to degrade him.

Alex had a flair for art and this was another source of annoyance to Dave. He didn't want to see anything of Lydia in him and he was pleased that the child was so like him in appearance. But ironically as, growing older, the boy's physical features resembled his even more strongly, so his personality became more like Lydia's. He was forever going off on jaunts into the countryside to paint and draw and he had a sketch pad full of drawings of plants, birds and other wildlife. And when he wasn't drawing and painting, he had his head stuck in a book. Dave was disgusted. As far as he was concerned, his son was an excuse for a man. He showed no interest in football. Alright so he would never make a footballer, but Dave had at least expected him to take an interest in the game, follow a team. It didn't have to be his team, in fact it would be better if it wasn't. It would cause some healthy rivalry between them.

Dave wondered if Alex was gay and, as he approached puberty, he looked out for signs of interest in girls. There were none that he could see. He covertly studied his son. Certainly he looked manly, well he resembled him so strongly, he could hardly look anything else. But Dave had met many gay men in his time and he knew that they were as diverse as any other group of people. He had nothing against gays *per se*, being of the breed who claim proudly, 'some of my best friends are gay but…'

He certainly did not want his son to be in that category.

He began to suspect that there was something going on between Alex and his friend Pedro.

Alex and the Spanish boy had gravitated towards one another on their first day at school. It was not in Alex's nature to need many friends but he was loyal to those he did befriend and the two had been inseparable ever since. Pedro was a good-looking boy with thick, dark curly hair and large dark eyes. Alex was six foot, so Dave reckoned, Pedro must be at least six-three. Both boys had beautifully toned bodies, for Alex's life was not entirely sedentary: he still enjoyed swimming and sailing.

Then Pedro wasn't around as often and when Dave questioned Alex he was told that Pedro had a girlfriend, Francesca and was spending more time with her.

'And what do you feel about that?' Dave queried. Alex shrugged his shoulders nonchalantly. 'Good luck to them I say, she's a lovely girl.'

'And what about you? No young lady on the horizon for you?'

Alex shrugged again. 'Nah, I'm not really interested in girls…'

'So you're a poofter! I knew it!' Dave cut in, thinking his worst fears confirmed. Alex looked at him, head shaking. 'Get a grip Dad. I was about to say, I'm not interested in girls at the moment. I'm too busy working for my exams. Plenty of time for that sort of thing later.' Though he felt a measure of relief, Dave was not totally convinced.

Alex did well in both the arts and the sciences and Dave hoped his chosen university course would be something that would give him a job with kudos and a good salary: a company director, a financier in the City, or a lawyer.

When Alex told him he was torn between applying for art or modern languages, Dave tried to discourage him from both, pointing out that with either an art degree or a languages degree, he would probably end up teaching a load of disaffected and abusive kids in some inferior school, struggling on a teacher's salary. He reminded him that he had a great head for figures and could make it big in the world of high finance.

But Alex wasn't interested and didn't go to the trouble of listing all the other jobs he could get with either degree. He finally decided on languages and he was delighted when he was offered a place on the course of his choice in Manchester.

Relieved to get away to England, Alex spent part of the holidays, when he wasn't working or travelling, with Minnie who had returned to live in her cottage when he had started university. When he did return to Spain, to visit friends, as much as to see his father, he was dismayed to find that Dave had the same sneering attitude to him and to his choice of course.

Unsurprisingly, Dave was 'too busy' to attend his son's graduation. Alex visited shortly afterwards and it was then he had decided to stay away.

Alex still hadn't made up his mind about the police and at any rate, he realised there was no point in informing them until he knew if Dave was still alive and what the prognosis was. He rang the hospital again, first thing in the morning to hear that there was 'no change'.

Alex worked from home and, since Minnie's illness and death, he had a backlog that needed to be dealt with; over the next few days he concentrated on that, ringing the hospital a couple of times a day to hear 'no change'. He knew that they were unlikely to tell him much over the phone and, after some thought, he decided to return to Spain and see for himself what was going on.

When Alex arrived at the hospital, he was told that Dave was still in a coma. A doctor explained that he had seriously injured the neck area of his spinal cord, resulting in paralysis from the neck down. It was uncertain if there would be severe brain damage. Alex would be allowed to see him but only for a few minutes.

As he entered the ICU, Alex thought he had been taken to the wrong patient for he did not recognise the figure in the bed, looking so small and vulnerable amongst the many tubes attached to most areas of his body, his face bruised and swollen. He had never known his father to be ill beyond a head cold or a mild stomach upset, had never seen him look anything less than strong and virile. He remembered the last time he had seen him: furious, fists clenched; how he had thought he was going to hit him.

As he stood looking down at Dave, feeling a strange mixture of pity and contempt, he suddenly had a strong urge to cry.

Chapter Twenty-One

John woke at 3 a.m. with a pounding headache and a mouth like the dry bed of a contaminated river. He gulped the remains of the pint glass of water on the bedside table and went in search of some more which he drank with two painkillers. Getting back into bed, he reflected on why he was so hungover. He hadn't had that much to drink: two glasses of white wine in the restaurant with Jess at lunchtime and two or three glasses of red in the evening with some friends and work colleagues who had come round to celebrate his sixtieth birthday. Not much, when he recalled what some of the others had put away. Still, he was unused to drinking. If he got through a bottle of wine a month, it was unusual.

It had been a lovely day. Jess had taken him to an upmarket place on the shores of Lake Windermere in Cumbria and the weather had been perfect for sitting outside, looking down over the blue expanse of the lake with its tourist cruisers and other water craft reflected in the calm water, and across to the Lakeland Fells.

He hadn't wanted any fuss but his friends had insisted that they were coming for drinks and that they would bring food and he was surprised at how much he had enjoyed himself. He soon drifted off to sleep once more and when he woke again it was nearly eight-thirty. His headache had almost gone but his mouth was still dry and he still felt somewhat under the weather. A good breakfast and a stint in the garden would be the best cure, he decided. The grass needed cutting and there was always weeding to be done.

John was emptying the lawnmower when he heard the telephone ring. Bother. He would finish what he was doing and then check the answer machine. If it was anything important, whoever it was would leave a message.

The machine was flashing and he pressed the 'Play' button. *Hello John, it's Hal Hawkins.*

Remember me? You'll no doubt be surprised to hear from me. Please give me a ring when you have time.

As he wrote down the number, John was puzzled. The last time he had spoken to Hal was when the man had heard of Anna's death and had rung to sympathise. He and Anna had never known him well, even though he and his wife had once been friendly with Anna's mother, Kate. When Anna had put *Sea Music* on the market, shortly after the tragedy, he had snapped it up. He had always loved the house, he said and when Kate had died and left it to her daughters he had hoped they would put it up for sale.

After he had bought the house, he had kept in touch by sending cards at Christmas, which he still did. What in heaven's name could he want?

Since her second visit to *Sea Music*, Jess had resolved to stop trying to recall any more of Lydia or of anything that may have happened on her last stay there to cause her to react to the cellar the way she had done.

It had been a busy ten months and she had no regrets about giving up teaching. In the autumn, she had had an exhibition of her work in the local library. She had sold most of her pictures and taken several commissions which had kept her busy over the winter. Now she was preparing for another exhibition and she was advertising a water-colour course for adults, due to start in September.

She had just finished framing her latest commissioned work, when the phone rang. It was John explaining about the call he'd just made to a man called Hal Hawkins, who was the present owner of *Sea Music*.

'He lives in a residential home now and he had a young man with him who was claiming to be a long-lost relative of ours. He obviously knew what had happened at *Sea Music* and he had gone to see Hal, as the present owner in the hope that he could give him our address – your mother's and mine, that is. He obviously didn't know that Anna was dead. Hal told him he couldn't give the information to a stranger but that he would ring me to see what I wanted.'

'And?'

'When I spoke to Hal, the man was still there, so I asked him what it was all about. He said his name was Alex, he didn't give me a surname, and he said he knew he was related to us but wouldn't say how he knew. Said he would rather talk about it face to face and could he come and visit me. He lives in London and will be on his way back down there tomorrow, so could do a detour to call here.'

'So did you agree to meet him?'

'I said I'd think about it and ring him back. He gave me a mobile number. I have every intention of meeting him. I'm intrigued. I stalled because I wanted to ask you if you'd be there as well and to find out if tomorrow would be suitable.'

'Yes, I have no plans for tomorrow. But who do you think he is?'

'Well the only long-lost relative I can think of is Simon,

219

Lydia's child but how, I wonder, would he have found out about us?

—m—

On his return from Spain, Alex had made an effort to catch up with his work, then he had travelled to Yorkshire, arriving late on Friday night, spent a night at the cottage which Minnie had made his, sometime before her death. In the morning he made his way to Barrowman's Point and *Sea Music*.

The first thing he noticed was the For Sale sign and it struck him that the house wasn't as friendly looking as it was in the newspaper cuttings; as it gazed out over the headland, it appeared to be frowning. Then he noticed that all the interior shutters were closed, so no wonder it was frowning; it couldn't see a thing. He smiled at his anthropomorphism of it.

He had a strange urge to see the interior of the house where his mother had lived and died. Was he being morbid? He asked himself. Well, morbid or not, he felt he needed to satisfy that urge.

He entered the back garden, sat for a while on a rickety seat and, as he tried to imagine Lydia, whose inadequate image he had from the press photo, pottering about here, weeding, picking fruit, pruning, he felt a great sadness. After some contemplation and tears, he wondered if seeing the interior would be such a good idea after all. Well he would go and see the estate agent anyway. They should be able to tell him something of the history of the house's owners and that might start him on the way to finding his relatives.

He walked along the cliff path, found some wooden steps and descended to a sandy cove.

Was this where Lydia had come to swim? To paint?

Returning to the cliff top he sat on a bench overlooking a choppy sea. It was windy and unseasonably cold for the second week in June but he neither felt the elements nor noticed the sea's mood. Two walkers, in boots, waterproof jackets and woolly hats passed by, greeting him and making comments about the weather and he answered mechanically, unseeingly.

Alex parked his car in the grounds of a red brick Victorian villa and walked up the ramp to the front door. By the time he had got to the estate agent's, he knew he definitely did not want to view the interior of *Sea Music* but he did want to know who owned it and whether they had bought it from Lydia's sister. He was told the present owner was a Mr Harold Hawkins. He had had to go into residential care about a year ago, because of severe arthritis. The house had been on the market since then.

Alex explained that he was looking for some long-lost relatives and that Mr Hawkins may be able to help him; asked if he could go and visit him and was told that they'd have to get his permission first. They'd rung the home, Mr Hawkins had agreed and now here he was at the reception desk.

Alex was shown into a large lounge, dominated by a huge television. Armchairs lined the walls, their occupants apparently engrossed in the programme but, anyone looking more closely would note that many eyes strayed away from the television, many staring at the screen were unfocused; some residents were asleep; some picked at their fingernails; one woman was shredding a tissue while gazing through the window. There was a cloying smell of air freshener, which failed to deodorise the atmosphere rancid with the residue of urine, cooking fat and cabbage.

Harold Hawkins was in a wheelchair, a dark blue blanket

over his knees. On being introduced by the care assistant, he smiled broadly and extended his hand. Standing, he would be a tall man; he was lean, almost gaunt, with a full head of silver hair and dark eyes under still dark, heavy brows. 'Let's get out of here,' he said to Alex as he propelled his wheelchair across the room. Alex followed him down a corridor and out into the grounds. 'Too hot in there, always too hot,' he said gruffly, coming to stop beside a seat overlooking a pond with ducks and geese.

Alex sat down. Harold parked the wheelchair facing him. 'By the way, call me Hal, everyone does. Now what was it you wanted to know?'

Alex explained that he thought he was a relative of the one-time owners of *Sea Music* and was trying to trace them. He wondered if Mr Hawkins…Hal, knew anything about them.

Hal's eyes widened. 'Know anything about them? I'll say I do.'

He went on to explain how he had grown up in the village and had known Kate Benton, later Kate Allan, mother of Anna and Lydia Allan.

'We played together as children, went to school together – we were the same age. I was very fond of Kate; I think I was a bit in love with her in those days but I had no chance. She went off to train as a teacher, got a job in Edinburgh, married a man called Eddie Allan and that was that.' There was a faraway look in his eyes.

'So how did you come to be the owner of *Sea Music*?' Alex asked as a sudden gust of wind made him shiver. Hal tightened the blanket round his knees. 'Not so warm out here, is it? Let's go in again, we'll sit in the conservatory. It's more private.'

Hal resumed his tale. 'I always loved *Sea Music*. As a boy, I often went there to play with Kate and her brother Alf. Alf and I were in the same regiment during the war but unfortunately Alf didn't survive.

'Kate came back here in the early fifties with her two daughters. I had married a local girl who'd been a friend of Kate's and the three of us used to socialise.' He sighed and shook his head. 'Kate died of cancer, terrible thing. She was only fifty-eight.' There were tears in his eyes. 'That was when I got to know Lydia better. She came home to nurse her mother. Anyway, as I said, I'd always loved *Sea Music*, and when Kate died and left it to her daughters, I hoped they'd put it on the market and I was determined to buy it but they didn't, they kept it as a holiday home.'

'So was Lydia on holiday there when she died?' Alex found it hard to believe he was hearing so much about a family he hadn't, until recently, known existed.

Hal shifted in his chair, threw off his blanket. 'Too damned hot again!' Then he laughed. 'You must think me a right grumpy old so and so!'

Alex got up. 'It is very warm in here, I'll open some of the windows.'

Hal continued. 'She'd been living at *Sea Music* for just over two years. I used to go and visit her. She wasn't sure if she wanted to make it her permanent home or not. She'd had a big tragedy in her life and she'd come to *Sea Music* to try and get back to painting – she was an artist. Her sister was a joint owner and used to come up on holidays with her husband and little girl.' He turned away and stared out over the pond for a moment. 'Anyway you haven't told me how you think you may be related to the family.' He looked quizzically at Alex.

Alex rubbed a hand across his face. 'It's a long story. I only recently found out about their existence. So was it Anna you bought the house from, after Lydia's death?'

'Yes, she told me she was putting it on the market and I made her an offer there and then. It might seem strange to you that I still wanted it after what had happened there but I'd had my heart set on it for such a long time, all my life really. I don't think my wife Jean would ever have agreed to live there after the tragedy but she had died the previous year – another untimely death from cancer.' He sighed again. 'I don't think I'm ever going to sell the old place. Been on the market for over a year now. Lots of interest but no takers.'

'So are you still in touch with Lydia's sister? Do you have an address or phone number where I could contact her?'

Hal frowned. 'Anna's dead; she died, let me think…' he stared at his clasped hands, as if for enlightenment, 'must be at least ten years. But as far as I know John's still at the same address – they moved from London to Manchester the year after the tragedy. I never knew John and Anna that well. As I say, I was closer to Lydia.' He looked thoughtful. 'Don't know how he'd feel about his details being given out to a stranger though.' Then he brightened. 'Tell you what, I'll root out the number now and ring him, see what he feels.' He moved his chair towards the door, beckoning to Alex as he did so. 'Follow me, the number's in my room.'

He led the way to a ground floor bedroom where he rummaged about in a desk drawer, producing a red notebook. 'Now have I got change for that damned pay phone?'

'No need for that.' Alex produced his mobile. Hal looked slightly alarmed. 'I wouldn't know how to use that.' Alex laughed. 'It's alright, you read out the number and I'll dial it for you, then you just hold it to your ear and speak.'

John and Jess sat waiting for their guest to arrive. John was trying in vain to concentrate on a crossword. Jess had a book but she was not taking anything in, she realised, as she read the same page for the third time. She looked at her watch: 2.35. He was five minutes late. The hands crept slowly: 2.41. She looked at John. 'Maybe he's not coming. Maybe it was a hoax.'

'Be patient love, it's a nice day for a change. The roads are probably busy and that route's busy at the best of times.' At that moment the doorbell rang. John raised his eyebrows at Jess as he got up to answer it.

Opening the door, John knew immediately that the man standing there was Lydia's son and he had to stop himself from gasping aloud for the likeness to Dave Collier was unmistakeable: tall, taller than Dave, he reckoned, dark hair, athletic build, same facial expression, same pale blue eyes. The man smiled and proffered his hand

'Sorry I'm late, the traffic was heavy. Thank you for agreeing to meet me Mr Allan.'

'Call me John please.' John led him into the sitting room where Jess too was struck by his resemblance to the man she had seen in photos.

Looking extremely ill-at-ease, Alex perched on the edge of the sofa.

'I'll get straight to the point,' he said, having declined John's offer of tea or coffee. 'I'm sorry if this is a shock to you but there is no other way to put it. I am the son of Lydia Allan and Dave Collier, who was abducted back in March 1975 when I was eight weeks old.'

It came out in a rush; then he took a deep breath and looked quickly from John to Jess and back again. Neither one reacted visibly and they sat in silence for what seemed like several minutes. John was the first to speak. 'So where have you been living and how did you find us?'

Still perched on the edge, Alex leaned on the arm of the sofa. 'I was abducted by my own father…' There was a sharp intake of breath from John, '…and taken to my grandmother's in Yorkshire. She brought me up with input from my father until I was four and a half, then we moved to Spain. I've only just found out. My grandmother died last month and she left me a letter telling me the truth. I've got it here if you want to read it.' He patted his pocket.

'Yes please.' John who had paled significantly, held out his hand and Alex passed over the blue envelope. Jess stood up.

'Well I'm going to make some tea. Sure you won't have a cup?' A faint smile flickered across Alex's face. 'I've changed my mind. Tea would be lovely, thanks. Milk, no sugar.'

Jess was relieved to escape to the kitchen. She was astounded by the young man's disclosure. When she returned with the tea things, silenced prevailed. John looked stupefied as he handed her Minnie's letter which she read with increasing amazement. As she handed it back to Alex, she looked at him with renewed wonder and interest. This handsome young man was her real flesh and blood cousin. It was a completely new concept for her. She had known him as a baby, played with him, been allowed to hold him; there were photographs of her doing just that. Yet he was a complete stranger to her.

At last John broke the silence.

'Incredible, totally incredible. To think that Dave Collier was capable of kidnapping his own son. I must say I didn't like him when he and Lydia were first together but I came to like and respect him after they lost Simon… I mean you Alex. You could see he was torn by grief but he was such a support to Lydia. I'm sure she'd have gone under without him. Anna and I had to admit we'd been wrong about him. What an actor. What a confounded, two-faced bastard. Oh I'm glad Anna didn't live to see this day.' He shot a glance at Alex. 'Not that she wouldn't have been glad to see you, of course.'

Alex finished his tea and set the mug down. 'I'm truly sorry to have sprung this on you. But I felt you had a right to know and I certainly needed to meet my long-lost relatives.'

John waved his hand. 'Yes, yes, of course, of course you did the right thing. We had a right to know and you had a right to meet us. But tell me, does your father know about this yet? Where is he anyway? Still in Spain?'

Alex nodded. 'Yes he's still in Spain but he is totally disabled, quadriplegic in fact. He is alert mentally and he still has speech, though it is impaired. He was involved in a serious road accident recently.'

'What?' John sounded both outraged and puzzled. 'So does that mean he never found out that you knew the truth about the abduction?'

'Oh no. I had gone over only the day before the accident and presented him with my grandmother's letter…'

'And what was his reaction?' John interrupted. Jess looked anxiously at her father. She couldn't remember when she had last seen him so agitated and angry.

Alex shrugged. 'Well, as you can imagine, he was quite staggered that I had found out. He told me the whole story about how Lydia wanted an abortion and he had said he would bring me up…'

'He what?' John nearly started out of his chair. 'That's a pack of lies. I can tell you what really happened.' And he launched into the true story of Lydia and Dave Collier.

As Alex listened, he felt he couldn't take much more. Who did he believe? His father who had told the same story to Minnie as he had to him, or this man? A relative by marriage, but a total stranger. One thing was sure: the abduction could not be excused under any circumstances. But had his father killed Lydia?

John finished his diatribe with, 'And then he goes and becomes totally disabled the next day, so there's no chance of him being brought to justice for what he did. Was he on his own when the car crashed? Sounds like it might have been an attempt to kill himself.'

Alex said nothing and Jess leaned over and put her hand on John's arm. 'Dad, this man has just lost his father. He may still be alive but he has lost the man he used to know and, no matter what he did, he was still his father.' She looked compassionately at Alex who responded with, 'It's alright. I can understand John's anger and frustration. I feel very angry myself.'

John nodded. 'When I think what he's put this family through,' and he told Alex about Lydia's years of grieving, Anna's alcoholism and early death. 'No,' he concluded, 'Anna never recovered from her sister's death. And at a time when Lydia was just getting her life back together...' He stared through the window, apparently lost in thought. Alex broke the silence.

'He swore he had nothing to do with Lydia's death. He was adamant she was already dead when he got there... but then he would, wouldn't he? He couldn't very well deny the abduction after my grandmother's letter but there was no proof of murder. How convenient that Lydia died, supposedly accidently, just when he was worried about police involvement. I was a fool to think even for one moment that he didn't do it.'

'But you were going to go to the police about the abduction? Maybe he killed Lydia, maybe he didn't. A verdict of accidental death was returned, after all. But there is no doubt he was responsible for taking you.' John leaned forward in his chair, eyes agog. Alex described his conflicting feelings to them, told them how his first reaction had been to inform the police immediately, then, when he had calmed down, how he'd had doubts when he thought of Dave spending years behind bars.

'It's not an easy decision to make, turning your parent, no matter how bad a parent, over to the police and if my abduction had been the only issue, if it had affected only me, then I would more than likely have left things as they were, but when I thought of how my mother must have been affected, not to mention the possibility that my dad was a murderer.

'So yes I probably would have turned him in but then I got the news about the accident and his serious condition. I decided not to make a decision until I found out more. After all he could have died or been brain damaged as well as physically disabled.'

'Yes, very convenient, very, very convenient,' John muttered, as if to himself. Then he looked at Alex. 'Are you sure you're telling us the truth. Your father is paralysed? You're not just telling us that because you don't want to see him go to prison?'

Alex stood up abruptly. 'I need to get going. I've taken up enough of your time.' He turned to John. 'Just one thing I will say. My father is completely paralysed. There's no way I'd make up a story like that. But if you need proof, I'll send you some cuttings from the local paper in Spain. In fact there's also a write up in a London paper – my father was well-known in the business world. You can have that as well.'

John was silent and remained seated as Alex made his way to the front door, followed by Jess. 'Sorry about my dad's rudeness. I guess your news has dredged up a lot of difficult stuff for him. But please keep in touch and come and see me sometime in my own home. Here I'll give you my address and phone number. I don't have a mobile.' She produced a pad and a pen from a drawer in the hall table. 'Here you are. My dad will come round in time and he does have lots of photos of Lydia and lots of anecdotes to tell about her.'

Alex didn't look convinced but he wrote down his own details and passed them over. Then he was gone.

Jess went back to the sitting room and faced John. 'Well, I know this hasn't been easy for you but there was no excuse for your rudeness. Just imagine what Alex must be going through.'

John began to pace about the room. 'I know, I know, I shouldn't have behaved the way I did but I'm an old cynic and he is so like his father, it felt like Dave was here in the room with us and I found it hard to warm to him once he told us what Dave had done. I still find it hard to believe that he could have done such a thing to Lydia. And to think I'd really got to like and admire him!'

'Even so, I can't believe you thought Alex was lying about his father's condition. Apart from anything else, he didn't have to come and see us; tell us any of this. Why would he do that and then lie about his father?'

John shook his head. 'I don't know. I guess he was delighted to discover he had some relatives apart from his father and was curious about us. But you didn't know Dave Collier; it's a shock to realise now how we were all taken in by his acting skills. When I think of how sincere and genuinely grief-stricken he seemed after the baby was taken. Thinking about it, lying about his father's condition is just the sort of thing he would have done and I'm sorry I won't see that bastard rot in jail after all the suffering he's caused.' He raised his voice and tore at his hair with both hands. Then he sat down again.

'I can understand that but I do think it's really unfair of you Dad, to judge Alex just because he looks like his father. Aren't you pleased that the mystery of his disappearance has been solved after all these years?'

'Well yes of course but it's so sad that Lydia is not here, or your mother.' His eyes filled with tears and Jess went to comfort him.

Chapter Twenty - Two

After his meeting with John and Jess, Alex drove home with a heavy heart. It was clear that John didn't like him and, on the one hand, he asked himself, what did he expect? He wasn't just a long-lost relative turning up but a long-lost relative turning up to reveal he had been abducted by his own father, a man his uncle had grown to admire and trust. It must have been a terrible shock to him and Alex had an idea that his likeness in appearance to Dave hadn't helped. And of course John wanted to see Dave brought to justice. It obviously hadn't occurred to him yet that his condition after the crash was probably a worse punishment than spending time in prison. At least then there would have been a chance of being released. There was no release from his paralysis: it was a life sentence.

When he got to his apartment, he immediately went into his study, photocopied the accounts of Dave's accident in both the Spanish and English papers and subsequent accounts of his resultant disability, put them in an envelope and addressed them to John. Going into the kitchen he reached for the kettle, then decided he needed something stronger and poured himself a double measure of brandy. Sitting on his balcony, overlooking the common, he took a sip and rolled the bulb of the glass between his palms, feeling that a heavy weight had settled on his head and was pressing him down into the chair.

Alex had caught up with some of his work since returning from Spain but there was still much to do, so the following day, he sat at his desk and contemplated the translation he had been working on before his weekend away. But he couldn't concentrate. Every time he got down to it, he felt like there were several threads which kept tugging him away from the work in hand to flashbacks of the past month's happenings: Minnie, feeble in her hospital bed, telling him about the letter, Minnie, fingers twitching at the bedclothes, gradually sinking into oblivion, taking with her a part of him. The blue envelope, addressed in that comforting hand, containing, not comfort, but the unravelling of the very foundations of his life. Anger, fear, uncertainty. The confrontation with his father; violent feelings he hadn't known he was capable of. His once virile father reduced to impotence. The house where his mother had lived and died, still standing stoically, gazing out to sea, seemingly oblivious to and unaffected by the tragedy that had occurred within. His excitement at meeting his newly-discovered relatives, dampened by John's hostility.

Alex shut down his computer and stood up. It was no good, trying to work here; he needed to get away but where? And would a change of scene make any difference? Would these images go with him wherever he went?

He decided to go for a run on the common. He'd not been running since before Minnie died and, next to swimming, it was the best thing to clear his head and give him a new perspective on things. Passing the post box on the corner, he threw in the envelope addressed to John. *Now maybe you'll believe me*, he thought.

By the time he returned from his run, Alex knew that he must get away, even if only for a short time; he needed to decide where to go. The cottage was out of the question. Too many memories and too near *Sea Music*: he would probably be tempted to drive up to it again. He considered going abroad.

Then he remembered his friend Tony had a place in Cornwall, a renovated fisherman's cottage. They had met at university and Tony now taught languages in a comprehensive school in Islington as well as giving private tuition to adults. Alex had never been to Cornwall but it was on his list of places to visit and he knew there was good sailing and surfing there. He would ring Tony and ask if it was available.

'Well Alex, this is a godsend. It just so happens that the people who had booked it for the next fortnight, have cancelled. They should have been in last Saturday, so you could have a whole twelve days there if you want. After that, it's booked up until the end of July when schools break up and then we're there for the rest of the summer.'

The whitewashed cottage stood on a hill, overlooking the harbour. The rooms were tiny and retained many of the original features, the kitchen well-equipped and, as well as central heating there was a fireplace and a good supply of coal and logs in the shed. Not that there was any need for heating with temperatures currently in the high seventies.

As Alex stood breathing in the sea air and watching the Atlantic breakers roll in to the beach by the harbour, he felt he had made the right decision. But that evening, as he sipped a pint in the pub, the heaviness descended once more and, dangerously near to tears, he abandoned his drink and returned to the cottage where he sobbed for several hours. He had shed a few tears after Minnie died but then he had read the letter and anger and incredulity had taken over. Now he was both relieved and exhausted after his long cry and he went to bed hoping for a good night's sleep but there was Minnie, smiling, saying she had a surprise for him. *I'm taking you to see your mum, she's in the next room.* He felt excited as she took him by the hand and opened a door. The room was in darkness and Minnie reached for the light switch.

That was when the dream turned into a nightmare. A woman was lying on the floor, a woman who had Lydia's face, Monica White's flared trousers and platforms; a knife was protruding from her chest and she was covered in blood. He opened his mouth to scream but he was powerless.

Alex awoke in a sweat and saw that it was 02.56. He sank back on the pillows with relief but the aftermath of the nightmare stayed with him and it was a long time before he dozed off again.

John rang Alex's home number. He had received the press cuttings and had felt instantly ashamed that he had doubted the young man: his nephew, for God's sake, Lydia's child. He knew that Anna would have been delighted to meet him, albeit appalled by his story and sad that Lydia had not lived to see that day. He was ringing to apologise but there was no reply, so he left a message to that effect.

Two days later, he had still not had a reply, so he rang Jess. 'I guess he's still angry with me and who could blame him?'

'I'll try him Dad. I've been meaning to ring him anyway to see if he wants to meet up.'

She dialled the number and got the machine, left a message. She tried his mobile but it went on to voice mail. *Maybe he's pissed off with both of us, she thought and felt sad.*

Alex spent the first few days in a whirlwind of activity: running, swimming, sailing in the boat Tony said he could borrow, teaching himself to surf. In the evenings, he got a take-away and got drunk on wine. Then he would sleep all night and waken with the most dreadful hangover. After six days and nights, he vowed he had had enough. Suppressing grief was understandable: it made life bearable, but it was not a good thing to do. Sooner or later, it would break through in one form or another.

And so, during the second week, Alex started each day with a swim, then he got down to his current work: translating a French novel into English. Sometimes he would sail or surf, late afternoon. He eschewed the take-away meals, in favour of home-cooked fare and he drank a lot less. When the traumatic snap shots appeared in his mind, he no longer pushed them away but instead welcomed them, crying if the need arose.

Two days before he was due to return to London, he was walking past a charity shop in St. Ives, glancing in the window as he did so, when a painting caught his eye. He stopped and stared. It was an impressionistic water colour of a house, situated on a cliff, looking out to sea: a squarely built, Georgian house of stone, covered in Virginia creeper. A ticket said *Original Water Colour* and named a price. Surely it was *Sea Music*? He looked for a title: *Cliff-Top Home*. No indication of the situation. Alex was excited. Could the artist have been his mother? He couldn't make out the initialled signature. FM? BN? CN? He couldn't even be sure that the second letter was an N or M. Was it his mother's initials, LA? The second letter didn't look like an A... or did it?

Shortly after discovering from Minnie's press cuttings that his mother was an artist, well-known for her illustrations of

235

children's stories, he had gone to a bookshop and asked about books illustrated by her. Then he had gazed at them, enthralled. They were beautiful with magical and ethereal qualities. And to think that he was holding part of Lydia in his hands. He could see nothing of them in this painting but he guessed that the style of a water colour should not be compared to children's book illustrations.

Entering the shop he went up to the young woman at the counter. 'Excuse me, do you know who painted the picture in the window?'

She shook her head. 'No I'm afraid not. It was handed in by someone who said she'd had it in the house for years but she didn't know who painted it.'

'May I see it?'

Alex studied it. 'I don't suppose you have any idea where the house is situated?'

'Sorry no. It could be anywhere round our coast couldn't it?' Alex agreed. But it was so like *Sea Music*.

'I'd like to buy it!' he said on impulse.

Chapter Twenty-Three

It was three months since Dave's accident and his fervent regret was that it had not been fatal. He had progressed from lying in a hospital bed to sitting in a wheelchair in his own home. He had two carers who alternated night and day shifts: both nurses and, at his insistence, both men, Manuel and Juan.

He had long ago stopped worrying about police involvement. He knew that after his accident, Alex had no intention of reporting but, at any rate, as far as he was concerned, his condition was worse than, more humiliating than any prison sentence and he wanted more than anything to fall asleep and never wake up.

At first he welcomed visits from his closest friends, Fred, Charlie and Derek and indeed they were the only people who were permitted to visit. It was humiliating enough that they should see him in his, as he saw it, useless state but he had no desire to be cut off completely from the outside world and he loved to hear about the world of business, both legal and otherwise, in which he had played such an important role for the past twenty-three years. Other friends, neighbours and employees, on ringing to enquire about him, had been told firmly that visitors were not welcome.

For a time, the men had made him laugh as they regaled him with stories of their exploits in both their working lives and in their private lives. But then he had begun to find their visits depressing. It was anathema to him that the once powerful and, he had thought, invincible, Dave Collier was reduced to the status of an infant: having to be fed, lifted and laid, bathed and changed, dressed and undressed. He couldn't even use the remote to change television programmes. He was thankful that he could still speak and he made sure that the nurses jumped to fulfil his frequent demands.

One day when the three friends turned up together and took him for a walk, as they often did, he asked them to assist him in ending his life. The men were not surprised at his request. They had watched him sink deeper and deeper into depression and had discussed what they would do in similar circumstances. They told him that they had no wish for him to die: they still cared about him and would miss him but they understood how he felt. It was too dangerous a risk for them to be personally involved in such an act but if he was absolutely sure it was what he wanted, they were willing to help. Together they devised a plan.

—⟋⟍—

Juan and Manuel noticed that Dave was more cheerful. His appetite had improved and he was generally more cooperative and amenable. He even apologised for his former recalcitrance. He was, he said, more accepting of his condition and prepared to work with physiotherapists and other therapists in order to reach his optimum potential.

This was Dave's outward face: part of the plan he had hatched with his friends. Inwardly, he was as depressed as ever about his condition but he also knew it was only a matter of time until he attained his much longed for state of oblivion.

He saw Alex as responsible for his present, unendurable circumstances. If he hadn't run off to stay elsewhere on the night

of their quarrel, or if he had returned in the morning, Dave felt
he would have been able to talk him out of informing the law
and Dave's life would have carried on as normal for he knew
that his accident had been the result of his extreme agitation and
fear. Bad enough to have to face the abduction charge but
infinitely worse to have to face one of murder.

Still, he had had a good life, overall. He'd used women for
pleasure and then discarded them like pieces of litter. He
castigated himself for his major mistake in getting involved with
Lydia. No woman had had that kind of hold over him, before
or since. He had no regrets about the abduction. So Alex hadn't
turned out to be the kind of son he'd wanted but he had had
some good times with him and, more importantly, he had got
his revenge on Lydia. He still relished how he had made her
suffer over the years.

He knew he had made the right choice in coming to live in
Spain. His car business had been thriving in London, but since
his sojourn in Spain, his new concerns had taken off in a way
that surpassed anything that had happened in London and he
was now a very wealthy man.

Yes, life had been kind to him, on the whole and a few
months ago, he would never have believed that he would await
death with such yearning.

Chapter Twenty-Four

New Year's Eve 2002, a moonless night, bright with stars. The wind had risen and Alex was walking along the edge of the turbulent Atlantic Ocean, its icy breakers churning about his bare feet. Checking the luminous dial on his watch, he saw that it was five minutes to midnight and moving away from the sea's reach, he sat down by a small fire he had lit earlier and picked up a spiral-bound note book. He had done a review of the past traumatic year and made a list of all the negative feelings that he wanted to eradicate from his life. As his watch hand moved towards midnight, he tore the page from the book and threw it on the fire, watching it jump and squirm as the flames engulfed it, reducing it to blackened ash.

He held himself in the moment, listening to the waves as they rose and fell, crashing against rocks and shore. And, as he watched the minute hand pass midnight, moving into 2003, he felt totally at peace with himself and with the world.

Last New Year's Eve had been the antithesis of this one. That was when the final split had come with Daisy, his partner of two years. It had been a tempestuous relationship from the start with several separations and reunions. That night they had gone to a party, drunk too much, rowed. Daisy had stormed off before midnight and when he got home at around two-thirty, she wasn't there. He had expected her to come round the next day, repentant and in want of a reconciliation, as was usually the case but she had sent her brother to clear out her stuff with a note saying that it was definitely over and that he wasn't to try to contact her. At any rate she left no address. Alex's first emotion was relief but that in no way alleviated the sense of loss he felt. A loss that turned out to be the precursor to a year of loss.

When he had celebrated Minnie's eighty-eighth birthday with her in February, he had not expected that she would be dead within three months. Yes she was a good age but she was very fit and active and mentally alert. He had thought she might well see a hundred. Then there was the shock of what her letter revealed when he had lost the sense of himself that he had had for twenty-seven years, discovering, at the same time, that the woman who had given birth to him was not only dead but had met with a violent death possibly at the hands of his father.

News of Dave's accident had been distressing. It was hard to believe that the once virile man was so incapacitated as a result. The final shock had come when, in September, he had been informed of his father's death.

Alex still wondered about that. He had been told that Dave's home had been broken into during the night and that Dave and his carer Manuel had been given injections of a drug which had proved fatal in both cases. The thief had made off with money, credit cards, an expensive sound system, computer equipment, several original paintings and many valuable artefacts.

When Alex had last seen his father, shortly after the accident, when he knew that he was paralysed from the neck down, the man had wanted to die. It seemed coincidental that, less than four months later, he had got his wish, and in a painless way. Alex knew his father had some shady friends and suspected that many of his business activities were not above board and he did wonder if a hit man had been paid to carry out the deed under pretence of burglary as the motive. It also seemed extreme that a lethal injection had been used on Manuel when a sedative injection would have been effective. And why inject Dave who was completely powerless? Not that the burglar would have necessarily have known that, of course. Also, at the time of his death, his three closest friends had all been conveniently out of the country; so far no one had been arrested for the murders.

Alex did not go to the funeral: he had long ago said goodbye to Dave as his father. Then a few days later, he received a letter with a Spanish postmark.

20 August 2002

Dear Alex,

I'm dictating this letter to my friend Fred who is being kind enough to type it for me and who has agreed to send it to you after my death, an event I hope will come sooner rather than later. The thought of my life continuing in this state for another ten or twenty years is enough to drive me insane.

I hope you realise it was your accusations that led me to the state I am in now, totally helpless and dependent on others. I still believe Lydia got what she deserved when I took you but I do not admit to killing her and I wanted to put the record straight. I know you despise me for some of the things I have done but I am not capable of murder and I want to tell you what really happened that night.

As you can imagine, it was a terrible shock to be confronted out of the blue by Lydia and accused of being the one who took you. I still believed in what I had done and I was very worried that she would go to the police. I remembered that her family home was in Northumberland and guessed she was staying there so I rang and she actually agreed to see me, said she found it hard to believe I had taken you and she needed to know the truth. But when she didn't answer the door, though her car was there and after knocking several times at both back and front doors, I became worried that something was wrong. I managed to get in through the kitchen window and I found her dead at the foot of the cellar steps.

I know I should have rung for an ambulance but I panicked. I just wanted to get out of there as fast as I could. I was in a terrible state, I can tell you. When I found myself outside the cottage where you and your gran were staying, I had no memory of how I got there. It was only when I stopped the car and turned off the ignition that I remembered where I had been and what I had found there. I kept asking myself if it was real. Was Lydia really dead?

You might think I was pleased that Lydia was out of the way but I wasn't, I was actually very sad. Whatever you might think I was telling the truth when I said I was in love with her and it was her rejection of me that led me to do the things I did.

I freely admit that I had a niggling fear that Lydia had already contacted the police and that I would be chief suspect in her death but thankfully 'foul play' was not suspected and a verdict of accidental death was recorded eventually.

*Well Alex, I don't know if I have convinced you that I am innocent. Unfortunately I can't prove it; you've only got my word for it. But **I know** what happened that night and I feel better for having got it written down.*

I still feel deeply hurt by your rejection of me at a time when I needed you most and for that reason I have written you out of my will so you can say goodbye to any hopes you had of becoming wealthy, and believe me you would have been a very wealthy man.

Yours,

Dad/Dave

Alex was perplexed. Why had Dave felt so strongly the need to declare his innocence? Maybe it was a coincidence after all.

Surely the police would have suspected something if it was murder, by him or anyone else.

The letter accused him of being responsible for Dave's accident. Well he knew he wasn't. Whatever had happened to Dave, he had brought on himself. He didn't hate the man; in many ways he pitied him and there was a modicum of regret for the way things had turned out between them.

As for being written out of the will, Alex was relieved. He didn't want his father's money and he certainly didn't want the house where Dave had lived so unhappily after his accident and where he and his carer had been killed. Nor had he any desire to become wealthy on the assets of a child abductor, abusive partner, possible murderer, and a dishonest businessman who, he suspected, was involved in drug dealing and goodness knows what else.

But good had also come out of his finding out his true identity. He had acquired a cousin and an uncle. On return from his holiday in Cornwall, he had been pleased to find on his answer machine an apologetic message from John and an invitation to his home in Manchester. There was also a very friendly message from Jess. He had gone to visit them soon afterwards, taking with him the painting he had bought in St. Ives. If anyone recognised it as *Sea Music*, it would surely be John who had stayed there frequently.

He also hoped that, if the painting was done by his mother, then John might recognise it or that at least they could verify the style by comparing it to her other work. He was pleased when John confirmed it was indeed *Sea Music* but disappointed to see that the style was very different to Lydia's and was unlikely to be her work.

After an enjoyable weekend where he had heard much about his mother and looked at photos of her, he had come away with some of those photos and with most of her work, including the originals for the books she had illustrated.

He had no doubt that he had done the right thing in coming to the west of Ireland for New Year. He had refused several invitations to parties and his friends had thought he was mad to even contemplate going away on his own, and to such a remote part of the world. Indeed, he too had, at times, wondered if he was doing the right thing: he had never before been alone at New Year. He could have gone to the cottage in Yorkshire but it had too many memories for him. He had needed to get away from all that and take stock of the past year and of his life in general.

Alex woke on New Year's Day feeling refreshed and clear-headed, something he had not felt on that day for many years. Getting out of bed, he pulled the curtains on bright sunshine and clear blue skies. The wind had died and the Atlantic was calm, the many islands clearly visible. He opened the window and took several deep breaths of the crisp, salty air feeling an exhilaration he had not felt for a long time.

After breakfast he drove inland towards the Maumturk Mountains where he planned to walk.

This was going to be a good year and, one thing he was sure of, he was going to have a birthday party. As a rule Alex didn't go in for marking his birthday but this year was different. It would be the first year ever that he would have his birthday on his true birth date, the thirty-first of January, instead of the day he had been led to believe was his birthday, the twelfth of February.

It so happened that the thirty-first fell on a Friday that year and he was pleased that both John and Jess were free and had agreed to come for the weekend. They insisted on coming on Thursday evening so they could help him with the food.

It wasn't a large party, just close friends and spouses/partners.

The only person he didn't know well was a woman called Amy. He had met her recently at a friend's house, had taken an instant liking to the petite woman with the cropped dark hair and elfin features and, on the spur of the moment, he had invited her to the party. He didn't think it was a romantic attraction and, at any rate, since his break-up with Daisy, he was being cautious about involvement. She had seemed pleased but he didn't think that she would turn up and was pleasantly surprised when she did.

Alex was going round, with a bottle of white wine in one hand, a bottle of red in the other, topping up the guests' glasses, when he noticed Amy standing in front of the painting of *Sea Music*, staring intently at it.

'Do you like it?' he asked.

'Yes, yes I do.' Her eyes didn't move from the picture. 'And I think I know where you got it.' She turned towards him, smiling.

'Oh?'

'A charity shop in St. Ives?'

'Yes, as a matter of fact. How did you know?'

'I know who painted it. It was my dad, Luke Matthews. As far back as I can remember, that painting was in the house, but it was never on display, just stored in a room with a lot of his other work. Finally, my mother persuaded him to part with it and she took it to that shop.'

Alex was immediately interested though the name meant nothing to him. 'Your dad? Well, well, fancy that. I know the house; it's called *Sea Music*. It's in Northumberland.'

Amy nodded. 'Yes I knew it was painted in Northumberland. My dad is from that part of the world though he's lived in Cornwall for a long time.'

'So have you been there – to the house, I mean?'

'Oh no, I don't know anything about the house. My dad doesn't talk much about his life in Northumberland but he did tell me he painted it there. It's one of his very early pictures. He has become quite well-known over the years.' She moved closer to the picture and scrutinised the signature. 'Hard to make out the initials, isn't it? He doesn't sign his work like that anymore. He signs his full name.'

At that moment their conversation was interrupted as the music changed to Happy Birthday and Jess came in from the kitchen bearing a cake with lighted candles, followed by John carrying two bottles of champagne and there was much cheering and clapping and popping of corks. The next time Alex saw Amy was when she came to say goodbye and to thank him for the party.

'Well, I found out who painted the picture of *Sea Music*.' It was the following morning and Alex, John and Jess were having breakfast.

'Oh?' John and Jess said in unison as they looked at him quizzically.

'Yes. I noticed Amy taking a great interest in it and when I asked her if she liked it she told me that it was painted by none other than her father. I was stunned. Apparently he is from Northumberland but has lived in Cornwall for some time.'

John laid down his knife and fork. 'Well what a coincidence.'

'So did she say what his connection to the house was? Had she ever been there?' Jess buttered a slice of toast and reached for the marmalade.

'No. She didn't know anything about it other than where it was painted.'

'So at long last you know the name of the artist.' John proffered the coffee pot and Alex and Jess both nodded their acceptance.

'Yes, someone called Luke Matthews. Apparently he's quite well-known now…'

'Luke Matthews?' John set down the coffee pot and turned to Jess in astonishment. 'You remember who he is, don't you?'

Jess nodded, looking equally astonished. Alex looked from one to the other with raised eyebrows as John leaned towards him. 'Alex, Luke Matthews was the man who found your mother's body – I think I told you his name but you've obviously forgotten – this may not be the same Luke Matthews of course but it seems too much of a coincidence to be otherwise.' He slapped his forehead with the palm of his hand. 'Of course. It's all coming back to me now. Luke Matthews was a painter and decorator by trade but Lydia did tell Anna and me that he painted both oils and watercolours as a hobby and landscapes and seascapes were his great passion. That was part of the attraction between them, I guess.'

Chapter Twenty-Five

Sarah Matthews carried a tray with two china mugs, a milk jug and a pot of coffee into her husband's studio and laid it on a small table. Luke turned from the easel where he was putting the finishing touches to a painting.

'That smells good.' He smiled at his wife, then made his way to the sink where he began to wash his hands. Sarah looked appreciatively at the picture.

'Nearly finished, is it?' Luke accepted a cup of coffee and sat down at the table.

'Yes, and just as well. Will Jones is coming to collect it tomorrow. I think I told you, it's a surprise for Jenny's fiftieth.'

Sarah nodded, took a sip of coffee and leant back in her chair.

'Anyway Luke, I've just had a phone call from Amy.'

Something in Sarah's tone made Luke feel apprehensive. 'Oh? Everything alright?'

'Yes, yes, she's fine but she's recently met a man and woman who claim to be related to Lydia Allan and who would like to talk to you about her.'

Luke felt the blood drain from his face as he hastily put down his cup.

'What? Who were they? And how did they make the connection between Amy and me?' His voice shook. Sarah put an arm round his shoulder and drew him to her.

'Sorry it's been a shock to you love but Amy did ask me to

tell you and to find out if you would agree to speak to them. It was a big shock to her as well, hearing something she knew nothing about.'

She went on to tell Luke about Amy seeing the picture of *Sea Music* at the man's apartment and mentioning that she knew the artist, not for one moment realising what she was unleashing, and about her subsequent visit from Alex Collier and his cousin Jess Cooper.

Luke was dumbfounded. 'I know who Jess is. She's Lydia's niece. But Alex Collier? The name means nothing to me.' His face puckered in a frown.

'He told Amy he's Lydia's long-lost son who was abducted when he was a few weeks old.'

Luke's frown deepened. 'But Lydia called him Simon.' Sarah rolled her eyes. 'Yes but whoever took him wouldn't have known his name, would they? And even if they did they would have wanted to change it.'

Luke spread his hands. 'Yes, of course. I'm just so shocked, I wasn't thinking. Did she tell you anything else about them?'

'Just that Jess lost her memory of Lydia and of her stay at the house before she died. She hopes that talking to you might trigger something. Alex would like to know more about his mother.'

'So nothing about who abducted him or how he found out about Lydia?'

Sarah shook her head. 'Amy just said it was a long story.'

After his horrific discovery on the afternoon of the sixth of August 1978, Luke felt a desolation he had never known before and to this day he wondered how he had got through the days immediately afterwards. He remembered the police arriving, his distraught phone call to John and Anna, the ordeal of being grilled by detectives, his relief on being told that, they believed the death to be accidental, the heartbreak of the funeral.

In the aftermath, Luke couldn't sleep and ate little. He threw himself into his work but was grumpy and taciturn. Finally his partner, Mike suggested that he take a holiday, have a complete change of scene.

'A holiday,' he said scornfully, 'And how do you think that would help? If working hard day in and day out doesn't help, how do you think I'd feel with nothing to occupy me?'

Mike sighed. 'You'd have to find things to do Luke. What about your painting? Go somewhere far away from here. Somewhere with beautiful scenery and good light and do what you love doing best. The boys and I can manage here for a week or two.'

Luke thought about it and decided it was worth a try. He booked a week in southern Italy and spent three days wandering around in a daze, feeling lost and lonely. He wanted to get on a plane and go home but instead he got out his materials and began to paint. The light was amazing, the scenery idyllic and if he had ever had doubts before, he knew now that this was what he wanted to do full time. But, he told himself, that wasn't practical. Even if he sold his share of the business, he would not be able to live on the proceeds for long. No he would still have to follow his trade, for a time at least. He wanted to get as far away from Northumberland as possible, but not abroad, he decided. Italy was beautiful, but he knew he wouldn't be able to stand the heat of a southern climate at the height of summer. He considered more northerly options but knew in his heart that he didn't want to leave Britain.

—⚈—

On his return Luke told Mike and their two employees, Bob and Joe, of his plans. Then he spent some time poring over maps and researching the far-flung reaches of the country. Bob put in an offer for his share of the business and, having decided to give Cornwall a try, Luke rented a cottage there to get a feel for the place, keeping on his house in Northumberland. He became absorbed in his artwork, also advertising himself as a painter and decorator and soon work was coming in. After six months, he decided it was the place for him, put his northern home on the market and set about looking for a house to buy.

In the summer of 1980, Luke had been living in Cornwall for fifteen months and had recently settled into a house overlooking the ocean. After the sale of his business and his home in Northumberland, he was in the lucky position of not needing a mortgage. He had enough work to keep him going but he made sure he left plenty of time to indulge his passion for painting. It would soon be the second anniversary of Lydia's death and his life was still overshadowed by profound sorrow. He knew, however that he had made the right decision in leaving the North-East; that the memories that haunted him here would be starker still in the place where he would have been in close proximity to *Sea Music* and the other places where he had spent happy times with Lydia.

When he wandered round art exhibitions in the Cornish towns, he longed to display his own work but he still did not have the confidence to approach anyone about it.

On a hot July day, Luke parked his car and made his way down the steep path to a deserted cove which he had not visited before. Positioning himself in the shade of an overhanging rock, he set up his easel and looked towards the lighthouse, its black rock a stark contrast to the calm jewelled waters: turquoise and sapphire. Before starting work, he took a moment to absorb the peaceful atmosphere, where the only sounds were the gentle lapping of the sea and the cry of sea birds.

He had just begun to mix his paints when he heard shouts and laughter and a woman ran down the last of the steep incline, a child on her hip and one by the hand. Luke sighed. He had hoped to have the cove to himself. Well as long as they kept their distance and weren't too noisy.

The family settled down at the other end of the beach and, as Luke became absorbed in his work, their sounds faded into the background and he started when he heard a small voice say, 'Painting's my favourite thing, you know.'

He looked down at the small boy with dark brown eyes, tanned skin and incongruously blond hair who was staring earnestly at his work.

'Is it now? I'm very glad to hear that.' He smiled, amused at the boy's serious expression.

'Yes, I do lots of painting and drawing at home and at nursery but I'm going to big school in September and I hope I'll still be able to do lots.'

'I expect you will,' said Luke as he noticed that the woman was now at the water's edge, paddling with the younger child.

The boy folded his arms and turned his attention from the painting to Luke, his eyes widening. 'What's your name? Are you a very famous artist?'

Luke chuckled. 'My name's Luke and I'm not at all famous. I just paint for fun. What's your name?'

'I'm Paul West and that's my mum and my sister.' He pointed to the figures in the water. Just then the woman turned and, shading her eyes with her hand, peered at them, lifted the toddler and called, 'Paul, what are you doing?' Come away and leave that man in peace to get on with his painting.'

'It's all right,' Luke shouted, 'he's not bothering me. We were just having a chat.'

The woman began to walk up the beach. She was early thirties, of medium height and blonde with very blue eyes, her hair pulled back in a ponytail. She was dressed in shorts and a bikini top. Luke smiled at her. 'Paul was telling me how much he loves drawing and painting.'

'Yes, he's never happier than when he has a brush, pencil or crayon in his hand. Isn't that right?' She ruffled the boy's hair. 'Now are you hungry yet? I am. I think it's time for our picnic.' She looked at Luke's painting. 'Oh I like that. I really admire people who can paint. Paul doesn't take after me I'm afraid but I do have a good eye for art and I'm building up a collection of work by local artists. Do you exhibit locally?'

Luke grimaced and shook his head. 'No I'm afraid not. I've never had an exhibition in my life. I'd like to though.'

She looked at him curiously. 'So why not then?'

Luke shrugged and looked away. 'Not sure I'm good enough, I guess.'

'But that's such a shame. Your work's really good and I know someone who would be only too happy to show it, if it's all like this. Oh I'm sorry, I should introduce myself. I'm Sarah West and this is Amy.' She indicated the child in her arms. 'Paul you've already met.'

Luke extended his hand. 'Luke Matthews, pleased to meet you Sarah and Amy.'

'Now do you live locally or are you on holiday?' Luke explained his situation and it transpired that Sarah lived in St. Ives and Luke accepted her invitation to meet for a drink so that she could tell him about her contact in the art world.

Two nights later, they were seated in a pub garden and Sarah was explaining that her close friend Diane, a sculptor, had recently opened a gallery of contemporary arts and crafts near Penzance and was looking for people to exhibit there. She was sure Diane would be interested in Luke's work.

'But you've only seen one of my paintings and that wasn't finished,' Luke exclaimed. 'Why don't you come along to my home and see some of the others. Better still, bring your friend.'

Sarah did just that and, as Luke's work went up in the gallery, he found it hard to believe that it was on show at last, that maybe he was on his way to realising his ambition of becoming a professional artist. And to think that it was due to a chance meeting on a beach with a woman who admired his work and realised its potential.

But something else was happening. For the first time since Lydia's death, Luke found himself attracted to another woman. He still mourned Lydia but, as he continued to see Sarah, he found that his periods of sadness were fewer, his periods of laughter more. Once or twice, he even felt something akin to happiness bubble through.

He was able to tell Sarah that the last woman he had been close to had died and that grief had driven him to leave Northumberland and take up residence in Cornwall. But he could not bring himself to talk about the details of that death or to disclose the tragedy of Lydia's life.

Sarah, on the other hand, was quite happy to talk about her life. Born and brought up in Cornwall, she had qualified as a nursery nurse and worked in that area for a year before realising it was not for her. She then did a course in horticulture and had set up her own gardening business. She had married a barrister, Geoff Winter, in 1974 and Paul was born the following year. Two years later, she was pregnant with Amy. Geoff did a lot of work in London and, not far into the pregnancy, he began spending more and more time there and less and less time at home. When challenged, he became angry and verbally abusive. Then two months before Amy was due he came home to announce that he was leaving to live permanently in London with another barrister named Ellie and was filing for divorce.

That was difficult enough but the worst thing was, he wanted to cut all ties, didn't even want to see Paul, didn't want to know about the new baby.

Devastated, Sarah had picked up the pieces as best she could with the help of her parents who lived nearby and she had continued to make a success of her business. Fourteen months after meeting Luke, they were married and Luke legally adopted the children.

They had had twenty-one happy years together and Luke was now a full-time artist; Sarah's business was still thriving.

Chapter Twenty-Six

Alex was driving along the M4 on his way to Cornwall. A week before, Amy had been in touch to say that Luke had agreed to meet with him.

'Oh that's brilliant. When?'

'Next weekend ok? He'd like to meet you on Saturday afternoon. If you name a time, I'll pass it on to him.'

'Did he say anything about meeting Jess?'

'Yes he's agreed to meet her too, when it's convenient for her. I'm going to ring her next.'

As much as he looked forward to his meeting with Luke, Alex was also anxious about reopening a tragic time in the man's life. He had been surprised to learn that Amy had known nothing of that traumatic time.

'He talked very little about his life in Northumberland. Uncle Phil, Auntie Sally and our cousins James and Richie came to stay with us but we never went there. When I asked him why, he just said it was a long way to travel and when I said it was just as far for them, he muttered something about him not liking to drive long distances. "But what about Mum?" I said, "She doesn't mind driving, or we could go on the train". He had no answer to that and I suspected that something had happened there that he was keeping from us. And then there was that picture that he'd painted of the house. I loved it but he wouldn't let us hang it up, yet it remained there, collecting dust in a room with other paintings, until finally Mum persuaded him to let it go.'

Since he had received the letter from Dave, reiterating that he had had no part in Lydia's death and describing what had happened that night, Alex had decided to give him the benefit of the doubt and had not told Amy or anyone else since that he was there that night. He had decided not to tell Luke either. Bad enough to find the person you love dead but to find out there was a possibility they were murdered didn't bear thinking about, especially as the possible perpetrator was now dead so nothing could be done about it.

Luke was nervous as he awaited Alex's arrival. He had no desire to talk about Lydia and that happy, turning to unhappy period in his life but he had agreed to the meeting for two reasons: he was curious to meet Lydia's son and to hear from him the circumstances of his abduction, knowing by now from Amy that his father was the abductor. And he felt the man had a right to find out as much as possible about his mother.

He was happy with Sarah certainly, very happy, but for many years after their meeting he had continued to be haunted by nightmares from which he would awake crying, sometimes shouting. He had done the painting of *Sea Music* the summer before he had met Lydia. Luke had no desire for it to be on show so he kept it in a room with some of his other work and at the beginning of their marriage, Sarah had often found him in there staring at it, his eyes full of tears. The first time it happened, it took him all his time to persuade her that it was her he loved and that it was not Lydia he was pining for but the tragedy of her life: the loss of her child, her desertion by the man she loved and how when she was on the verge of finding some measure of happiness with him, her life had ended violently and possibly painfully. Sarah said it wasn't healthy and encouraged him to take the painting to one of the art shops but he wouldn't hear of it, though as time went on he looked at it less and less often and then finally stopped. He still wouldn't part with it though, not until last year when Sarah was doing some clearing out and he had actually asked her to take it to a charity shop.

'Just hand it in. Don't say who painted it.'

He had known Sarah for nearly a year before he had been able to tell her of the circumstances of Lydia's death and life. And he'd felt much better for unburdening himself. But he had never been able to talk to the children about it as they grew older. Had never felt the need for them to know. Now Amy had found out from none other than Lydia's son and she had relayed the details to her brother Paul.

Alex and Luke were sitting in the conservatory at Luke's home. Sarah had appeared with a tray of coffee, introduced herself and left them on their own. As Luke poured the coffee, Alex studied him. A handsome man with dark, sensitive eyes, thick wavy hair, prematurely white for his fifty-six years, dark eyebrows.

This is the man who was in love with my mother. My father never really loved her, I am convinced of that. This is the man who found her body. This is the man who believed they had a future together, until that fateful night. The man who was afterwards so traumatised that he exiled himself from his Northumbrian home and those he loved to live at the other end of the country. No he could never tell him that there was a possibility that Lydia had been murdered by Dave or anyone else.

There was an awkward silence. Luke cleared his throat. 'It's hard to believe I'm sitting here with Lydia's son.'

As Alex began to speak, it was Luke's turn to study him: at

least five inches taller than he was, strong build, dark, spiked hair, pale blue eyes. He could see no resemblance to Lydia – except maybe his open candid expression. *This is Lydia's son. The son of the first woman I ever truly loved. This is the boy she lost when he was eight-week- old – and to his scoundrel of a father. A despicable man who, from Amy's account, had hidden his crime under the cloak of going out of his way to support Lydia, even in the supposed throes of his own heartfelt grief. A man much admired by those who had previously distrusted him and wished him out of Lydia's life.*

Jess was on her way to Cornwall. She was excited about the prospect of meeting Luke and would have done so weeks before had it not been for her classes. Now it was half-term.

She had no picture of Luke's appearance in her head. Alex had told her about his meeting with him, how he had liked the man, had found him open and sincere and how the meeting had helped him to a greater understanding of his mother and what she had gone through after his disappearance but he had given no physical description.

She knew that, since receiving his father's letter, Alex no longer told people that Dave had been there on the night of his mother's death and, at any rate, for the same reasons as Alex, she had no intention of informing Luke of that. The man had suffered enough.

John had made no further accusations against Dave but she believed he was still convinced that he had murdered Lydia. She was unsure. After all, she'd never known Dave as John had and yes, from all accounts, he was a bad'un but, having read his letter, she was, like Alex, inclined to give him the benefit of the doubt.

Her main reason for wanting to meet Luke was to find out

more about Lydia's life at *Sea Music* thereby, perhaps, stimulating some more memories in her.

Now that she knew the answers to the questions that had puzzled her over the years, she felt that the void was not as gaping but she knew that it would never close completely if her full memories of Lydia did not return.

As Luke waited for Jess to arrive, he recalled his mood as he drove to *Sea Music* on return from his holiday. He had had a wonderful two weeks cycling in Holland and Germany and was feeling healthy, fit for anything and very much looking forward to seeing Lydia. He had said he might call on the way back from the ferry but had made no promises. He wondered if her niece was still with her. She was supposed to be staying for another few days but Lydia had said she wouldn't be surprised if her parents cut short their holiday through missing her.

As he drove along, Luke asked himself why it was that, at the age of thirty-three, he had failed to maintain a happy relationship, and he wanted children. His only serious relationship, with a woman called Liz had ended more than two years ago; he was devastated when he found out she was having an affair while at the same time still declaring her undying love for him. When challenged, she had laughed scornfully and said, 'A woman has her appetites, just like a man. He meant nothing to me; it was purely a physical attraction and I still meant every word I said to you. Don't you ever feel attracted to other women?'

Luke had admitted that at times he did, but only in a superficial way. He knew he would never be unfaithful and jeopardise a relationship that was important to him.

He thought then of Lydia: so beautiful, so vulnerable. He had found her tragic story about the loss of her son shattering. Yet there she was, carrying on, picking up the pieces, pouring all her emotions into her paintings and book illustrations, ever hopeful that one day she would be reunited with her beloved Simon. How he admired her. And for the first time, he had found someone who took his art seriously. Everyone else: Liz, family, friends seemed to see it as a hobby to be indulged. But then none of them was really interested in art. For the first time, he knew he had met a soulmate and that he loved Lydia in a way he had loved no other. He believed she loved him and he understood her reluctance to commit herself as a lover. He would wait, albeit with covert, never overt, impatience for that day. As he neared *Sea Music*, his heart gave an upward lurch.

Sarah opened the door, greeted Jess warmly and ushered her into the conservatory, asking if she preferred tea or coffee. Moments later, Luke entered and she immediately felt at home with him.

He was concerned that she was sure she wanted him to tell her the details of that time.

'Absolutely,' she replied, 'some memories have come back but I'm desperate for something to trigger more, however painful they may be. Otherwise I can never lay the whole thing to rest. So please don't spare me any details.'

'Well if you're sure.'

Luke began his tale:

'As you probably know, on the Sunday, I was returning from a cycling holiday abroad. I'd told Lydia I might call round en route, depending on how tired I was feeling. Well I was tired but

I couldn't wait to see her. I always used the back door so I went round there. I was surprised to see a light on in the kitchen as it was early afternoon and a very bright day. I knocked a few times but there was no answer. Lydia had given me keys to both back and front doors but I wouldn't have dreamt of letting myself in. It would have seemed impolite and I would only do it in an emergency. So, I went to the front and knocked. There was still no answer. I was becoming a bit worried. Anyway, I went to the back again and tried the door handle. I knew that Lydia had a habit of not locking it but it was locked, so I went to use my key, but couldn't because there was already a key in the lock. Well I can tell you I was getting seriously worried now, so I unlocked the front door and went in, calling Lydia's name. There was an eerie silence. By this time I was frightened. I called her name again as I went towards the kitchen.' Luke stopped abruptly and put his face in his hands, then looked up again, 'Sorry. That was when I made the discovery. Lydia was lying at the foot of the cellar steps, her eyes were open, staring. I went down and felt her pulse but I knew she was dead. I phoned the police. And that's about it.'

He sat back in his chair and spread his hands. It was plain that the recounting had been painful for him. Jess leaned towards him, 'I'm sorry to have brought up distressing memories for you.'

He smiled at her, 'Please don't worry about that. Admittedly it's still not easy, after nearly twenty-five years but I don't mind if it helps with your recall. It must be awful to have lost your memory like that.'

'Yes.' She proceeded to tell him something of her childhood, how she'd always had this sensation of an absence in her life; her discovery of *Sea Music* and her initial reaction to the cellar.

'Dad thinks it was because I must have overheard a

conversation about where Lydia was found but I wonder if something else fearful happened there – oh it's just a niggle I get sometimes.' She waved a hand dismissively, continued. 'I wonder why she was going down the cellar that night? Did she keep fuel for the range down there?'

Luke shook his head. 'No she kept it outside, in a shed. I think it was something to do with an old doll's house. When you were coming to stay, she told me about it. It belonged to her and your mother and it had been in the cellar for years. She said she'd been meaning to do it up for you and your visit would spur her on.

When I came into the kitchen that afternoon, I noticed it was sitting on the table but I didn't pay it any attention. There was a toolbox sitting near the cellar door, so obviously she had been down for that so maybe she was going down again to get some paint or something.'

After her meeting with Luke, Jess felt unsettled. Something he had said was bothering her but she couldn't put her finger on what it was. The afternoon was breezy but not cold and she decided to go for a cliff walk to try and clear her head.

Parking her car, she changed into her walking boots, began the steep walk to the cliff-top and was dismayed to find that, after only a few metres, she was quite breathless and her calf muscles were aching. When she'd lived with Max, hill and mountain walking had been their passion and she realised that, in the almost two years since their break-up, she had been leading a largely sedentary existence. She felt unexpected pain then as she remembered the five good years with Max and even deeper pain as she thought about the loss of her child who would have been seventeen months now.

Relieved to reach the top after several rests, she noticed that the breeze was stronger here; white horses galloped on a sea of solid grey and as she set off along the cliff path she went over what Luke had told her. So it looked as if Lydia had gone down the cellar that night to bring up an old doll's house which she was intending to repair and give to her. Doll's house? Some fragment of memory was needling her brain. Doll's house? Of course! It was coming back to her. Suddenly she had a clear memory of the house and of the first time she saw it.

She has been forbidden to go down the cellar on her own because the steps are dangerous and indeed she has no desire to go there. But one rainy afternoon shortly after her arrival at Sea Music, Lydia asks her if she would like to go down with her and sort through some boxes. 'There are some toys and books that belonged to your mother and me.'

Jess falls in love with the doll's house, a four-storied Victorian dwelling, as soon as she sees it. It had been a present to Lydia and Anna from their Scottish grandfather not long before his death. A family of dolls already lived there but it was sparsely furnished as their grandfather wanted them to get to know the family and then have the fun of choosing items for them.

Over the years, they had collected many bits and pieces and their mother had helped them to make curtains and other soft furnishings. As the girls got older they lost interest and it had been relegated to the cellar where it had fallen into a state of disrepair and was almost forgotten.

Jess runs over now and goes to open it. 'Leave it Jess, it's very dirty and probably falling apart.'

Jess is dismayed, 'Oh can I not play with it?'

'Yes of course you can but it needs a good clean and maybe some repairs. Leave it now and I promise I'll sort it very soon. Now let's see

what's in these boxes.' The child is soon distracted by the discovery of many toys in good condition: dolls, furry animals, games, a large spinning top, cars and other vehicles. There are many broken toys as well, and books that are falling apart. Lydia puts these in a bin liner and says she will burn them soon. They spend a happy afternoon, washing the dolls, animals and other toys and dusting the games and books.

Happy as Jess is with these new treasures, she keeps thinking longingly of the house and on the evening before their trip to Newcastle, she asks when she can play with it.

'I'll bring it up soon and we'll see what needs doing to it.'

'Tomorrow?' Jess is hopeful.

'Not tomorrow, remember we're having a day out tomorrow? But what about the day after?'

'Oh yes, oh goody!' Jess jumps up and down in excitement.

Then another memory, not so pleasant.

On their return from Newcastle, Jess goes to play in the garden and after a while, Lydia comes out and asks if she is alright, says she will be painting in her studio if she needs her. At that point Jess is happily engrossed in a game but later she has a bout of homesickness. She is lonely and fed up playing on her own. She misses Cathy and her mum and dad. She has a sudden longing to play with the doll's house.

She goes indoors and climbs the stairs to Lydia's studio to find that she isn't painting but pacing up and down with a strange expression on her face. She jumps when Jess speaks, asking her if they can start work on the house tonight, instead of tomorrow. She looks annoyed, says that she doesn't feel up to it this evening, they will definitely work on it tomorrow, as promised. Jess begins to whine. 'Oh please let's do it this evening Lydia!' Her aunt shakes her head but before she can speak, Jess has burst into tears. 'I'm fed up having no one to play with, I want to see my mum and dad. I want to go home.'

Frustratingly the memory stopped there.

Chapter Twenty-Seven

On return to Manchester, Jess spent the rest of the week preparing for the new term of her water-colour class. She would think no more about Lydia in the hope that the memories would return fully in their own time.

One thing she was determined on, she was going to get fit. She had been appalled at her lack of fitness on the walk in Cornwall. She signed up at a local gym and began the relentless round of weights, treadmill and exercise bikes. All, she found, extremely boring; she hated the closed-in feeling of the windowless room, the air redolent of stale perspiration. So as soon as her first month's subscription was up, she didn't renew it and instead bought a pair of running shoes and set off first thing every morning.

She had never been a runner before and she found it very hard going at first but she took her time, it wasn't a race after all, and she delighted in being out at dawn when the roads were quiet and there were few people around. Just other joggers and the odd dog-walker. She appreciated the smells, sights and sounds of spring. It was warm for mid-April but, at that time of the morning, it was comfortably cool. She liked to vary her route but it always included her local park, abundant with the whites, pinks, creams and yellows of apple and cherry blossom, magnolia, forsythia. Sadly the daffodils were past their best but the tulips had come into their own.

One morning, just as she entered the park, she noticed a

runner ahead stumble and fall and, as she approached she heard him moan as he clutched his right ankle.

'You all right?' she asked, extending a hand to help, at the same time thinking, *What a stupid thing to say when it's obvious he's anything but.* The man gripped her hand. 'It's my ankle, I've gone over on it. At least I hope that's all it is…' He broke off as she helped him up and recognition dawned on both of them. 'Jess!' 'Max!' they said simultaneously.

They hadn't laid eyes on one another since the breakdown of their relationship two years before. Now Max tested his foot and finding that he couldn't put weight on it, put his arm round Jess's shoulder and leant on her as she led him to a nearby bench. Max dropped on to it with a sigh of relief.

'Well, well, who would have believed that Jess Cooper would have become a runner?'

'Never mind that. Let's have a look at that ankle.'

Max was wearing knee-length shorts and he leaned over, extending his foot and they examined his swelling ankle. 'I hope it's not sprained. I had a bad sprain about a year ago and I've had a weakness there ever since. It's not the first time this has happened but luckily I've not had another sprain.'

Jess unzipped a bag on her belt and produced a small brown bottle which she opened, carefully emptying a tiny white pill into the cap and giving it to Max. 'Pop it straight into your mouth and let it dissolve under your tongue.' Max looked at it suspiciously. 'What is it?'

'It's arnica, a homoeopathic remedy, brilliant for sprains, strains, soft tissue damage in general,' she laughed, 'don't look at it like that, it won't poison you.'

Max looked at her through narrowed eyes. 'Just as well I know you,' he said as he put the pill in his mouth.

Jess sat down next to him. 'Now, about getting you home.

Where are you living these days?' Max named an address, about two miles away.

'Well there's no way you can walk that distance. As you know, I'm only about a quarter of a mile from here. I'm going to go home, fetch my car and deliver you to your door.'

'Oh no, honestly, I couldn't put you to that bother. I'll ring for a taxi.' He pulled his mobile from his pocket. But Jess wouldn't hear of it. 'I'll be back in no time.' She thrust the bottle of arnica into his hand urging him to take another in about ten or fifteen minutes and ran off.

It turned out that Max lived on the first floor of a recently built block of flats and, on finding that he lived alone, Jess helped him upstairs, insisted that he sat with his injured ankle propped on a footstool and asked if he had any ice. Finding the cubes, she put them in a freezer bag which she wrapped in a tea towel and applied to the ankle. 'Now shall I make us both a cup of tea?'

'How does it feel?' She returned with two cups.

'It's not as painful as I would have expected.' Max had a look under the ice pack. 'And not as swollen either. I don't think it's a sprain.'

Jess examined it. 'Mm, not so bad. Did you take another pill as I suggested?' Max nodded.

'Well take another one now, arnica's wonderful stuff. I don't think it needs a bandage but you must rest it, keep your foot up as much as possible and keep on taking the remedy until the swelling goes down. You can keep that bottle; I have some more at home.'

Now that the immediacy of dealing with the ankle was over, there was an awkward silence. Max cleared his throat. 'Well Jess fancy seeing you after all this time and, doing what I would least have expected to see you doing – running! You were always so against it.'

'Against it is a bit strong. I never minded anyone else doing it; I just thought it wasn't for me.' But as she said it, she knew that wasn't strictly true. She had always thought there was something unsavoury about people who passed her, panting for breath and sweating profusely. Bad enough in winter but in a heat wave they were still at it. And when Max came in after a run, she could not bear to be in the same room until he'd had a shower.

'So what made you change your mind?'

'I was away in Cornwall last month, went walking and realised just how unfit I was. So, when I came back, I joined a gym but I hated it and I decided to give running a go.'

'And?'

'And what?'

'You're enjoying it?'

'I wasn't sure at first. I found it very hard but I do love being out in the open air, especially first thing on these spring mornings. I've only been doing it for a couple of weeks but it's getting easier already.' She stood up. 'Now would you like me to get you something to eat before I leave? You need to rest that ankle.'

Max shook his head. 'No you've done enough already and my ankle feels much better.' He went to stand up, gripping the coffee table and testing his right foot on the floor. He winced, then tried again. 'It really isn't as painful.'

'Do be careful Max. Sit down and put that foot up again. It's no trouble to make you some toast or get you some cereal. In fact, if it makes you feel any better, I'll join you. I'm a bit peckish myself.' She went into the kitchen and returned with two more cups of tea and some toast.

'Thanks Jess. I do appreciate all you've done.'

As they ate their toast, they lapsed once more into an awkward silence which was again broken by Max.

'So where did you learn about homeopathy? I never heard you mention it when we were together.'

Jess chewed slowly on her last piece of toast. 'I read an article about it in a health magazine and, shortly afterwards I saw an ad for a short course in homeopathic first aid and I enrolled.'

Max had another look at his ankle. 'Well it looks like the arnica's doing something. I've never known the swelling to go down so rapidly.'

'Yeah, well you still need to rest it.'

'But I'll have to move sometime. I can't sit here all day. I'm dying for a shower apart from anything else.'

'You need something to lean on. What about a broom? You must have a broom.' Max indicated a cupboard, Jess found the broom and together they improvised a crutch.

'You will let me know how you go on, won't you?' Jess said as she turned to leave. 'I'm still on the same number.'

As she drove home, Jess was surprised to find herself thinking how good it had been to encounter Max again and she was even more surprised to find that the anger she had once been harbouring towards him seemed to have dissolved. Not that she had given him much thought recently, so caught up had she been in the discovery of relatives she had known nothing about and in trying to retrieve her memories and to piece together the jigsaw of her life.

She recalled the good times. They had met as teachers at the same Manchester comprehensive but they'd only been acquaintances. Then he'd moved to another school and she had forgotten about him until they'd met again at a party given by a mutual friend. They had got talking properly for the first time and found they had much in common. He had invited her out and soon afterwards he'd moved in with her.

They were both keen hill walkers and, as Max was the proud owner of a well-equipped camper van, they had easy access to places where they could indulge this pursuit while Jess also indulged her passion for painting and sketching. It was an insouciant existence and, work permitting, they were rarely at home.

Her feelings for Max had been so strong and their life together so enjoyable that she had naively believed that it would continue forever. *And if it hadn't been for the unplanned pregnancy, it may well have done.* But her only regret about the pregnancy was that she had lost the baby. She couldn't wish that it had never happened and it had certainly shown her a side to Max that she'd not seen before.

Less than two weeks later, Jess was surprised to find herself sitting opposite Max in a restaurant.

Several days after the accident he had phoned to say that his ankle was almost better.

'I can't believe it. It's never healed this quickly before. I did strap it up for a while to give it support but I removed the bandage two days ago. The swelling's gone and all that's left is the odd twinge. I'll be running again in no time.'

She warned him to be careful. 'Anyway Jess,' he continued, 'I'd like to repay you by taking you out for a meal.' He sounded tentative. Jess was silent. She wanted to say yes, but realising that she still had feelings for Max she was cautious.

'Are you still there Jess?' He sounded anxious.

'Yes I'm still here.' She decided to take the plunge. What was the harm in sharing a meal?

'Thanks Max that would be lovely.'

Expecting to be taken for a pizza or a curry, she was surprised to hear him suggest the upmarket restaurant in the city centre where they now sat.

Over the meal, she discovered that not much had changed for Max: he was still teaching maths and physics at the same school, still went walking. She was surprised to hear he had sold his camper van.

'But why Max? That van was your pride and joy.'

He looked away, fiddling with the stem of his wine glass, muttered, 'It was never the same after we finished Jess. When I went away in it, I just thought about you all the time.' He looked at her now. 'This is awkward but you may as well know the truth. I don't go walking as often either. Going away with the lads is not quite the same.'

'So no girlfriend then? Or maybe one who isn't interested in walking?'

He shook his head. 'No, no one. Oh I've had a couple of flings but they didn't amount to anything. We had nothing in common. Anyway, how about you? What have you been up to in the past two years? Apart from going on homeopathy courses that is.' He laughed.

She told him that she'd given up her job at the school and was now freelance and running some art classes for adults, how she had got out of the way of hill walking altogether. 'I'm afraid I've led a rather sedentary existence, which is why I found I was so unfit when I was in Cornwall.'

Part of her wanted to tell him about *Sea Music* and her discovery that she had an aunt and a cousin but she held back, not really sure why.

Max shifted in his chair, looking awkward again. 'I was wondering…eh…would you ever come walking with me again Jess?' Then seeing her bemused look he added, 'Oh just occasionally I mean – as friends.'

Jess pushed aside her plate and folding her hands together on the table leaned forward, looking directly at him. 'Do you think we can be real friends again Max, after what happened?'

'Oh Jess I want to talk to you about that but I don't think this is the best place.' He looked around as if fearful of being overheard, though the tables were placed at discreet distances apart.

'Would you agree to come to my place sometime soon? There is so much I want to say to you and,' he scanned the room again, 'it feels too private to be said here.'

Jess shook her head, 'I don't know Max. Is there any point in stirring up the past? That awful, painful time.'

'Please Jess. I've spent a lot of time thinking and in self-examination and I believe I've changed. I'm not asking you to take me back, just to give me a chance to explain myself.'

He looked so contrite and sad that Jess found herself relenting but she said, 'I'll think about it Max. Now let's enjoy the rest of our meal. I'm in the mood for a rich, gooey pudding.'

Back home, Jess reflected on how much she had enjoyed the evening, once they had got off the subject of their relationship. She had forgotten what good company Max was and how he made her laugh. But was it wise to begin seeing him again – as a friend? And indeed was it possible for them to be friends? She felt sure now that he still had feelings for her. She would need to give it some very serious thought and she was too tired now. She would think about it another time.

—ww—

Over the next few days, painful memories made an unwelcome intrusion but she knew she had to face them if she was to give Max's suggestion serious consideration.

They had never discussed the possibility of children so, when she missed a period, she bought two pregnancy testing kits to be sure and, as she watched the blue lines materialise for the second time, she was astounded at the confusion of feelings within her: shock, horror and disbelief giving way to belief, apprehension, fear, hope, and finally delight.

She was worried about telling Max but, surprised at her own reaction, she hoped that he too would be pleased when he got over the shock.

'You're not serious.' Max was visibly appalled. He put down his knife and fork and gaped at her open-mouthed.

'Couldn't be more so. I've done two tests, both positive. I'll have to get it confirmed of course, but I'd say our baby is due in October.'

Max pushed his half-empty plate away. 'You're not going through with it?'

It was Jess's turn to be appalled.

'Well of course I'm going through with it. What else would I do? I know we've never considered children, but since I did the tests, I feel differently. I really want this child, Max.'

White-faced, Max slumped forward, head in hands.

'I can't believe I'm hearing this. What about our walking holiday in Spain at Easter?'

'There's no reason why I can't do that, as long as I'm careful. Pregnancy is not an illness after all.' Smiling, she reached out and touched his hand, but he shook her off.

'But when the baby's born, it will change our whole way of life and we have a good life Jess. Please consider a termination.'

'Look Max, I know this child wasn't planned, but it was meant to be. It's already a living, growing being and I'm not putting an end to that.'

'Jess, I want our lifestyle to continue as it was. I'll go mad if I can't get out into the mountains. No child could ever give me the sense of freedom and fulfillment I get there.'

'Max, I'm happy to stay at home with our child while you go off. Besides it won't be that long until we can take him or her with us.'

'Walking wouldn't be the same without you Jess. We're in this together, it's our life.' His look was pleading.

'Sorry Max, I won't even consider a termination. This child is here to stay.'

He pushed his chair back, stood up and left the room, slamming the door.

She let him go. There was no use trying to reason with him while he was in his current state and she still believed he would come round, given time.

But the weeks went on and the arguments continued, sometimes well into the night. Then she had a threatened miscarriage. Max didn't say much, but she felt he must surely be pleased. They saved the baby, but she was advised to rest. After a couple of weeks, she went back to work, but took it easy as much as possible. April came and despite Max's protestations about walking on his own, he went off to Spain. He sent her a card from the Sierra Nevada: *Missing you, not the same without you.*

By the time she received it, she had just come out of hospital, having lost the baby at eleven weeks.

When Max came home, he was loving and attentive.

'I'm truly sorry Jess; I know how much the baby meant to you.'

She was aghast.

'How can you be so hypocritical? You begged me to have a termination. You must be delighted now the baby's gone.'

'I never wanted it to happen like this. And I had come to accept it. I didn't tell you because I didn't think you would believe me.'

Jess had had enough. She told him the relationship was over and she wanted him out as soon as he found somewhere else to live. Within weeks he was gone. She missed him and the life they'd had together but she had never doubted that she had done the right thing. Until now that was. Maybe it was time to hear what he had to say.

Since his chance meeting with Jess, Max had also been thinking over their relationship and what had brought it to an end, two years ago.

He had been deeply in love with Jess and they were so compatible and had such an enjoyable life together that, like her, he had imagined it lasting forever. He had never wanted children, partly because he felt they would curtail his freedom but mainly because he didn't want to assume responsibility for the happiness of a vulnerable human being. His own childhood had been anything but happy. He had vague memories of a violent father who had abandoned them when Max was four, shortly after his brother Christie was born. Then his mother had died when he was six and Christie was two and, having no interested relatives, they had spent a miserable four years in care before going to a loving foster home.

During the years in care he had felt responsible for his little brother who, small for his age and prone to nightmares and bed-wetting, was bullied both in the care home and at school.

He and Jess had never discussed being parents and he had made the assumption that she felt as he did and he recalled the shock he had felt when she had told him that, not only was she pregnant, she was actually looking forward to being a mother. He had felt at the time that it was as much his right to decide on a termination as it was hers and he was appalled at the thought of the freedom he felt in the mountains being restricted.

Now he felt differently: how difficult it must be for a woman, with a living being growing inside her to make the decision to terminate it. Difficult enough for her to make the decision but to have someone make that decision for her. He was disgusted at his selfishness.

And, in fact, by the time Jess had the threatened miscarriage, he had actually been coming round to the idea but he didn't tell her because he didn't think that she would believe him, so unwavering had he been in his opposition to the pregnancy.

He remembered his relief when they saved the child and the happy daydreams he had had about his son or daughter when he was in Spain; the dismay and sorrow he had felt on return to find that the child was no more. His sympathy had been genuine but Jess, in the throes of grief and anger was in no mood to see him as anything other than a hypocrite.

In the past two years his life had felt incomplete and his heartfelt hope now was that Jess would give him a chance to explain himself and how he had changed.

Chapter Twenty-Eight

Amy and Emma were sitting outside an Italian restaurant in Islington enjoying the sunshine and the excellent food.

'This is great,' Emma smiled across at her friend, 'just what a girl needs. Three unbroken nights, good food, good wine, good company and a chance to spend time in my favourite city.' She raised her glass in a salute, using one of the few phrases they both knew in Cornish, 'Yeghes da!' Amy returned the salutation. Each gave a sigh of pleasure and they were quiet for a moment as they savoured their starters. Then Emma looked at Amy.

'So how's it going with Alex?'

Emma and Amy had been friends since nursery school. They had been to the same university, albeit to study different subjects, Amy doing physiotherapy while Emma did languages. That was when she met Sam and they had been together ever since, getting married just after they graduated and moving to his native Norfolk where they had both got teaching posts. But Emma had not taught for long: Arthur was born within ten months and Isabel eighteen months later. With Emma busy with motherhood and Amy working full-time and extending her repertoire of therapies on several part-time courses, their phone calls and emails were few and far between and when Amy had finally managed to persuade Emma to take some time off and come to London for a weekend, they had not seen one another for two years.

Now Amy was telling Emma just how good it was with Alex.

'I know we've only been together for five months but it feels...' she hesitated, '...*right*. How can I explain? It never felt quite like that with Mark... well for a few weeks maybe, but after that...it felt like I was trying to make it alright a lot of the time...oh I don't know, it's hard to explain...' She looked imploringly at Emma.

'I do know what you mean. I had exactly the same feeling with Sam and I still feel the same, five years later. If anything the children have brought us even closer.'

She topped up both their glasses, took a sip of wine and leaned back, folding her arms.

'So have you finished studying at last?'

Amy nodded, 'Yes, the reflexology course was the last one – for the time being at any rate. Who knows what I might decide to do in another year or two?'

While on her physiotherapy course, Amy had started to do yoga and that had led to an interest in complimentary therapies. After finishing her degree and getting the job in London, she had done a diploma in aromatherapy and massage, trained as a yoga teacher and she had just qualified as a reflexologist. Now she was telling Emma of her ambitions.

'I want to set up a centre of healing where I live in south London. It would offer meditation, yoga, counselling and a whole range of complimentary therapies, not available on the NHS. I would want it to be available to everyone in the local community,' she said, fiddling with the rose quartz pendant she wore on a silver chain, 'so I would charge on a sliding scale according to people's income. I would work there, of course; other therapists could work on a self-employed basis, just pay me a percentage for the use of the place.'

Emma leant on the table, chin cupped in her right hand.

'Sounds like a lovely idea; people would really benefit from a place like that. Do you have any premises in mind?'

'No, not really, it's a bit of a pipe dream at the moment. It would need to be a sizable property and even the price of smaller properties is daunting in London.'

Emma lifted the wine bottle and scrutinised it before tipping the remains into their glasses. 'Shall we get another bottle?'

Amy shook her head. 'If I have any more, I won't be fit to walk round the shops.'

'Oh come on, I'm on my holidays. Besides it's too hot for shopping. I'm quite happy to sit here and gossip. I'll order a bottle of water as well.' She beckoned to the waiter.

Jess and Max were driving to Northumberland. When they had met up back in May, each had listened carefully to what the other had to say and a renewed sense of understanding had resulted. There was no big reconciliation but Jess had agreed to accompany Max on some walks and those had been easy and enjoyable times. Now they were a couple again but they were taking things slowly and they were both determined to hold on to their independence by continuing to live separately.

After some weeks, Jess had come round to telling Max about her new-found cousin and the aunt who had died just after she had been staying with her.

Max had looked at her sympathetically, putting his arm round her and drawing her close. 'Well no wonder you always had that sense of incompleteness and no wonder your mother turned to drink. But if only your parents had seen fit to tell you. It would have made your life so much easier and maybe bringing it out into the open would have helped your mum to cope better, who knows?'

'Who knows indeed,' Jess snuggled against him, then straightened up, 'but you know they did what they thought was right at the time. They wanted to protect me.'

Max had no doubt of that but he was also aware that in so doing, they had caused Jess to have a very difficult childhood. He knew better than to voice that opinion.

Now, on this hot July day, they were on their way to *Sea Music* en route to a walking holiday in the Cheviots.

'You know it's almost exactly two years since I embarked on this same journey. The long school holiday had just begun and I'd decided to go off on my own to try to sort my head out. It had been a terrible year: losing the baby, finishing with you; I'd resigned my teaching post and on one hand that was exciting but it also felt very risky.'

Max leaned over from driving to hold her hand.

'Anyway,' she went on, 'little did I know what a journey of discovery it was going to be.'

Since the return of some memories after her meeting with Luke back in March, Jess had recalled nothing further and she wondered if she ever would.

They were going to *Sea Music* for two reasons: Max wanted to see it and she still held out some hope that being around the place again might help her recollection. She wondered if it had been sold yet and thought that, surely after all this time it would have been, but if it hadn't, she had decided she was going to brave another viewing. Given what she now knew from Luke's account, she felt that if only she could go in and imagine herself in the scenario he had painted, absorb the atmosphere, she might just recall something.

They decided to approach the house on foot by taking the cliff walk and, as they neared the bend in the path where *Sea Music* would come into view, Jess felt a mixture of excitement and trepidation. As they rounded the bend, she stopped abruptly. 'Oh,' she said in dismay. There was something different about the house. It looked bare, exposed. Yes of course, it was completely devoid of Virginia creeper and, what's more the stonework had been sandblasted. There was an air of sterility about it and there was no For Sale sign to be seen.

On approaching she saw that the front garden had a perfectly tended lawn and symmetrical flower beds, a tree had been cut down. There was no chance of seeing the walled back garden but from the scaffolding behind the house, it was obvious an extension was in progress.

Max put an arm round her shoulder, 'It's certainly not as you described it.'

Jess sighed, 'No it's completely different. I don't think there's any chance of me remembering anything here. Let's go back to the village and have some lunch. I think it's high time I put all this behind me.'

Chapter Twenty-Nine

It was Christmas Eve and Alex had invited Amy round for a meal. On Christmas morning they were to drive down to Cornwall to spend the next two days with her family. Just Luke and Sarah on Christmas Day; they were to be joined by Paul and his partner Tim on Boxing Day.

Alex put the finishing touches to the table, lit the candles and looked round the room. Even though he was not at home for the festival, he had gone to the trouble of buying a real tree which he had decorated in red and silver. Red-berried holly adorned the mirror and pictures and mistletoe hung near the centre of the room. The savoury smells from the kitchen mingled with that of pine resin and mulled wine. *True Christmas smells,* he thought.

He glanced at the two beautifully-wrapped gifts for Amy that he had placed under the tree with a mixture of excitement and anxiety and at that moment the doorbell rang.

Amy kissed him lightly on the cheek and handed him a bottle of red wine. 'Wow, what a wonderful smell. I'm ravenous!' She headed for the sitting room and was about to seat herself in one of the armchairs.

'Not so fast.' Alex took her in his arms under the mistletoe and gave her a lingering kiss.

'I know we don't need mistletoe to do that,' he said as he released her, 'but it is my first Christmas with you...'

Amy laughed. 'Oh Alex, you old romantic,' she touched his

face gently, then seeing the candles, the tree and holly, 'well you have gone to a lot of trouble. This looks lovely.'

Alex came and stood beside her, put an arm round her. 'Before we eat, I want to give you a present.'

'A present?' She sounded flustered. 'I've left yours in the car. I thought we were doing presents at Mum and Dad's tomorrow.'

Alex squeezed her shoulder. 'Oh we are but this is a special present I wanted to give you in private, well two actually but we can leave the other one until after dinner. Now do sit down.'

He stooped beneath the tree and picked up the smaller of two square packages and handed it to Amy. The paper was so beautiful that she opened it carefully, reluctant to tear it. Inside she found a small midnight blue velvet box. With sudden realisation, her hands began to shake as she opened it to find a solitaire diamond, set in platinum. She gasped involuntarily. Alex knelt before her,

'Amy Matthews will you marry me?' Amy burst into tears. Alex slapped his forehead in mock horror. 'Oh woe is me, my benign request hath caused the lady much distress!'

Amy laughed through her tears. 'Oh Alex you fool, of course I'll marry you.' She produced a tissue and began to dab at her eyes. Alex kissed her. 'In that case, let me put the ring on your finger.'

Amy held her hand at arm's length to admire the ring. 'It's a perfect fit. How did you manage that?'

'I borrowed a ring from your jewellery box, measured it and put it back one morning while you were still asleep. Now let's eat before the dinner's ruined, but first, a toast.' He disappeared into the kitchen and returned with a bottle of champagne in an ice bucket.

After the meal, Alex leaned across the table and covered Amy's hand with his own. 'And now for your second present.' He rose and lifted the other box from under the tree. It was about the size of a shoe box. *Surely he has not bought me a pair of shoes. Checked my size while I was sleeping.* But on lifting the lid, she found another box, then another and another. Mystified, she opened the last box to find an envelope with what felt like a card inside. *Is this an elaborate joke? Extreme wrapping for a Christmas card? No Alex would never do that.*

Tentatively she tore open the envelope. The card had a picture of a white dove holding the word Peace in its beak. She opened it to reveal a cheque made out to her. When she saw the amount she was so stunned she almost dropped the card. She read the words:

This should go a long way towards helping you realize your dream of a centre of healing; a centre of peace.

With much love,

Alex

She turned to him. 'But I don't understand. Where on earth did you get so much money? Have you had a win or something?'

Alex sat next to her on the sofa and gently pulled her towards him, so that she nestled her head on his chest. 'Let me explain what happened.'

Alex sat back from his computer, stretched and rubbed the back of his neck, stiff from spending too long without a break. He had been working on this translation since eight o'clock and it was now eleven. Time for a coffee.

As he went through to the kitchen, he heard his mail drop on to the mat. He was in no hurry to pick it up. In these days of emails, there was rarely anything of interest.

It was a dark November day with thick penetrating fog, one

of those days when it never brightened enough to turn off the lights. While he waited for the kettle to boil, he looked out over the common where the bare trees had taken on the form of emaciated giants peering at him through a silvery veil and thought that, even at the grimmest time of year there was always something of beauty to be appreciated. He gave thanks, as he often did that, five years ago, he had had the good fortune to find a relatively inexpensive property in this area. Carrying his cup through, he put it on the desk and went to see what junk mail had been delivered. A solitary cream envelope lay there, addressed by hand. Puzzled, he picked it up, not recognising the spidery writing and he was even more puzzled to see a Spanish stamp and postmark. He turned it over. *If undelivered please return to Fred Lee,* a Marbella address followed. *Fred Lee. Dave's friend, now why is he writing to me?*

Alex had known the man when he was growing up but, apart from the message about Dave's accident and seeing him briefly at the hospital when he went to visit, he had had nothing to do with him for years. He sat down at his desk, took a sip of coffee, opened the envelope, withdrew the writing paper and unfolded it. He was surprised to see that it contained a cheque, but he nearly fell off his chair when he saw the amount and that it was made out to him.

Dear Alex,

I wanted to write this by hand but I knew you would have difficulty making out my terrible scrawl. No doubt you will be very surprised to hear from me and very puzzled by the cheque.

Let me explain. Your father left a large proportion of his estate to me, including his villa. He never told me the details of his will, only that he had written you out of it. I told him it was unfair and tried to persuade him to change his mind but there was no reasoning with him and I hated having to write that letter for him when he told you he was leaving you nothing.

He told me about how he took you from your mother when you were tiny, also some stuff about you thinking he might have had some part in your mother's death and I know that's why you were so angry with him. I also know you were estranged before you found all this out and I'm not sure what that was about.

Dave was my closest friend for a lifetime but I know only too well what a difficult man he could be. I felt really sorry when he told me he wasn't leaving you a penny and when I found he had left so much to me I felt even worse. I actually sold the villa a few months ago and I wanted to send you the proceeds then but I wasn't sure how you would react so I have given it a great deal of thought before sending it. I hope you won't think it feels like charity or that you will be beholden to me in any way. I just believe it is money that is rightfully yours. After all it was Dave and not you who caused the problems between you. I don't need the money, I was a wealthy man before I received Dave's legacy and I'm sure a young man like you could put the money to good use, so please accept it in the spirit in which it is given.

With kindest regards,

It was signed with Fred's indecipherable signature, his name typed underneath.

Alex let the letter flutter to the floor. He picked up the cheque from the table and stared at it, mesmerised. He had never seen, never mind held, one for such a large amount. He knew he should have felt elated but was it right to accept money from a man he'd had nothing to do with for many years. He did recall that Fred was someone he had liked when he was growing up. Most of Dave's friends had joined with him in his put-downs of his son but not Fred. He had been encouraging and, on a number of occasions he had taken Alex's part when he and Dave had had a disagreement. But it was incredible that he was now holding in his hand a cheque for a more than generous amount of money. In spite of what Fred had urged, he knew he would feel beholden to him and he still queried the morality of accepting money which had probably been largely acquired through dubious dealings. He wanted to discuss it with Amy but she was going to visit her parents that weekend. He would miss her, not that they lived in one another's pockets: she still lived in her house in south London, which she shared with a lodger. But they did spend most weekends together. They had been together for nine months and he had plans for asking her to marry him. Alex decided he would see if Tony was free for a drink and discuss it with him.

Tony listened attentively to Alex's account of his surprising windfall and whistled when he heard the amount.

'That's incredible Alex. I can understand your reluctance to accept but, at the same time, you've heard the saying, *never look a gift-horse in the mouth.*'

'Of course but to tell you the truth Tony, I was never all that sure what it meant.' He smiled looking somewhat abashed.

'It means don't look too closely at a gift, accept it in the spirit in which it is given.'

Alex shrugged, 'That's just it. I don't know what his motives are. I don't want to be beholden to one of my father's friends. I used to like Fred but at the end of the day, I think they're all just a crowd of crooks.'

Tony laughed. 'Oh come on Alex, now you're being fanciful. What could the man possibly want from you? It's clear from the letter he feels bad about your father cutting you out of the will and he wants to make amends.'

Alex made patterns with his index finger in a spillage of beer.

'Okay, well apart from all that, do you think it's right to take a gift of money that was probably largely made by devious means?'

'Oh Alex.' Tony sounded exasperated. 'Look I'm going to the bar. Another pint?'

Minutes later he returned and set the two pint glasses on the table.

'Honestly Alex, you're being too scrupulous. Are you as scrupulous about what the government chooses to fund with your taxes? Just remember you are not responsible for the way your father chose to make his money, nor have you proof that he was involved in any shady dealings. And besides, surely you are owed some recompense for what the man did to you – abduction, lies, showing you a photo of a stranger and telling you she was your mother. Just think of the good you could do with the money,' Tony took a long draught from his pint.

Alex had thought over what Tony had said and concluded that the worthiest cause he could think of was Amy's dream of a healing centre.

Amy, who had listened to his tale with rapt attention, now sat upright. 'Oh Alex, are you sure you want to do this? It's your money by rights. After what your father did, he owed you that and a lot more. And, as we're getting married, we'll want to buy a house, won't we? Surely it would be better to put it towards that.'

Alex cupped her face in his hands, looked directly into her eyes. 'Amy, Amy listen to me. Yes we will buy a house together. When I sell my apartment and you sell your house we will have more than enough to do that. I see this money,' he held up the cheque, 'as something separate. Call it a godsend if you like; I see it as an opportunity to do good with some of Dave's money, after all the harm he has done to me and others.'

Amy finally conceded that he was right and grew excited at the prospect of looking for suitable premises for her centre. Alex was relieved. 'Good, now that that's settled, can we start to make plans for our wedding?'

Part Four

Chapter Thirty

2004

In the sixteen months since Jess and Max had been reunited, their relationship had got back to the footing it was on prior to Jess's pregnancy and miscarriage. The only difference being that Max was now keen for them to have children. Neither of them wanted to get married but, after nearly a year, Max had moved back in with Jess and they were looking for a bigger house.

It was Friday night and Max had gone out with some work colleagues to celebrate a fortieth birthday. Jess could have joined them but she hated socialising with people she hardly knew. She found the talk of work, the in-jokes, tedious, though she tolerated Christmas meals when people were expected to bring their partners. It was Max's birthday the following day and she decided to use the opportunity to make him a cake, his favourite Lemon Drizzle. Although she enjoyed cooking, Jess didn't often bake and, as she turned on the radio and lined up the ingredients on the kitchen table, she looked forward to the task in hand.

Putting the cake in the oven, she became aware of a pleasant odour drifting through the open window: burning leaves, one of her favourite smells, evocative of frosty autumn nights like this one, Halloween fun, bonfires, apple pie. She stood for a moment, recalling happy times before her mother's drinking got the better of her. Then she cleared up, made herself a cup of tea and sat at the table to listen to the rest of her programme and wait for the cake, which was already giving off a delicious smell, to cook.

After about ten minutes, she got up, peered through the glass oven door and saw that it was rising nicely. At that moment another smell mixed with the cake's aroma: the acrid and, to her, loathsome smell of burning rubber. Had someone added rubber to the fire of leaves? Or was it one of the many bonfires lit in anticipation of the fifth of November?

As she inhaled the smell of burning rubber and baking cake, she felt nausea creep up on her but, superseding that was another, most peculiar sensation. It was similar to the sensation she had felt at the top of the cellar steps at *Sea Music* when Mr Winton was showing her round: something flapping and clawing at the back of her mind. She put both hands on her head and shut her eyes, floating, unreal. She leaned against the cooker for support, then found her way to a chair, put her arms on the table and rested her head on them. That was when the pictures started to come; snapshots at first.

She wakens from a bad dream where there is a lot of angry shouting. The shouting is still going on downstairs. She is frightened.

Jess lifted her head, put her elbows on the table and leaned her mouth against her closed fists, her eyes wide and staring straight ahead. She had broken out in a cold sweat and she was shaking, her mouth as dry as dust. She must get a drink of water. Weakly she got to her feet then sat down again abruptly. More pictures were coming.

She gets out of bed. The shouting is still going on. As she starts to go downstairs she is assailed by the very unpleasant odour of burning rubber. She recognises it from last year's Bonfire Night when one of the boys was scolded for throwing a tyre on to the fire.

That smell is bad enough but mixed with that of the cakes Lydia let her make earlier, it is intolerable and suddenly she feels queasy. She knows she should go to the bathroom in case she is sick but she wants Lydia so she carries on. The shouting stops. Silence. The kitchen is empty. She crosses to the open cellar door and looks down. Lydia is lying there in a heap, unmoving; her head is twisted; her eyes are open, staring, glassy, like a doll's. A man and a woman are hovering over her.

When Max returned, an hour later, he found her asleep, still seated at the kitchen table, head on her arms once more. He shook her gently, noticing when she raised her head, that her eyes were red and swollen.

'What's the matter Jess? Why have you been crying?'

Mesmerised, she looked around wondering where on earth she was. Then she saw the cake on its wire cooling rack and it all came back to her: the smell, the memories, the fear, the grief. She had no recollection of having taken the cake out of the oven.

'Oh Max I'm so glad you're home.' He sat next to her, took her in his arms and she clung to him.

'What's happened Jess?'

She was silent for what seemed like an age, then just as he was about to ask her again, she spoke.

'I've remembered. The night of Lydia's death. I was there, not at home in London. It's all come back to me, clearly as if it has just happened.' She tensed her body and shivered as if trying to ward off something horrible. 'It was awful Max. It *is* awful! I feel like I'm still there, seeing Lydia's body; her glassy stare. But it's worse than that: much, much worse.' She buried her face in her hands.

'Do you want to tell me about it?'

'Yes I think so…yes I do.' Hesitancy became resolution.

Max released her and stood up. 'Shall I make some tea or would you prefer something stronger?'

'No, no, tea is fine. Let's go and sit somewhere more comfortable.'

Chapter Thirty-One

5th August 1978

'Lydia can we look at the doll's house now instead of tomorrow?' Jess found her aunt in her studio but she was not painting. She was pacing about the room with a very odd look on her face. She gave a sharp intake of breath and turned swiftly to look at Jess, hand on her heart, as if something had frightened her.

'No Jess not this evening. Apart from anything else, it's getting late. Time you had some supper and a bath. We'll sort it tomorrow, I promise.'

Jess began to whine. 'Oh please let's do it this evening Lydia.'

Lydia shook her head but before she could speak, Jess burst into tears, telling her how fed up she was playing on her own, how she wanted to see her mum and dad, 'I want to go home.'

Lydia sighed, crouched down to Jess's level and gave her a hug.

At that moment the phone rang in the hall below. Lydia's spirits lifted. *Oh I hope this is someone I can talk to about this predicament I'm in.* She took Jess's hand.

'Come down with me Jess. I'll try not to be long on the phone and then I promise we'll do something nice together.'

Jess waited in the kitchen and when Lydia returned she seemed brighter.

'Well Jess, how would you like to make some fairy cakes all on your own?'

Jess's sulky expression turned into a beaming smile. 'On my own? Really?'

'Yes really. I know you know exactly what to do and I promise I will sit and watch and I won't interfere unless you ask me for help.'

'Can I make rock cakes instead Lydia? They're my favourite and I know what to do.'

Lydia agreed and Jess was thrilled. She loved helping her mother and Lydia to bake but she had never made anything completely on her own. She felt very mature as she put on an apron, got out the ingredients and utensils and began her task.

Lydia opened the oven door, put her hand in.

'Hmm, I need to stoke up the range before the cakes go in, so I think you should have your bath now and I'll put them in when the oven's hot enough.'

Jess looked disappointed. 'Oh can I not put them in myself Lydia after my bath? I'll be ever so careful and you can watch me.'

Lydia sighed in mock exasperation. 'Oh all right then. Now bath!'

Lydia was feeling guilty. She was aware that her preoccupation since her encounter with Dave had been noticed by Jess. No wonder the child had been fed up.

So, when the cakes were in the oven, she announced that she had a surprise.

'Why don't we go down the cellar and bring up the doll's house…' As Jess interrupted with cries of excitement, she put her hand up. 'Hold on, we're not going to work on it tonight but we'll lay everything out ready to start on it first thing tomorrow.' To her relief Jess didn't demur.

Together they went down the cellar and Lydia gave Jess the

task of getting some newspapers out of a cupboard, to spread on the kitchen table. Then she carried the house up and tried to show her where spiders had moved in with the dolls, weaving lace curtains over the windows but Jess squirmed and backed away. Lydia laughed. 'Don't worry I'll evict them and put them outside. Then we can start work in the morning.'

When the cakes were cooked and sampled, still warm, with butter, Lydia looked at the clock. 'My goodness we are running late tonight young lady, it's well past your bedtime.'

Chapter Thirty-Two

'She read me a story as usual and that was the last time I saw her alive.' Jess stood up suddenly and walked to a shelf, lifted a framed photograph and stared at it. 'Oh Max what am I going to do?'

'There's only one thing you can do, must do, you must confront him. Ask him what happened.'

She sat down again, still clutching the photo. 'Oh my God Dad, all these years of knowing you and I never really knew you at all, or you either Mum. Is it any wonder I lost my memory of that night? It wasn't just the trauma of finding Lydia dead; it was the shock of seeing both my parents bending over her body. I thought they had killed her!'

Leaning her forehead against the photo, she began to weep softly.

Max was at a loss as to how to comfort her, impotent as he was to eradicate or change the devastating recollections that had at last come to her after twenty-six years. *Oh that the memories had remained locked away.* As if reading his mind, Jess lifted her tear-stained face, blew her nose and said, 'And to think these horrible memories have returned because I decided to make a cake and someone decided to burn some rubber. Smell is such a powerful sense where memory's concerned.'

—〰—

'I've remembered everything about the night of Lydia's death Dad.' Jess faced her father across the coffee table, a grave look on her face.

'Lydia's death? You mean you remember saying goodbye to Lydia and some of the journey back to London with me and your mum? You slept most of the way.' He sounded calm but, watching him carefully, Jess could see a wary look in his eyes.

'No,' she said, 'I remember being there just after she died. You know perfectly well we weren't on our way home. No wonder I was freaked out when I saw those cellar steps. I had seen Lydia lying dead at the foot of them and you and Mum were there, bending over her. I don't want any more lies. I want to know what happened that night.'

John felt a prickle of sweat under his arms, shifted uncomfortably in his chair.

'So you really have remembered all of it.'

'Well the next thing I remember after that is being at home in London and not going back to school, Mum teaching me at home. So why have you kept the truth from me? Was it because one or other of you – maybe both of you, caused Lydia's death or was it because you witnessed it? Or you found her dead and did nothing about it? Why? If it was an accident why did you run off and leave her there? Why did you not ring the police? Why have you told me a pack of lies about the whole thing?'

John put his elbows on his knees and covered his mouth and nose with his hands and, rendered speechless by Jess's words, contemplated a spot on the carpet, for what seemed to her like an age. Then he straightened up.

Well there's no point in denying it Jess. We were there that night but neither of us killed Lydia, she fell. It was an accident.'

'But why did you go off then? Dad I'm heart sick of your lies. I want the truth. Now.' She thumped the table.

'It's a long story Jess. I'm going to get a brandy. Let me get you one. You may need it.'

'No I want to keep a clear head for this.'

John went to the sideboard, poured a measure of brandy, returned to his seat, took a sip, looked at the glass, threw the rest back and went to get another. 'Sorry about this Jess. Dutch courage.'

'Exactly. Now leave it after that one Dad, I want you to have a clear head as well.'

He sat down again and took a deep breath.

'Well, as I said, it's a long story and before I tell you what happened that night, there is something else you need to know, sure you don't want a brandy?'

Jess rolled her eyes, shook her head. 'Just get on with it Dad.'

He took another deep breath.

'There's no easy way to break this to you Jess. Lydia wasn't your aunt, she was your mother.'

Jess gasped. 'What? You mean you and Mum are not... Oh my God! Why have you never told me this before? No, no, what am I thinking?' She held up her hand as if repelling something undesirable. 'Why would you have told me this when you've kept so much from me? I wonder what other 'surprises' you have in store for me.'

John leaned across and covered her hands with his. 'Jess, Jess...' She pulled her hands free and wrapped her arms around her upper body.

'If your mother had been a stranger, we would have told you but it was difficult with her being Anna's sister and living so near. We had every intention of telling you when you were older but then we were overtaken by events – Lydia's death and the need for us to keep her existence a secret from you.'

Jess opened her mouth to say something, closed it again and

sat back as if resigning herself to what she was hearing and was about to hear.

John continued. 'Back in 1970, your mother and I had been married for five years and had wanted a family almost from the start. When Anna failed to get pregnant, she had some tests done and she was devastated to be told that she would never conceive. I was pretty cut up about it as well. We discussed adoption but we weren't sure we wanted to go down that road. Then Lydia told Anna she was pregnant. She and the father had finished before she found out and he had moved away but at any rate, she didn't want him to know. She didn't want a baby. She'd been teaching for less than a year and a half and she loved her job. There was no way she wanted to give it up and she was frightened at the thought of bringing up a child on her own. She asked Anna if we would adopt the baby. Well we thought long and hard about it. We were afraid that, if we agreed, Lydia might change her mind when she saw her baby. We also wondered if it would be a good idea bringing up her child while she lived nearby and spent so much time with us. But we were desperate and in the end we agreed.

'Well Lydia kept to her word and when you were born, she handed you over straight away and we legally adopted you. She was always very involved with you, as you know, and it was clear she loved you very much. She just didn't want the responsibility of bringing you up single-handed.'

John finished his second glass of brandy. 'Are you still alright with hearing this Jess?'

'I've not got much choice, have I? And I'm dying to hear how you're going to explain what happened to Lydia.'

John's shoulders slumped; he looked like a little boy who had just been told off but he went on to tell her that, by the time Lydia got pregnant with Simon, she was in a different position

– in a relationship with Dave Collier and about to leave her teaching post so there was no question of not wanting him, even after she threw Dave out.

'Then when the worst happened and she lost Simon, your mother and I felt guilty for having you and we were also afraid that she might want you back. We knew that she couldn't of course: you were legally ours, but it was a highly emotional time and we weren't thinking rationally. Anyway, she never gave the slightest hint that she resented us for having you and I think she got great strength from seeing you and playing with you...'

Jess cut in. 'So I'm still waiting to hear what happened that night.'

Chapter Thirty-Three

5th August 1978

When Jess was asleep, Lydia decided to burn the old toys and books they had sorted. She got the bag from the cellar, tipped the contents into the range and returned to the cellar to get her toolbox in readiness for working on the doll's house in the morning. But first it needed a good clean. She filled a basin with warm soapy water, added a few drops of disinfectant, pulled on a pair of rubber gloves and began work. But she couldn't settle to the task. She threw the cloth into the water and walked round the kitchen, head in hands.

She wondered if she had done the right thing in agreeing to see Dave. She had been shocked to hear his voice when she had answered the phone, full of hope that it was a friend she could ask advice from. She recalled the conversation.

'Dave? I don't want to talk to you! But how… how did you know I was here? And how did you get this number?'

'Well I guessed that, as you were in Newcastle, there was a good chance you were staying at *Sea Music* and I got the number from Directory Enquiries. But listen Lydia please don't hang up on me. I'm really sorry about the way I spoke to you before. I was just so shocked that you thought my son was Simon…'

'Well what did you expect me to think? It was such a shock seeing that child – so like you – and then seeing you after all this time. And him running up to you. My mind's still

307

preoccupied with Simon a lot of the time, so…' She broke off, near to tears.

'Lydia, Lydia, listen to me. I'm sorry you were so shocked. I think about Simon all the time too but at least I have Alex… sorry I shouldn't have said that. It's a long story – I didn't know he existed until fairly recently. Listen, can I come up and talk to you? Explain about Alex. I know I was a right bastard, having those affairs. You never deserved a dickhead like me and you must never think that the child you saw today is Simon. Please give me a chance to explain.'

Lydia was in a quandary. Some part of her longed for the boy to be Simon; another part wanted to believe that Dave was incapable of taking their child and putting her through the years of anguish. It could surely do no harm to hear what he had to say?

While absorbed in these thoughts, she became aware of a noxious odour coming from the range. *Damn. I forgot to take out the rubber toys.* She got up and opened the back door and windows.

Anna and John were driving towards Barrowman's point and *Sea Music*. They had had an enjoyable week in Scotland: sightseeing and going round Anna's childhood haunts in Edinburgh, walking in the mountains above Fort William. Their plan had been to stay for ten days but Anna was overcome with loneliness for Jess and when she mentioned this to John, he said he was missing her too, so they agreed to surprise her and Lydia by turning up three days early.

As Lydia sat down again and attempted to focus on cleaning the doll's house, she was puzzled to hear a car crunch on the gravel drive. *Surely that can't be Dave so soon. He said he wouldn't be able to make it until later.* Throwing the cloth into the basin, she peeled off her gloves and went out just as John and Anna were approaching the back door. She made an attempt to calm herself.

'Oh Anna, John, this is a surprise. How lovely to see you.' She embraced them both.

As they entered the kitchen, Anna wrinkled her nose. 'God Lydia, what on earth are you burning?'

'Some old toys and books that belonged to you and me. Jess helped me to sort them the other day and I decided to burn the really tatty ones. I just tipped the contents of the bag into the range forgetting that I meant to take out the rubber toys. But I've opened the door and windows. It should soon clear.'

'Oh and the doll's house! You've been working on the doll's house! Gosh I've not seen this old thing for…I don't know how many years. Remember how we used to love it?' Anna went to examine it.

'Yes, Jess and I are going to start work on it tomorrow. She'll be disappointed if we don't get a chance before she goes home.'

'Well we don't have to rush off, in fact, as we're still on holiday, there's no reason why we couldn't stay here for a couple of days. If you'll have us, of course.'

Lydia smiled. 'Oh yes that would be great.'

John looked at his watch. 'I guess Jess is in bed. We meant to get here a bit earlier but the traffic was heavy.'

'You know, you've just missed her by fifteen minutes or so. As it happens she was up later than usual.'

'Oh so maybe she's not asleep yet. Shall we go and see?' Anna started towards the door.

Lydia shook her head. 'No she was out like a light when I was only half way through the story.'

'Oh what a shame. Never mind we'll see her in the morning. How's she been?'

'She's been good as gold, just one little blip this evening when she was missing you but I've loved having her here. She's good company. And look.' She indicated the rock cakes on the cooling tray. 'She made those all by herself. She was so excited and pleased with herself.'

'By herself, really?' Anna's examined the cakes. 'They look very professional.'

Lydia moved to the range, lifted one of the lids and moved the kettle on to a hotplate. 'Tea or coffee? And have you eaten?'

'Tea please,' John and Anna said in unison, 'and yes we ate before we left, though some of Jess's rock cakes would be nice,' finished John.

'Just let me clear this away and make some room on the table.' Lydia pushed the doll's house to the side and took the bowl of water through to the utility room.

As she set out mugs and milk and put some of the cakes on a plate, Anna noticed that her hands were shaking slightly.

'Are you alright Lydia?'

She looked up. 'No, as a matter of fact. I'm anything but.' She slumped on to the nearest chair and Anna was dismayed to see she was near to tears.

'So what's up? You're not ill are you?'

'No, no nothing like that. I went into Newcastle today and I had a tremendous shock.'

And she recounted the events of the afternoon.

'Oh Lydia, what a terrible shock for you.' Anna put her arms round her.

'Yes, I'm still very shaken by it all. Maybe I should have rung the police as soon as I got back but part of me wanted to believe Dave; I can't bear to think that he could have done that to me and to Simon. And the boy was so like him. I could see nothing of myself in him and I certainly wouldn't put it past Dave to have fathered two children at around the same time.'

Anna was about to say something but Lydia held up her hand. 'The thing is, shortly after I got back here, the phone rang and it was Dave, the last person I expected to hear. He apologised for his behaviour earlier, swore he had nothing to do with Simon's disappearance, said he only found out about Alex fairly recently and asked if he could come here later this evening and explain things.' She paused and closed her eyes.

'So? What did you say?'

'I agreed. I didn't think it could do any harm. But I'm so mixed up. One minute I want to believe him and I can't wait for him to get here, the next minute I want to believe I've found Simon. Anyway,' she brightened, 'it's great that you two have turned up. I feel stronger and it'll be good to have your point of view.'

John went to fetch the kettle which was whistling madly. 'Let's have that cup of tea.'

Anna stirred milk into her tea. 'Now let's think about this rationally. How likely is it that Dave Collier would have taken your child away from you? Remember how very supportive he was of you at the time though it was obvious he was grieving just as much?'

'Yes,' said John, 'Anna and I certainly had a lot of respect for him after the abduction; his care of you was immense. And it helped us to cope as well.'

'I know, I know. He was wonderful then but maybe he was just a very good actor. Oh I don't know, he had his bad points and he didn't always treat me well but I never thought he hated me.'

'Well, we'll just have to see what he has to say for himself. What time is he due?' Anna glanced at the clock on the mantelpiece.

Lydia shook her head. 'He just said it would be later on. He had some phone calls to make, to do with work.'

'I think if you have any doubt at all about his plausibility when he gets here, you should inform the police,' John reached for one of the rock cakes.

'One thing he did say which I found very difficult. When I told him I still think about Simon constantly, he said he did too, then added "But at least I have Alex." Straight away he admitted he shouldn't have said it but I can't get it out of my mind.'

All of a sudden she stood up. 'Of course he has that child, whoever he is and if he's who he says he is, he'll always have him.' Her voice bordered on hysteria. 'I don't want to believe Dave took him but at the same time I so want that child to be Simon. I want my baby, my Simon back.'

Anna looked anxiously at John as Lydia began to tear at her hair and to move about the kitchen erratically – range to table, to back door, to table. They hadn't seen her behave like this since the early days after losing Simon.

Anna went to try and calm her but she pushed her away and continued to pace, finally stopping by the open cellar door.

'It's great isn't it? Dave Collier's got his child, maybe *my* child, you've got Jess who *is* my child. Oh how I wish I'd never let you have her. I've loved having her here and I think she needs to know the truth.' Her voice had risen to almost screaming pitch.

Anna tried again. 'Come on Lydia, let's sit down and finish our tea. We can discuss this when you are calmer.' She put both hands gently on her shoulders but once more she shook her off, this time with greater force.

'Don't patronise me and don't touch me. Jess needs to know the truth and I am going to tell her first thing in the morning. You can't stop me.'

She lurched towards Anna, hands raised as if she was about

to attack her. Anna ducked and, covering her face with her left arm, hit out blindly with her right hand. The blow landed on Lydia's chest, sending her reeling down those precarious cellar steps. There was a loud crack as her head hit the wall. Silence. Anna and John exchanged a look of fear and disbelief as Anna went down the steps and looked for signs of life. As John followed, she shook her head.

Chapter Thirty-Four

John stood up. 'I'm going to make a cup of tea. My voice is hoarse with all the talking and the brandy hasn't helped. Will you have a cup?'

'I couldn't drink or eat a thing until I know the rest of what happened.'

John returned with a mug of tea and sat down. 'Well it was bad enough to realise that Lydia was dead but when we looked up and saw you there watching, we were shocked to the core.

'Can you remember how you came to be there? I suppose you must have woken up and heard the shouting?'

Jess recounted her new-found memories.

'Anna went up and carried you away from the scene, into one of the front rooms. You were quiet and staring straight ahead. When she spoke to you, you didn't answer. She went upstairs and found a blanket, wrapped you in it and sat cuddling you.

'She was in a terrible state herself. Her whole body was shaking. My first reaction was to phone the police but she wouldn't hear of it. "I killed her." She kept saying. "I killed my own sister." I tried to reason with her, pointed out that it was an accident but she was having none of it and when I went into the hall to use the phone, she followed me, physically restrained me. I never knew she had such strength but it's amazing what physical strength we can find in a crisis. Anyway I began to see she had a point. The death might well be seen as suspicious and either or both of us could be charged with murder. We were also afraid that Dave Collier would arrive at any minute. We needed to get out of there. We wanted to make things look as normal as possible so I went up and made your bed, gathered up your toys and clothes. I checked around to make sure there was nothing to suggest we had been with her when she died, locked the outside doors but left the light on in the kitchen and we left.

'We felt terrible about leaving Lydia's body but we were hoping she would be found soon. We had no idea that we'd left a window unlocked and that Dave would get in. We assumed she'd be found by Luke Matthews because when we'd dropped you off the previous Saturday, Lydia had talked to us about him, how he'd gone on a cycling holiday, due back the following Sunday and how he'd said he would probably call with her on his way back from the ferry. She'd told us he had a key. I was so surprised, on the day we first met Alex, to hear that it was actually Dave who first found her.

'The journey to London was horrendous. I drove fast but I was careful as well. I didn't want to get pulled over. We knew we should have taken you to hospital but we didn't want to be questioned about what had happened to trigger your state. Anna knew that once we were home she would be able to treat you herself. You fell asleep on the journey but you were very restless and you kept muttering things which were unintelligible to us. Anna said you were burning up. You were feverish for a couple of days and when your temperature returned to normal, you had no memory of Lydia or anything that had happened.'

—∽∽—

'So you see, you and I are half-brother and sister, not cousins as we were led to believe.' Jess put down her cup and sat back in her chair. After John's revelations, she had wanted above all to see Alex, tell him what had happened. She felt that, as he had been through a similar crisis of identity, he would have more understanding than anyone else.

Now they faced one another over a pot of tea in the sitting room of his London home and she had just finished reiterating John's account of the events of that fateful night.

'And I am very pleased about that. It was great to find I had a cousin but to find you're not a cousin but a sister, well that's pretty amazing…isn't it?' He looked at her as if doubting that she would feel the same.

Jess smiled. 'Oh yes, it's wonderful. Let me give you a hug, my long-lost brother.' She stood up and held out her arms.

'It must have been as big a shock to you finding out that Anna and John weren't your parents, as it was to me finding out that Monica White, whoever she was, wasn't mine.'

'You're telling me, it was. And to discover that Anna was responsible for Lydia's death, though unintentionally.'

'So my dad was telling the truth about that night after all.'

'Yes, he must have turned up shortly after we left.'

Alex frowned. 'Well I wonder what would have happened if Lydia had still been alive when he turned up – on her own I mean – if John and Anna hadn't come back early. If he hadn't managed to convince her that I wasn't hers and she'd still been threatening him with the police. Would he have killed her?'

'We'll never know that Alex so I think you should give him the benefit of the doubt. From what my dad has told me about him, he would probably have talked Lydia round, promised to show her your birth certificate.'

They were silent for a few moments, then Alex spoke.

'What a family of lies and secrets we come from Jess. How do you feel about Lydia being your mother?'

'Like you I've had to reassess who I am. At least you now know who both your parents were. I have no idea who my biological father was. But I've got over the shock and I've come round to the idea. I did love Lydia very much and I have no doubt that she loved me. I bear her no grudge for not wanting me when she found she was pregnant and in a sense she didn't really give me up. She was very involved with me until she went to live at *Sea Music.*'

'And you never had the slightest inkling that you were adopted?'

'No, none at all. I never had any need to see my birth – well in my case – adoption certificate. I got my first passport when I was eighteen. My friend Tanya and I went to France to celebrate our A level results and getting places at university. Dad paid for my trip and also bought my passport. I had to sign for it of course but he never showed me my 'birth' certificate and, to tell you the truth, I wasn't interested. I was too excited about going abroad.

'Since then, when I've needed verification of my identity, I've used my passport or driving licence.'

'And you remember Lydia quite clearly now?'

'Oh yes, she was an exceptional woman: kind, gentle, patient, good fun. Sorry Alex you must miss never having known her.'

'Of course but I do love to hear about her. It was great talking to Luke that time. So you can tell me as much as you like about her.'

'Dad told me that she and my mum, eh...Anna, were very close and that Anna would never have intentionally done anything to hurt her. He said Lydia had never stopped grieving for you, never would. But she told him once, it was like chronic pain: you were always aware of it but you learned to live with it.

And then seeing Dave with you that day brought it to the fore again. He guessed it was almost as acute for her then as when it happened. Certainly, he said, he had never seen her lose control like that since shortly after the abduction. In retrospect, he didn't think Lydia would have attacked Anna or told me the truth. She cared too much about us both but at the time Anna had felt threatened and acted reflexively.'

'And you believe him?'

'Yes I do. I can now recall seeing Lydia and Anna together and I think there was a lot of love there.'

'Of course. I wasn't doubting what John told you. I was just making sure you believed him. He's kept the truth from you for so long.'

Jess brightened. 'Anyway, changing tack completely, how's married life?'

Alex and Amy had got married in June. They had sold their respective properties and bought a house together.

Alex smiled. 'It's great. It's good to think something positive has come out of this whole web of deception. I'd never have met Amy if the truth hadn't come out.'

'No and I don't suppose I'd have got back with Max if I hadn't gone to Cornwall to see Luke and realised how unfit I was. If I hadn't taken up running, chances are I might never have seen him again.'

'I'm so glad my gran found the strength to write that letter. I feel so much better for knowing who my mother was, even though I never got to meet her. And I've found a sister and an uncle. Bless John. Don't be too hard on him. I'm sure he only did what he thought was best.'

'Humph.' Jess sat back and folded her arms. There were a great many things she understood: her parents' wish to protect their young child from the horror of what she had seen; why her mum had hit the bottle as hard as she did. She used to think it was grief for Lydia but now she realised that the guilt she would have felt, coupled with the grief, must have been unbearable. She understood why they hadn't told her she was adopted. As John had said, if they had adopted her through an agency, they would never have made a secret of it but with Lydia living nearby and having so much to do with her, they had thought it unwise.

She voiced all this to Alex, finishing with, 'Two things I don't understand. How could they run off and leave Lydia's body lying there? They didn't know for sure when she was going to be found. How disrespectful. And what cowards they were. They were innocent, so why were they so frightened? The second thing is, why didn't they follow up what Lydia had told them about seeing Dave Collier with a child she thought might be you? It wouldn't have done any harm to involve the police even if she was wrong. And as we now know she was right.'

Alex clasped his hands on the table in front of him and leaned towards her.

'Jess can you imagine for one moment how they must have felt? Bad enough that Lydia was dead, but that she was dead as a result of a shove from Anna. And then to find you looking on. It must have been their worst nightmare. They were both in a state of extreme shock and people often don't act rationally in that state. And John is right, they might well have been suspects. The police would certainly have wanted to know how Lydia came to fall. God knows how he managed to drive all the way to London, the state he must have been in.'

A hint of a smile flickered across Jess's face. 'You're so understanding Alex. I guess it's all too raw for me at the moment. I'm probably still in shock myself. But what about this business of them not telling the police about Dave?'

Alex shrugged. 'Well there could be several reasons. I guess they wanted to stay clear of the police after what had happened. But also, they didn't think my dad was that bad. They knew he was a womaniser and had been unfaithful to Lydia but there was a lot they admired about him as well. They wouldn't have thought he had it in him to do something like that. Even Lydia had come round to doubting that the child was me.'

'Yes, that's exactly what my dad said and they were very impressed with the letter of sympathy they got from him.'

Jess knew Alex was right. People who were shocked and frightened did sometimes behave uncharacteristically. Who was she to judge John and Anna? She had no idea how she would behave in a similar situation. Nevertheless, her anger remained and she had no wish to see John at present.

John rang to invite Jess and Max for Christmas. Max took the call.

'I know Jess is still angry with me Max but we've never been apart at Christmas. It's my turn to cook this year so I hope you will join me.'

'Don't worry John, we will.'

Jess was annoyed. 'You had no right to accept without asking me. I thought we could have a different Christmas this year, just the two of us.'

'But you and your dad have always spent Christmas together. Don't you think it's time you stopped blaming him. He's been through a terrible time as well and you can't deny you two have always been very close. So he and your mum ran off in a panic. So what? We all make mistakes. You might have done the same thing in the circumstances.'

—⁂—

Jess had not seen John since the night of his disclosure. He'd rung her a few times but she had kept the conversation brief and cool, so it was with trepidation that she turned up at his house on Christmas Day. As she parked the car, Max looked at her anxiously.

'Don't worry Max, it will be fine. I have no intention of creating a scene; I'll be perfectly pleasant.'

As they approached the front door, she straightened her shoulders and fixed a smile on her face. Max raised his hand to ring the bell but the door was ajar so he pushed it open, calling 'Hello-o. John.'

'Come in, come in.' John came out of the kitchen to greet them, wearing a striped apron. Max hugged him, 'Happy Christmas John,' and went to leave their presents under the tree. Jess gawped. She was appalled at the spectacle that John had become. In the intervening weeks he had lost a lot of weight, his cheeks were sunken and there were dark shadows under his eyes. If she hadn't known he was sixty-two, she would have taken him for a man of at least ten years older. Her heart went out to him and, without hesitation, she opened her arms wide, her face beaming with a genuine smile.

'Happy Christmas Dad. It's so lovely to see you.' She clung tightly to his bony frame, drew back and looked up at him. 'Sorry Dad, I've been a stupid, stubborn fool.'

—⁂—

Jess and Alex were in a hired sailing boat headed out to sea. It was a hot day with just enough of a breeze to keep the boat going. Reaching a point where there was a good view of *Sea*

Music, Alex turned to Jess. 'Will this do?' She nodded. 'Ideal, I would say.'

Alex gazed at the house that he had never entered. It was as Jess had described it the last time she had seen it, devoid of creeper and sandblasted, looking naked and bleak, nothing like the welcoming structure of Lydia's time. The first time he had seen it, he hadn't thought it friendly-looking but he had acknowledged that his perception of it was probably influenced by his mood at the time.

Alex turned the boat directly into the wind, the sails fluttered lose and they came to a standstill. He loosened the sheets to make sure the wind would not catch them and make them sail off again. They had rehearsed what they were going to do. Jess recited one of Lydia's favourite poems: Emily Dickinson's *'Hope' is the thing with feathers,* opened the casket she had retrieved from under the rose bush in John's garden, scooped up a handful of ashes and scattered them into the North Sea. Alex followed suit with another favourite: *No man is an island* by John Donne.

They lifted the casket together and scattered what remained. It was the fourteenth of May, Lydia's birthday. She would have been fifty-eight.

Epilogue

On the evening of the summer solstice Carrie Martin's art gallery in Dulwich was buzzing. The coffee shop had closed, as it always did, at 5.30 and the crowd milling around the gallery were all invited guests. A table covered with an immaculate white cloth was set out with wine, tea, coffee, fruit juices, as well as a selection of canapés and other nibbles.

On the dot of seven, Carrie took the floor at the front of the room. Now in her early sixties, she looked elegant in a jade silk dress, her hair still pale blonde, pulled into a French pleat. Jess looked admiringly at her, wondering what Anna, who would have been the same age, would have looked like now. And Lydia, her mother. What would she have looked like?

Carrie tinkled a little silver bell and immediately the chatter and laughter ceased.

'Good evening ladies and gentlemen. May I welcome you all to *Indigo* art gallery and say how proud I am to be putting on an exhibition of the work of a woman who first exhibited here just after the gallery opened in 1976. But I will detain you no further, I will now hand you over to the man who is opening the exhibition: the renowned artist Mr Luke Matthews.'

Amongst the applause, Luke took his place on the dais. He was sixty-one now, a distinguished-looking figure with thick white hair and a tanned complexion. His address was succinct:

How he had met Lydia in the spring of 1978 and they had become friends. How she had encouraged him in his art. How their friendship had been cut short by her untimely death.

'If I had not met Lydia, I would never have got to the place where I am today in the world of art. But that is not why I am here this evening to open this exhibition. I am here because Lydia was a dear friend and, in the twenty-eight years since her passing, I have never ceased to miss her.'

Jess studied Lydia's photo, read the résumé of her tragic life and death. Though she knew it by heart, she felt her eyes fill with tears. She mustn't cry, not tonight, she would go and see how Max was getting on with the twins.

She found him at the back of the room with two fractious babies in their buggy.

'I'm just going to take these two for a stroll in the hope they'll go to sleep.'

'No let me take them. You go and have a look at the paintings. I've seen them so many times and, to be honest, I'm not finding it easy.' She gave a rueful smile. 'It'll do me good to get out.'

It had been a hot day, the temperature well into the eighties so evening had come as a pleasant relief. Jess lowered the buggy's backrest and pulled up the hood in the hope that the babies would soon fall asleep. As she walked through the park, she reflected on the twenty months since her total recall. She still felt saddened by the loss of Lydia and particularly by the nature of her death but the hollowness had gone completely. And there were now two more very important people in her life. She sneaked a peek under the hood and was relieved to see that two pairs of eyes were closing, Megan sucking her thumb, Daniel stroking the base of his nose with a little furry duckling.

Back in January of last year when the pregnancy testing kit

had indicated positive, she had been suffused with a mixture of joy and anxiety. She had no doubt now that Max wanted a family as much as she did but she was frightened that this pregnancy would go the way of the first one. She rested as much as she could and her first scan revealed that not only was the pregnancy going well but she was expecting twins. There had been no complications; she had carried them to term and they were now nine months old.

Retracing her steps to *Indigo* she noticed a familiar figure leaning on the fence, looking out over the pond. It was John, looking fit and well.

'Had enough Dad?' He started and turned round smiling. 'Yes, well I've seen Lydia's work many times and to be honest coming here has brought up a lot of difficult memories. But apart from that, it's so hot in the gallery, I just had to get out.'

He nodded towards the pram. 'It's very quiet in there. Are they asleep?'

'Yes, thank goodness, they were getting really crotchety.'

Alex watched the crowd milling about the gallery, saw the *Sold* stickers go up by the paintings and felt both proud and pleased: proud of his mother's work and pleased that his idea of exhibiting it was such a success. The proceeds were to go to an art project for vulnerable young people aged between thirteen and twenty-one. The original sketches for *Tom and the Pterodactyl* had made a considerable amount at auction recently and that had gone to a charity for parents whose children were missing or dead.

'Isn't this wonderful Alex. What a good idea.' Amy appeared from the crowd and put an arm round his shoulders.

'Yes, I'm so thankful it's been a success but to be honest, I'll be glad when it's nine o'clock, I'm whacked.'

—⚋—

By ten o'clock, the family had gathered in Alex and Amy's sitting room. Daniel and Megan had woken briefly when they were changed for bed and were now sound asleep upstairs.

John was the first to raise his glass. 'Here's thanks for a very successful evening and may the exhibition continue to draw the crowds – and money.' There was laughter and cries of 'Here, here.'

Sarah followed with. 'And here's to Luke who opened the exhibition so eloquently and succinctly.'

Luke put an arm round his wife and turned towards Alex and Amy. 'To a continued healthy pregnancy and to our first grandchild.' All eyes were on the couple and there were shouts of 'What?' and 'Really?'

'Yes really.' Amy was beaming. 'We decided not to tell anyone until after twelve weeks, apart from Mum and Dad that is, and Mum and I gave Dad permission to break the news himself. He's been so excited.' She pulled a face at Luke who appeared embarrassed.

'So you're due in…' Jess counted on her fingers, '…December.'

'The fifteenth to be precise,' said Alex, 'maybe it will be a Christmas baby.'

'Oh don't say that, Tim here was born on Christmas Day and he's always felt he's missed out, not having a proper birthday. Isn't that right Tim?' Paul nudged his partner.

'Yes but it's not the end of the world. I always got more presents than anyone else. It caused a certain amount of friction with my younger brother and sister.'

Jess picked up her glass again. 'Well as long as everything

goes well, that's the main thing. I'm thrilled for you.' She looked at Max. 'Our two are going to have a cousin and I am going to be an auntie for the first time.'

Alex proposed the final toast.

'To Lydia, my mother and Jess's mother. A great artist who has touched us all one way or another. An inspiration.'